ORIGINAL BLISS

A. L. Kennedy was born in Dundee in 1965. Her first collection of short stories, *Night Geometry and the Garscadden Trains*, won the Saltire Award for Best First Book and the *Mail on Sunday*/John Llewellyn Rhys Prize. This was followed by the novel, *Looking for the Possible Dance*, which won a Somerset Maugham Award, a second collection of stories, *Now That You're Back*, and a second novel, *So I Am Glad*, which won the Encore Award and was joint winner of the Saltire Scottish Book of the Year Award. In 1993 she was chosen as one of the twenty Best of Young British Novelists. She wrote the script for the BFI/Channel Four film, *Stella Does Tricks*, and is working on a number of film and drama projects. She lives in Glasgow.

BY A.L. KENNEDY

Night Geometry and the Garscadden Trains
Looking for the Possible Dance
Now That You're Back
So I Am Glad
Original Bliss

A. L. Kennedy

ORIGINAL BLISS

VINTAGE

Published by Vintage 1998

2 4 6 8 10 9 7 5 3 1

Copyright © A. L. Kennedy 1997

The right of A. L. Kennedy to be identified as the author of this work has been asserted by her in accordance with the Copyright, Designs and Patents Act, 1988

Some of these stories have previously appeared in *Arena*, *Back Rubs* (Serpent's Tail), *Fallen Angels* (Pavilion), *GQ*, *The Junkie's Christmas* (Serpent's Tail), *Soho Square VII: New Scottish Writing* (Bloomsbury)

First published in Great Britain by
Jonathan Cape Ltd, 1997

Vintage
Random House, 20 Vauxhall Bridge Road,
London SW1V 2SA

Random House Australia (Pty) Limited
20 Alfred Street, Milsons Point, Sydney
New South Wales 2061, Australia

Random House New Zealand Limited
18 Poland Road, Glenfield,
Auckland 10, New Zealand

Random House South Africa (Pty) Limited
Endulini, 5A Jubilee Road, Parktown 2193, South Africa

Random House UK Limited Reg. No. 954009

A CIP catalogue record for this book
is available from the British Library

ISBN 0 09 973071 5

Papers used by Random House UK Ltd are natural, recyclable products made from wood grown in sustainable forests. The manufacturing processes conform to the environmental regulations of the country of origin

Printed and bound in Great Britain by
Cox & Wyman, Reading, Berkshire

In memory of
Joseph Henry Price
1916–1996

Contents

ROCKAWAY AND THE DRAW

She was thinking, only thinking. Because it felt good.

You can make someone deaf with a pencil. Just put it in their ear and shove.

Suzanne was feeling good and thinking and looking off and into the dark of a doorway, not particularly attempting to see anything, only looking off and entertaining thoughts.

Bang, bang, you're deaf. But why would anyone let you? And why would you want?

Ben progressed beneath the kitchen lintel and broke her line of sight. Ben was not the kind of man to walk. Ben simply and inexorably progressed within a familiar, steady range of speeds. She was used to thinking of his body bearing patiently down across the environment like tarmac, or a desert railway line. Ben would correct that to 'blacktop' and 'railroad track', but she was used to thinking in English, because that meant she could remember who she was. Ben, of course, was Ben, and in any language he would be broad and smooth as a gunsight, tempered and accurate. Whenever he came to a standstill anyone could be sure it was only because Ben had reached the most suitable point for the optimum comfort of Ben.

As he passed her, he patted her shoulder softly and unleashed a smile she still found unnerving. Some Americans simply had too many teeth, or too good, or too big – they were too obviously a later and better version of what the human being could be. They seemed almost dangerously well-prepared for feeding.

She watched as Ben snibbed a little door behind him

and left her alone with the passageway. Soon, she knew, Rochelle would come searching for her and make her enjoy herself again. Or maybe Ben had been sent to fetch her. She didn't mind. For the moment, she could overhear the party and contemplate.

I believe the human will and spirit are outstanding and can triumph both over pencils and dangerous teeth. I know of a girl, for instance, whose whole leg was taken off by alligator bites, but she never contemplated giving up – neither during the blood and ferocity of the attack, nor later in her amputated life. If I was cornered by a flesh-eating reptile I hope I could fight. If I was threatened by a thug with a pencil – a torturer with a pencil – threatened with being deaf in a couple of spikes, I hope I could remember there are few trials that humanity cannot surmount.

From behind the little door came the sound of flushing, a minor disturbance, the bubbling grind of a cistern, a pause. Ben unsnibbed and loomed forward, began approaching her with an odd intensity. When he paused and then gradually knelt beside her chair, she couldn't help but see his frown.

'Ben? Is something wrong?'

'Damn thing doesn't work right. Nothing I could do.'

'The damn thing . . . ?'

'Doesn't work. It was there when I went in and it still hasn't gone. I don't know – nothing is any good any more. It's terrible. Are you coming back to the party, Rochelle thinks she's offended you, or you're sick, or something. It's her birthday and she's feeling isolated . . .' Ben softened his face into an expression so understanding that no one could mistake his attitude towards Rochelle for anything less than loving concern.

'Ben, it's not my fault she didn't invite any other women.'

'She doesn't like women. But she craves female company, it's a big problem for her. Please come back through.'

4

'I was coming anyway, I just needed some air and to think.'

'There you go with that thinking again.' His tone suggested he might be about to playfully ruffle her hair. He didn't. He didn't have to. She felt she'd been ruffled anyway.

'I'll follow you. But I need to . . . I've drunk too much coffee.' Ben stood but failed to depart, doubtful. 'I'll be along. You go ahead.'

'Well, you remember it doesn't work. That thing had nothing to do with me.'

She smiled, not understanding, but smiling all the same in a poorly-nourished, poorly-hungry, European way.

And it was there – in Rochelle's bathroom, waiting – the thing that Ben had found himself unable to remove. This was understandable, because it must have been more than capable of withstanding the average flush. Long, fat, solidly put together and the sweet colour of caramel, or milk chocolate, it swayed very slightly in the ceramic curve and shadow of the lavatory pan: a wonderfully monstrous light-brown shit. But not Ben's. Not of his making. He'd been clear on that point.

As if in all these years, she'd never guessed why Ben went to the washroom, restroom, lavatory, toilet, WC. As if it had been a big mystery to her and always should stay that way. When Ben said he was 'going to freshen up' that was absolutely and only what he meant. He was going away for a while to become fresher; more soap- and cologne-scented; more agreeable to be with, although anyone would tell you that he was consistently agreeable in any case.

Ben had no bodily functions. He progressed and he loomed and he was perfectly attentive to all his acquaint-ances' mental states, and he was a good listener, one of the best, but he wasn't a bodily functions kind of man. Unless you counted screwing; although he actually had a way of doing that which made it seem no more than sporting, healthy and cathartic. You could guarantee catharsis with Ben. He found out *everything* you liked and told you *everything* he liked and then practised until both the sets of *everything* were as perfect as they could be. He constructed love faultlessly, as if it had never been a bodily function.

For the hell of it, she turned round after flushing and took a peek. All clear.

Back in the living-room, the guests had arranged themselves much as she'd thought they would do. They were all around Ben. He wasn't holding forth in any way but all the same, Ben was the heart of the room's attention. At the moment he was listening to Carter and Daniel and they were talking to him in the manner of lost children, or medicated patients, or applicants for extremely substantial loans. Rochelle and Peter, Herman, Max, all chatted to each other convincingly enough, but if Ben had any need of their presence, even a tiny change of tone, or a modest call of beckoning laughter, would mean they delivered themselves to him completely. It would happen as predictably as nightfall. Ben was a draw.

Rochelle swirled her scotch up dangerously close to the rim of its glass and glanced at the door. She performed an exquisite double-take. 'Suzanne, are you okay? Ben said you were fine. But you're not tired are you? Are we being dull?'

With a pencil. Deaf.

'No, I'm fine. I was just getting some air. Things were peculiar at work today.'

'Well that's fine, then. Come sit with me.' Rochelle patted the space beside her on the bright, woven rug and Suzanne squatted obediently into position. Remembering how Rochelle liked to avoid any actual use of her furniture Suzanne had dressed herself with an eye to reclining on floors. She had chosen a loose silk Indian-style trouser-suit. Indian from India, not Native American. Had

Suzanne dressed in the manner of a Native American, Rochelle would have offered her blankets and beads. That would have been her best appropriate gesture. As a British citizen in the costume of a former British colony, Suzanne knew she still presented a tricky choice between a welcoming martini and a Wampum trade. Every time Rochelle observed her, they both heard the inexpensive tinkle of coloured glass.

'You sure you're okay? You look a little pale, dear.'

Rochelle, like many other people, treated Suzanne as if regular contact with Ben must render her somehow frail or sickly. Occasionally Suzanne would even catch herself pausing before a flight of stairs or stumbling through a sentence as if she really were an ambulant invalid.

'You don't have a drink, sweetheart.'

'That's all right. I'm not thirsty. Not right now.'

'Whatever you want . . .'

Rochelle turned back to Peter with a smile that meant their conversation could recommence. Abandoned to herself, Suzanne did not smile but examined the geometry of the carpet with some contentment while Rochelle settled in to ignoring her thoroughly. Rochelle ignored with flair; she did it with an élan and conviviality many people failed to exhibit in full-blown intercourse.

If you chose something stronger than a pencil, like a pilot pen, a powerful blow could force it clear into the brain causing cataclysmic damage, if not death.

Over by the draped baby grand, Ben was tilting his head to the left which meant he was trying his hardest to hear, getting a better angle on the sound, or the sense. Ben's surprisingly dark blue eyes were cold, open and hungry as an infant's; Daniel laced and relaced his fingers helplessly under one knee, his mouth letting out thin sentences with which his face patently disagreed. Carter seemed bewildered, but Ben was being generously intent. He listened the way a Russian icon listens: absolutely.

Under the piano, in a nerveless sprawl, was Rochelle's cat. Everybody knew about that cat. Something like a Siamese, it was expensive and took off for months at a time leaving Rochelle distraught or sedated, depending on which of her doctors had gained her confidence. The cat had been christened Shelley, but people called it Prozac.

When Prozac was home it might sulk in the kitchen, or make an additional scratch of shadow in the margin of rooms. On some days it would circulate, screaming, at head height like a death-wall cyclist – nothing to keep it up and moving but the physics of speed and hate; or it might only bide its time, the ghost blue of its eyes willing an approach. Prozac drew blood. Prozac had put two people in A&E, one of them requiring facial sutures. If Prozac had been a dog, it would have been shot years ago.

Naturally Ben's favourite cat in the world was Prozac. He never would understand why nobody – even Rochelle – could like it.

'Here you go, Shelley, here you go.' Almost the first thing Ben did, 'That's a good cat, that's the best cat I know.' Standing in the hallway, not even stooping forward the way that anyone usually might to call an animal, Ben would murmur and smile and watch for Prozac, 'That's it. You're doing great. You're doing just fine.' Until the little creature, because Prozac only was a little, mushroom-coloured creature, would stutter forward, stiff-legged, head low, tail breaking from side to side in an effort to be away from the man with the voice that was wires pulling over its skin. 'Good to have you back, Shel.' Ben waited until Prozac froze at his feet and then scooped her up like a scalp.

Suzanne would look at Ben's hands closing massively around the cat's particular arrangements of pelt and bone. Ben would close his eyes for a moment, perhaps concentrating, and Prozac's astonished body would suddenly fall into itself. Muscles lolled, its head dropped back to Ben's arm and a low purring began. Suzanne hated the purr. It made her nauseous. It made her think she had never seen every thought and independent intention so thoroughly drawn from a living thing. The effect could last for days.

So Prozac, anaesthetised and under the piano, would be perfectly safe to approach this evening, although Suzanne was careful not to go near it herself – she didn't like to take unfair advantage. She also remembered that in Prozac's gaze she could often see something not unlike despair.

'What are you talking about?'

Growling softly back home inside Ben's indecently spacious car, she discovered she had spoken out on behalf of the cat.

'I thought you might want to leave it alone.'

'Shelley? I hardly go near her. Are you jealous of a *cat*?'

Suzanne could almost see that last word, bouncing out in the darkness beyond the dashboard display. Its single syllable had a greenish shine about it – the colour of gently teasing incredulity.

'I'm not jealous. I just don't think it likes to be held.'

'Oh, Suzanne, she comes to me. I call her over, she comes, I pick her up, she purrs. She wouldn't do that if she didn't like it. Come on now, lighten up.'

'I don't think it can help itself.'

'Yeah, look, I'm sorry you don't like Rochelle, but she does like you. We don't have to visit so often. And it does mean that she buys from me – a tiny picture, a talking-point lamp, something she'll enjoy, even if she thinks she doesn't care. Rochelle hasn't the faintest idea of what she likes unless *someone* helps her. All she thinks she's looking for is another way to spend her money.'

No one but Ben could make selling pointless objects to the impractically wealthy sound so much like a vocation to one of the lesser-known caring professions.

'I have some Lakota grave-goods; they're very hard to

get and I know that she'll love and enjoy them if I say she will. She needs that kind of help.'

'Maybe she should just invest in better plumbing.'

'Huh?'

He really did say 'Huh?' like a person in a strip cartoon. That one tiny noise could make him seem like her very own illustration. 'Suzanne?'

'I was thinking out loud. God, I'm tired. Are you tired?'

'Tired? Ten minutes, we'll be home. I don't want to hurry – the cold's making things a little greasy. I'm sort of tired. But not *so* tired. Are you *so* tired?'

There was a kind of orange shine, all along those last two sentences. Ben set his hand briefly on her thigh, ran his middle finger from somewhere slightly above her knee to somewhere slightly below where it wanted to be. One of Suzanne's more rhythmical body parts – the one whose peculiarities and demands Ben had made his particular study – gave a beat or so and then subsided. Ben was rapidly ceasing to be any kind of artwork. He felt nothing but three-dimensional. His hand withdrew to make the gear change he needed for a turn.

In perhaps half an hour's time, he would lick her wrists and suck at her earlobes and then quite systematically take her apart, shake out the beat he wanted and then bolt her back into sleep. While he performed their mutually agreeable overhaul, she would find herself holding him and being once again surprised that she could be so intensely loving with a man who was so little more than mechanical. Then one of his technical spot-checks would find her arching and stretching herself against his strangely unattractive body, with the ache he'd so neatly installed slowly howling between her throat and that perfectly snug and moist little space he'd made for himself inside her.

At other times and in another country, that space had been her cunt. Ben called it his beaver. She supposed beaver was a nicer word than cunt. Ben's beaver. She didn't mind it being a beaver, she only found it odd that it wasn't hers. Ben's own genitals were quite attractive, but nothing on which she would wish to stake a claim.

In the thick, heavy unconsciousness that unfailingly followed Ben, Suzanne would dream. Arid, hollow-skied dramas would cyclone and suck around her, almost as if the impossible and usually tasteless bodily fluid she had learned to drink from Ben could guarantee both sleep and hallucination.

A young woman shimmers up out of a desert full of hungry reptiles and survivalists – a place of bad premonitions and un-American, unaccidental deaths. I see her as a kind of pioneer: a fine example, walking through miles of open, panting white with only her smile and her determination to sustain her. Then she comes to a place called Rockaway where there is nothing but an old gas station and a man who waits.

Something about the man slows her, stems her progress, until she discovers that, quite without warning, she has started to live at the Rockaway Gas Station, to live with the man. As a couple, they are quite unsuited, but something here keeps them together, fixed. At times I can nearly see it slither and bend and dribble in the roasting, mindless air. It brings a faint but unmistakably mineral flavour to the mouth.

I watch the woman repeatedly counting through the sad collection of pointless goods the man has gathered to sell any passing drivers – although, naturally, no drivers pass. She tallies up jump-leads and pliers, gas cans and savage loops of wire, unexplained and oddly enticing little knives. She finds a matchbox full of milk teeth, an old diary and half a dozen yellow pencils, nicely sharp.

Suzanne noticed wakefully that the gas station partly offered the contents of her grandmother's kitchen drawers. Her grandmother had married in wartime, married a man who had no chance of living for more than a few weeks beyond their vows. Like thousands of others, she had flung herself on the mercy of the future and found it to be momentarily distracted. Grandmother's first and never-mentioned husband had lingered for a while in a hospital near Stratford upon Avon. He had been sad to discover the bomb blast had left him deafened and blind, unable to move. He had died calmly.

If the young woman caught in Rockaway has repeating dreams of blood and murder she might wake up one sudden morning and long to ask the man beside her how calmly he would die.

Ben woke Suzanne and then woke his beaver at around nine a.m. She struggled slightly against his chest, still dreaming of bleached bones and dust.

'Ben?'

'Who else. Good morning. How are you?'

'Oh. Groggy I think. My God, we've slept in. Why didn't you wake me?'

'I just did. You've forgotten, haven't you?'

'Forgotten?'

'Today we're taking time out. Nothing to do but schmooz before I have to go away. It's the healthy thing to do. Now you rest for as long as you want to and then I'll fix you something good. It's been snowing since dawn. A lot. Picked the best day to stay at home.'

'How long will you be gone for?'

'Oh, two days – three at the most. Don't worry.'

Suzanne didn't worry, she waited until the bedroom door swung to and then slipped up from under the covers and walked to the window. Down in the street, everyone knew exactly what to do. Pedestrians slithered perfectly against soft sugar snow, leaping and tiptoeing the banks and reservoirs of icewatered slush at every kerb. Mr Beck from the fruit shop had bounced out a kind of mowing machine to chew up the hard packed surface in front of his store. His son was shovelling slabs of it neatly away. Seasonal changes were barely tolerated here, they didn't stand a chance. The subway gratings had already thawed themselves back to normality and monstrous pillars of steam were completely obscuring the roadworks at the far end of the block. The sky was set for a freeze – the palest, most merciless blue – but the city was still shifting, simmering under its surface, riding up on an invincible, buzzing heat.

In a desert place called Rockaway, the young woman is trapped by the heat. It is plain that she can never leave the man or the gas station unless something very terrible happens first. She is given free food and lodging in return for her work, but there is hardly any work to do. Her wages are subsequently very small. As each night swoops in below zero and shatters rocks, the young woman owes the gas station man more money. There is something unjust about this, something that tries her determination and sharpens her smile.

Had it been anything like a hot day, Suzanne would have had to go walking with Ben and maybe sat in the park. Far enough into the park and the ceaseless passing of traffic could be mistaken for something like a tidal swell, or the wind in a great many trees. Suzanne could sit on a bank or a bench and convincingly picture the Thousand Islands and the Finger Lakes where she and Ben had gone once when they were freshly married and he did not yet know quite completely how to please her. They had sneaked away to practise each other in a place where they could concentrate.

And certainly they could concentrate out of doors, but they couldn't be alone. If they both paused for too long with the warm weight of Ben's arm laid out across her shoulders, or tucked in at the small of her back, or in any other posture they might attempt, then it would happen – the draw. As if Ben had thrown out food, or called, or scattered pheromonal substances by the handful, bird upon bird would come drooping down. Every time she went out with Ben into anywhere like the country, the same happy,

Hitchcock rush would start. With animals, too: everything wanted to be near him.

It was embarrassing. People would stop and look and then they, of course, were also pulled on in. Ben would squint at the sun and scratch modestly through the hair just above his ears while the grass quietly peppered with docile bodies. Dogs would tug at their leashes, or trot freely forward until their heads dropped and they lay down over their folded paws, oblivious of any other calls on their attention.

Pigeons came the closest – like doves to Saint Francis, she supposed. They were almost frightening. Completely silent handfuls of breathing feathers, they watched Suzanne with their golden-ringed, blood-coloured eyes as if she was the one point in their world that was out of place.

So she loved when it was cold and inhospitable outside their apartment. Today there could be no question of their stepping out and upsetting the balance of nature again.

A person, traumatically deafened, loses vital clues to his or her surroundings. The patterns and rhythms of reality subside. Moving into one room from another may be almost unbearable, walking out of the house, an impossibility.

'Let's take a walk.'

Ben frowned at her elbows where they leaned on the kitchen table. Suzanne made sure she kept them exactly as they were, even though her position was not entirely comfortable and seemed, in fact, to put an odd kind of pressure on her lower back. She knew that Ben's mother had kept both his elbows strictly under decades of savage control. Ben's elbows had never leaned, or even loitered. Even now, he could react quite oddly to certain expressions of physical ease.

'Suzanne? I said, let's take a walk. We can go to Reuben's, you like Reuben's.'

Every single thing she liked: he remembered them all. Yes to fellatio – if you don't shove, no to rye bread – however you hide it. Yes to cotton and 'Disaster Chronicles' and latkes. No to Gingrich, no to ragtime, no to lox. No to ever changing your mind.

'Reuben's. I don't know. They give you so much there, I hate to waste all that food.'

'Everyone gives you that much. We all eat over here, remember?'

'Yeah.'

'Come on. We can get dressed up warm and hold hands in our mittens, it'll be great. We did it last February, right? I didn't even think we'd have snow. Not this year. I'll go look for my boots.'

Ben preceded her down the front steps and onto the street. Up above, their apartment windows were a blank dark, as if there were no glass there and no successfully co-ordinated furnishings behind, as if where they lived had become an interval between floors.

The streets were trudging and stumbling with figures very much like Ben. Men and women wore ear-bands and woollen hats, insulated parkas and rubber hoof shoes, as if this was their perfectly natural winter coat. They were nothing but sturdy and courageous. Although Suzanne was kitted out in much the same way, the hallway mirror had already proved she looked more than averagely out of place. She did not seem sturdy, only clumsily fat. Her hat reduced her face to imbecility while she wore it and when she took it off, she knew, it left her with an elasticated forehead scar one might very easily associate with recent and major cranial surgery. She didn't want to be outside like this.

'Come on now, better keep moving. Minus thirteen. You're not in motion, it'll bite. We've got time to make a loop – explore some.'

'You can't make loops here, you can only make rectangles.'

'Yeah. You're right. But you know what I mean.'

She didn't want to walk with him, but she did, all across Midtown and down into Murray Hill. The ice wind scalded her ears and made every colour ache and soar under the empty, frozen light. Suzanne sweated and slithered, oddly cosy between intersecting walls, the safe and solid slabs of Hudson River Gothic or blinding glass. Ben right-angled their route according to the well-patterned hopes of buildings that a New World, a world without conscience, loved to produce. An odourless death by refrigeration was snapping in wait for the unsightly, but there was nothing unsightly to be seen. All was suddenly, numbingly clean.

'Like to check out your favourite terminal?'

She would have liked to. Attentive Ben, considerate Ben, omniscient Ben, was right; Grand Central Station was somewhere she truly and unreservedly loved. She had never changed her mind about it, or grown tired of its peculiar, marbled intimacy. Despite its utter lack of visible trains, Suzanne had been nowhere quite so much to do with transportation. She could not walk into the concourse, look up at the clock, without feeling something pump underfoot. The whole place was a licking and breathing and hauling Westward compulsion. The indicator board alone could make her long for covered wagons, for a licence to drive recreationally, for any way to be away and never mind if it ended in tears.

Among its many clacking revolutions, the indicator sometimes showed a train was due to leave for the best-sounding place in America, for Far Rockaway. It wasn't Far: only beyond the airport, out at the ocean's side, but she'd never been there. The idea of it was too lovely to risk visiting.

'Want to step inside? Out of the cold?' Ben began to steer her down Vanderbilt without waiting for a reply.

Pioneering and migrant hardships – forces which nourish a need for self-defence – have shaped the American character in both lovely and ugly ways. I am an immigrant. My hardships are negligible, but I may still learn to develop an interest in certain forms of personal protection. I can become a survivalist.

'I'm not really all that cold yet, Ben. We can walk some more.'

'You don't want to go in? We're right there? It would be no problem. Are you feeling okay?'

'I'm feeling great. They've cleared the streets so well, we could get down to the Village and back.'

'Streets.' Ben squeezed her hand as if a wife who spoke a mildly different language was exactly the quality artefact he had been longing to acquire. But as they passed the Terminal building without a pause, he didn't speak.

'Ben?'

'Yes? We can turn back if you'd like. You want anything? Anything I can do?'

'Well, maybe if you let go my hand. There isn't really a path here for two of us side by side. Could you go ahead?'

Quick on the draw. In the context of pencils rather than pistols, this could still be a considerable threat.

'Yes, I could go ahead. Are your legs tired? You want to stop? We could go back and get a coffee and fat-free cranberry muffins. You like them.'

'No. That's fine.'

Ben slid very slightly as he repositioned himself on the ice. He caught at her arm.

'Careful, Ben.'

'I'm fine, I'm fine. You do still want to go to Reuben's? Suzanne?'

'Oh, I don't know. I hadn't decided. I'm enjoying the walking so much.'

Attack need not always be attack, it can be pre-emptive defence.
This is an American lesson and quite easy to learn.

'Ben, I was wondering – '

'What?'

'Have you ever been in a desert? Somewhere with sand
and lonely highways and motels here and there, maybe gas
stations.'

'Gas stations?' He was finding it hard to turn back and
speak to her without losing his balance. Plumes of breath
and heat moved around his head.

'Mm hm.'

'No, I'm a city boy. I was out in Akron once, that's
about as far West as I've gone. One of the old rubber-tyre
families was clearing a house. For sure, there's nothing
there, but it isn't a desert. Why? Would you like to see
a desert? Vacation out there?'

Vacation in Far Rockaway. Alone. Come back with a pencil.
Bang. Bang.

'No. No thank you. I didn't mean anything personally.
I was only thinking.'

'You think more than anyone I know.' He tried a
smile.

'I really can't help it. That's how I am.'

ANIMAL

Everyone turned a blind eye to this, but he still wasn't sure if he should. It was theft.

Kind of. In anyone else, this definitely would be stealing, but this was him and he'd never taken anything illegally in his life. The spirit was more important than the act and because he wasn't a thief, he couldn't be thieving. But then maybe that was how thieves always thought, he couldn't be sure. Mark only knew this whole procedure was making him smile, with his mouth and then his thinking. He was imagining all of larceny's possible possibilities taking him far and away out of character.

Not that he didn't have help, a partner in crime. From somewhere in the storeroom, Sally would be watching him smiling and making up his mind when actually, he didn't want her to watch – not if he couldn't watch her back.

'Sally? I don't know what to take. Now I'm here, I think there's too much for me to pick. I can't decide. Where are you?'

Mark pulled another few shirts along the rail and waited. He was hoping that Sally would feel she could give him advice. Sally never said much, but whatever she managed did tend to be good. He supposed she might talk more in other places, but here was where she did her job and part of her job was silence. Back at home she probably rattled on. He liked to think of her rattling on.

'What do you reckon? Help me out.'

In the concreted and ducted stillness, all those hard cold surfaces, he could hear a comfortable noise. He didn't need to look, Mark was absolutely certain without checking that he felt Sally and no one but Sally, walking up closer to stand in snug at his shoulder and slightly behind.

This move could look quite intimate when she made it with anyone else, but she made it with almost everyone else quite often and meanwhile her manner was only formal, expressing a rigidly business-like interest. No nonsense, not a bit. She set herself democratically, unpassionately close, as if she were a coffee table or a sewing machine. Except, of course, that she would watch and stroll – and speak a little, now and then – which made her not like a coffee table or a sewing machine at all, and also her positioning meant her sentences touched your cheek and warmed your hair, as if the inches between your body and her mouth had been abducted suddenly. Sewing machines and coffee tables never made him feel the way she did.

The way that would hit just a little before you expected.

'What about his shoes?'

That felt close, that felt drowningly close.

'Hm?'

'His shoes.'

She could be so ideally excruciating.

And you never could be in a position to see if she was any nearer with you than average. No one would give an opinion on that because either they didn't notice the times when you were together with her, or else were considering nothing except her distance away from them. You got no help.

'He wasn't like you as a character, but he wore nice shoes.'

'Fuck, you're right.' Mark noticed the beginning of a shudder in his neck. 'I mean – sorry – you're right. He had great shoes. What about the black pair?'

'Over there, but I don't know about them ... You definitely want the black?'

Wanting to see how she meant that, Mark began to execute a turn. Naturally, somebody standing so close to his back was not really a problem, but if they came face to face, the lack of space dividing them would really start to seem quite odd, so as well as spinning round, he tried to ease himself away. Politeness was important and he intended to stay polite, not to brush her with — for example — the inside of his arm, the nakedest, softest part where his elbow folded and where sometimes he would have the sensation of lack, or want, a kind of rodent shiver that no one else should touch.

The shirt-rail blocked his retreat and made him clumsy. As he stepped against it, the whole of the structure squealed and swayed and he turned and returned and began to think of blanket apologies for being generally the way and the type of man he was, but Sally had already gone to look out his shoes.

Nice that she said the character wasn't like him. People — even people in the business — would see you playing this utter shit once a week; every episode, something worse. They would see you in the studio, trying to be fine around people *as yourself*, but trying to remember the way that *he* would be, and they would get confused. Even the other week, that make-up girl — admittedly the stupid one, but even so — she'd said, 'You laugh just like Dr Barber.'

Well, Mark didn't laugh like Dr Barber; Dr Barber laughed like Mark. And never the twain should meet. Sally, he was sure, understood that far better than anyone. She would know that roles could change, but Mark would have to be there underneath them, every time. He had to be consistent. He was all he'd got. Keep that straight, or everything went.

'Did you hear me? Mark?'

'I'm um . . . the black would be wrong? Black shoes?'

'Nothing to do with me, but how often do you wear dark clothes?' She was so good with continuity, picked up every consistency and every change.

'*He* did all the time. Barber.'

'I know he did. I made sure he did. I'm asking about you. Like now – you're in browns and greens. Added to which,' She knelt and opened a cardboard box, 'He wore the black shoes a lot. These,' She lifted a pair of brown brogues he was sure he hadn't seen before, 'Can't have been on him more than once.'

'I don't remember them.'

'Episode in the country-house hotel where he's banging that nurse.'

'Oh, my God, that's hundreds of years ago. Were you here then?'

'Of course. You just hadn't noticed me.'

'Oh.' A good script could have put words to say there which would have been witty and complimentary and able to stop the round, acid pain he now had, eating at his chest. 'Well, my loss, eh?'

Eh? He hadn't said that since he was at school. In fact, he hadn't said that *at school*. The big fuckwit with the monkey eyebrows had said it all the time and for five years it had annoyed Mark horribly. Five years. *Eh?*

Sally didn't look horribly annoyed. She lifted one shoe by the heel and tried to let it swing from her thumb, rather jovially, but instead it slipped and battered to the floor.

'Oh.'

'I'll get it.' Mark began to step forward.

'No, I'll get it.'

He really should try for it. 'No, let – '

'Not at all.'

It was sometimes hard to be effectively polite. 'I coul – '

'I'm closer.' Sally dipped smartly down and retrieved the brogue while Mark concentrated on avoiding a clash of foreheads, or of anything else. There was no need to be too insistent about half a pair of shoes.

'That's fine then. You're right.'

'I was closer.' She spoke with her eyes lowered, examining sides, heel, stitching for signs of harm.

'You were, yes, you were closer.'

'No damage done.'

'Damage?'

'To your shoe. I wouldn't want to have scratched it.'

'I wasn't thinking of damage. I mean, I would probably deserve damage. These aren't my shoes I'm taking, they're Barber's shoes, the company's shoes.'

'Don't worry about it.' Sally slipped his stolen good beside its partner in the box and handed the whole assembly across to Mark. 'That's that, then. You can go?'

'I suppose I can, yes.'

Not in any way the answer Mark had hoped to give. For some reason, he had supposed this might all have taken longer. Theoretically, they could have skulked around Wardrobe for ages. Perhaps Sally would have had to go and be busy somewhere else, but she naturally would have trusted him not to run off with the whole of her inventory and possibly would have nodded to him reassuringly before she slipped upstairs. It would not have been out of the question for her to tell him he shouldn't go – at least not until she'd come back to be nicely curious about whether he'd found out a good souvenir; whether he was sad the series had finished, or happy to be moving on.

In the pause they seemed to be sharing, Mark stared at the box, hoping it might suddenly assume a new significance that he could talk about. Then she spoke. Sally spoke.

'You must feel strange, knowing it's all going on without you, upstairs. Different people, different sets.'

'It's not going on without me, it's going on without Dr Stuart Barber the all-purpose bastard, finally killed in a glamorous but economical, off-screen skiing accident.'

'I never knew he skied.'

'No, neither did I. But they'd already had a car crash and a drowning. And I think a drive-by shooting would have been out. They were trying to be up-market, after all.'

'And the ladies wouldn't want you disfigured. Not their sexy Dr Barber. They'll like to take time imagining you breathing your last in the ice, all packed down neat and frozen. Like those vacuum-sealed joints of meat.'

'Charming.'

'You know what I mean.' She sounded slightly gentle there − trying to be sympathetic for him, or to him, or with him − so maybe he would push it. Not for any reason, just to see, just to play, just to be talking for a little while more.

'No I don't. How do you mean, *the ladies wouldn't want . . . ?*'

'I mean your lady fans.'

'What fans?'

'You get letters.'

'People will write to anyone.'

'Well, obviously. They write to you.'

That's what happens when you push, people push back. 'Yeah, anyway, it'll be good to get away.' Not the right thing, not what you're thinking. 'To be in something shorter. Theatre maybe for a while. There's this thing coming up . . .' He wanted to say a substantial phrase now, one that would count. 'I have enjoyed it here.' Feeble.

'Good.'

'I mean it.'

'Good.'

'It's nice to be a bastard at work. I think it makes me a better person, gets it out of my system. Any badness. Feel free to stop me and agree.'

'You haven't been temperamental.'

'Mh hm.'

'You haven't hit anyone. Stabbed anyone.'

'Mh hm.'

'Fucked anyone.'

He spent the longest time breathing in, as if someone had punched his lungs. 'Mh hm.'

'That was a guess.'

'Good guess. Yes indeed. On the nail. Easy going, that's me. To the point of invisibility.' Mark noticed the damp from his hands was mildly affecting the thin card of the box. It wasn't a great box, all round, not substantial. 'I wonder, do you have any string, I think this box could do with some string. I don't have the car today, so I'll be walking with it. Home. With the box.'

'I'll find you a carrier bag. There'll be one in the office. Come on, I can lock up here, now you've had your pick.'

'*Your* pick.'

'Whatever.'

He followed Sally through a succession of irrevocably closing doors and thought of the studio floor – it would be working while he was not.

'You know what I will miss?'

Her back was turned between him and an electronic keycode lock. Her shoulders were making nice, busy movements.

'Sally?'

'What will you miss.'

'The coughing. Did you ever notice how much everybody coughs?'

'No.'

'Yeah, all over the set: coughs and coughs and coughs. The nervous cough, the necessary cough, the preparatory cough, the prophylactic cough.'

'What, like a condom?'

'You'd cough if you swallowed a condom.'

'Serve me right.'

Mark laughed. Not intending to; only realising afterwards, in fact, that what she said had been funny. Or something that he wanted to laugh at which was probably the same thing.

'But as I was saying, I have never heard so many people

cough. Even the crew; everyone; you'd think we'd been limbering up for an opera. Fuck's sake.'

'I love to watch everything pointing the same way.' Sally paused with her arm across the office doorway. Inside there would be other people, Mark realised, and they wouldn't be alone any more and he would have to start behaving in a way he didn't want to at the moment. At the moment he wanted to find out more about being on his own with her. 'I love the way it flows.'

She wasn't even trying to go in, he noticed.

'Flows?'

'Mm. You would be there – for example – as Barber, caught in up against the set, the three walls out of four, and all around you there's the flow. Telescoping, sliding, gliding, swivelling, catching in everything you do. I always think – '

She thought about things, Sally, thought properly, that's why she didn't talk too much.

'I always think it looks as if the booms and cranes and cameras are all part of . . . I don't know . . . an animal, and sometimes it lets people inside amongst itself so they can play. It's very beautiful.'

'And you keep the animal running.'

'The animal runs itself. But I help.'

'It does feel good sometimes . . .'

Stop her opening the door. Be expansive. Be yourself. If possible, slightly better than yourself.

'Not really on this thing, but . . . well, there was the speech he makes about the hospital – about how much cheaper it is to build and equip a psychiatric hospital than a medical one and then you make so much money out of phoney therapies and all of that medical insurance and then when the suckers' cover expires, they're instantaneously cured? That was good. And I could look around while I did it. I could see your animal. I suppose.'

'You were watching my animal?'

28

'Yes. I was watching.'

'Go on, then.'

'Go on?'

It didn't sound as though there was anyone in the office. Either that, or they were being very quiet.

'Do the speech. I'll bet you can remember it.'

'No. Not now.'

'Do the beginning. Go on. Jesus *I* remember it. We had to do it often enough. The boom shadow was all over the place, like a fucking albatross.'

'Yes. Yes, that's right. You do remember things, don't you? Well, correct me if I'm wrong, then. Ah . . .

'. . . *I would like to say something, gentlemen, ladies. I would like to say something right now. Thirty-six per cent. I'll let you hear that again. Thirty-six per cent. Profit. Minimum. Remember the number, it's important.*'

He stopped.

'What?'

'Oh, just that I used to make him think *I am the centre of the Lord's Creation, I am, I am, I am.* And that morning, we both were. Me and Dr Barber, we were the en-tire fucking show.'

'Dr Barber and I.'

'Whatever.'

He'd been right, there was no one in Sally's office. She bent over smoothly, neatly and pulled a carrier bag from a drawer.

'There.'

Mark had forgotten he wanted one. 'Oh. Oh, yes. Thanks.' Of course, once it was in the bag, the box opened slightly and one of the shoes began to loll out which didn't matter particularly but was an irritation. He wanted to do something about it, but couldn't think what.

Sally perched at the edge of the desk and smiled at him. Mark thought he had never met a smile before which had been so remarkably at him.

'That's you, then. All fixed up.' She extended a hand, opened and ready for shaking. 'Mark? Are you okay?'

As soon as he touched her fingers, they would be over. His last chance for not too much that he could put specifically into words would have expired before its definitions could be framed. He reached forward to Sally and felt himself begin to descend an interior slope. The closer he came to her body, the further away she seemed to be.

She almost smiled. 'I'm sorry about the fucking.'

'Hm?' He felt a roll of sweat glove him in up to his forearm, unpreventable and unclean. In a thin, airless way, he said, 'About the . . . ?'

'My guess. I didn't mean I thought you couldn't have. You're professional, that's what I meant. You wouldn't go over the lines with someone at work.'

'At work?' They hadn't even started shaking each other's hands, they were just stuck in a frozen grip with no way to break it, because they were still talking and watching eye to eye and he was sweating from his elbow to his fingertips. When somebody touched you, sweat was so obvious.

'There are boundaries, aren't there? Chinese walls. Otherwise we'd have the personal thing, inside the professional thing, and the sexual thing and then that's all inside some other kind of thing again – it would be a maze. I couldn't keep up with the flow, with the animal, if that was going on as well, could you?'

'I've never . . . No.'

'You were very professional, Mark. Good to be around. Good.'

'Thank you.'

'We'll miss you.'

'Well, we'll miss – ' he coughed without being able to cover his mouth, '*I'll* miss you. All of you. Of the crew.'

'Good. Bye, then.'

'Yeah, bye.'

Mark didn't know if Sally was looking at him, because he himself was staring towards a far corner of the room. She let go his hand, stood and opened the door for him, held it while he passed. There was no opportunity for him to touch her again, other than accidentally, and there were no accidents.

Out in the passage, Mark let a kind of heaviness round his shoulders push him on and make him chill. He moved as if an odd music was breaking the rhythm of his step. This wasn't the proper finale, wasn't good, and the wrong tune to close their scene with had begun playing, somewhere near his hips.

GROUCHO'S MOUSTACHE

I always believed in Groucho's moustache. He had me fooled completely. I had never met a man who would simply colour his top lip black instead of growing bristles, so I looked at him in his pictures but never really saw. Instead of a monstrously obvious joke, I saw a face to believe in, a face I could trust.

I do so love to trust. I've passed many jolly years growing used to being made this way. When I was still a very little girl, for example, another very little girl told me that my rather unnoticeable nipples were really insect bites.

I had not yet given them much thought, but when I did, what she said seemed very sensible to me and so I spent a fortnight dabbing myself with disinfectant creams. On finding no sign of improvement in my condition I finally asked my mother what more I might do.

God, how she laughed. I don't think I ever saw her laugh so long and hard and truly joyfully at any other thing I said. It was a special moment for us both which I'm glad I was there to be part of.

Thinking back, I can see times like that helped me to find a different attitude towards deception. In fact, today there's nothing I would choose to class as a deception. Today I have Educational Encounters. That is to say, bad things happen, but they make me learn. And when very bad things happen very frequently I learn like anything, for which I am very genuinely grateful. Sometimes I will wake early in the morning and immediately, spontaneously, I can hear myself say 'Thank you.' Thank you: those two words will be up in the air when my eyes and thoughts are barely open. That's how deep my gratitude goes – it's awake before I am.

Think of it from where I'm standing and you'll know why. I have been allowed to benefit from decades of in-life, intensive, private education. Naturally, this is the kind of privilege one has to pay for and sometimes the fees have been painfully steep, but being gulled and fooled and tricked, cheated, hoodwinked, bamboozled, hocus-pocussed, befuddled, taken a loan of, generally misguided, sold a dud load of snake oil and just plain lied to, undeniably sets my neurones firing like nothing else will. Some days I won't even make it to lunchtime before I can feel my synapses fizz and shine with skullduggery.

I am, you must understand, a particular kind of person. I am the exact opposite of, or complement to, a Deceiver. I am a Receiver and my life has become quite wonderful since I've known that. Now I have a direct line, straight to my fundamental nature. I can go about my business in safety, unassailably certain that no matter what dangerous, stupid, superstitious, or hand-me-down nonsense I am offered, I'll swallow it whole and smile. In some situations, where I find myself inflamed by a particularly virulent faith, I can even withdraw without taking any especially disastrous action. I will still believe powerfully, but I need not act on my belief and, in the end, my whole situation, no matter how sad, will educate.

Better than that, the odds against all this lovely, gullible learning ever fading to a close are almost infinitely high. Public joy and social well-being may break out universally at dawn, galaxies may open their secrets to all red-headed men called Frank, while dodos sweep our sunsets in thousands of chirruping skeins, but I will remain no better than myself – as big a dope as ever.

The Receiver has a settled place, right at the bottom of the information chain – like those mud-coloured fish that flutter over the ocean bed, hoovering through the sewage drifts and liberated isotopes. To be honest I have not always relished this role. I still surprise myself with daydreams about choking this or that flagrant liar by pushing a hatchet into their windpipe. I can no longer eat taramasalata because of gently recurring fantasies that involve me ripping out the lungs of various statesmen, broadcasters, tobacconists, bar-room gossips, bus drivers and partners-for-life. I picture myself, spreading their warm and slippery lungs across enormous linoleum floors and then stamping them into paste. The paste looks uncannily like taramasalata, the very scent of which now always sets me wondering how hard it would be to clean ground-in lung paste out of shoes.

Of course, nothing terribly anatomical ever really arises during deceptions, other than the relationships. In relationships, the whole world sees me coming and, oddly enough, I can see it coming, too. Never mind the starter's orders, we are off. Receiver and Deceiver, both uncovered, we recognise each other instinctively, like lemmings rushing together so they can free-fall holding paws. Our essential natures are ready, beneath our actions and our minds, whimpering to nuzzle up and bend reality right around until it bites its tail.

I cross over a road, join a checkout queue, cast off into a party and within seconds I will be aware of a current, a kind of invisible psychic lasso. This force will catch me up like a rip tide and then drop me down face to face with the least suitable candidate available for intimate contact. We will have been made for each other. Intellectually I will be certain I am offering small talk to a practising necrophile bigamist, or exchanging pleasantries with a man far too recently freed from padded surroundings, but I will be powerless in the grip of my own nature. My new friend will wink up with his tiny red eyes, dab the stale baby's blood from his fangs and clutch my hand between his hairy palms, happy that we are already such a team.

Except it's neither as simple, nor as obvious as that. I do not continually wear a forehead tattoo, announcing

PERSON WOEFULLY UNREADY FOR ADULT RELATIONSHIPS

and none of my Educational Encounters have hinted their psychological good health by flourishing SS daggers or being unable to produce shadows and reflections when required. It is more than likely I will not know I am participating in a disaster until I am participating in a disaster.

For example, I am sure it is not a good idea to trust oneself to a person who bases their behaviour on a small repertoire of easily available video tapes. In that case, we parted primarily because of simultaneous ill-health, but I then spent several months discovering uncannily familiar dialogue in television weekend matinees. I had always suspected the doctor in 'The Railway Children' was working to a seamy, hidden agenda and I have to say my worst fears have been confirmed at a very personal level.

Naturally, a number of my encounters were also on intimate terms with other women. I had in no sense happened to see them out coaching a Peruvian exchange student through her Vocabulary For Evasively Illuminated Restaurants; they had not spent a dull evening away, comforting a tragically castrated school-chum; they had not at all woken before dawn to slip outside and telephone their auntie after a dream predicting the winner of the Cheltenham Gold Cup. These were tedious fibs that even I would see through, sooner or later.

Far more instructional were the men who presented themselves under completely false identities. In order to begin a liaison, they would impersonate quieter, cleaner, funnier, more tolerant, flexible, tender and even moustachioed men. Having secured their position as one man, they would then become another. Those who had cooked would stop and those who hadn't would start. It occurred to me that, as I gradually discovered an incompatible stranger in my life, some other bemused woman was probably waking up, stomach to stomach, with a man steadily revealing himself to be just the chap for me.

Finding this all just a little too much, I took to lying in the bath with my ears under water and breathing loudly while thinking of the Islands of Galapagos. I would see them from time to time on the television, every volcanic fissure packed with under-evolved misfits like me. I was beginning to feel real empathy with the mad, blue-footed seabirds and their waggling landings, not to mention the dim-wit flamingos. My place must really be out there with the iguanas, happily stuffing their toes under the rocks and rasping at seaweed, or floating off roughly in the direction of Chile. Even a tortoise could be contented down there and safe for centuries. As long it didn't meet up with too many people.

But I wasn't only in the bath to meditate on natural history. I was also avoiding going to bed with Matthew the body sculptor. He would be lying in wait, coyly horizontal, bronzed and glazed to the point where his skin tone was almost identical to that of a Chinese-style duck. It made me hungry just to look at him, but in all the wrong ways.

Matthew had never pretended to be anything other than a body sculptor, his honesty had been scrupulous on that point. He had, however given the impression that I would get a little more of his attention than his friends at the gym, or his mirrors. My first clue that all was not well arrived with the eight-foot-high triple mirror he gave me for my bedroom. This addition to our nights and days had nothing to do with eroticism and everything to do with marks out of ten for artistic impression and technique.

I was staying relatively sane throughout our affair by

39

taking long, late-night baths and then feigning uncon-
sciousness before I hit the mattress. Our performance was
suffering.

Matthew took this as a sign of athletic failure rather than
any lack of adoration on my part. He bought me my very
own membership for his second-best health club. At the
time, I didn't feel inclined to use it.

And as one of Matthew's baked and basted chums folded
his mirrors under one enormous armpit and waddled off,
I knew that another romance was over with no sign of a
positive pay-off even nudging the horizon.

Then I went to the gym and the dawn dawned.

Ladies' Days at the gym are nothing short of a spiritual
experience. Naturally, the rows of graded barbells and the
swinging, dipping machines to pull and push and press and
pump are all available. It is very possible to go there and
get fit. But the locker rooms, the locker rooms will change
the way you see the world forever. There is nothing quite
like them.

Women are amazing. The physical reality of women is
enough to turn your brain. Yes, being in a room full of
nude and semi-nude men would have a certain interest,
too, but it would be very limited, specific, sexist. The
Ladies' Locker Room, that's about me, about what I am.

You see, I had never – apart from Matthew – really
moved in sporting circles. The mysteries of mass changing
were a revelation.

I picked my way, pale and shuffling, through steam
and swimsuits, benches, limbs and quiet conversation.
Around me there were women like triumphant ice-cream
sundaes, scoop upon dimpled scoop of cellulite all balanced
above girlish ankles and tiny feet. Women the colour of
coffee tables bounded into the saunas, their entire body
surface one perfectly maintained tension. Glistening lady
pensioners strolled in towels, the flicker of serious muscle
stalking under every smile. And all of us there to uncover

a touch more power in ourselves with every worked-out hour. There were days when I felt I was showering with the start of a master race.

And then I realised what made me keep on coming back – it was me. I had begun to need the calm, the almost post-coital training afterburn that would leave even me stepping languidly back from the showers and towelling down without a fragment of self-consciousness. I had also developed an appetite for uncut determination, mainline focus, the crackle in the air above a room full of women who are doing only and precisely what they want. I enjoyed being there. I enjoyed being myself.

I was looking good. That's the kind of thing they say in these places. 'Looking good!' they shout, as you fold yourself around one or another machine and tease a muscle group until it pops. I could almost see what Matthew had seen in Matthew. Looking good.

Then a funny thing happened. Part of the gym's little extras are provided in the form of classes where row after row of bodies watch their mirror image thrusting and kicking and twisting in uncanny unison. Thanks to Matthew, I was more than a little at home with the general scenario. Suitably rhythmic music bumped and ground while we simultaneously did what we were told, trusting that it would be good for us in the long-to-medium-distance run. Our wonderfully healthy situation was only unusual in one respect. The ladies and the gentlemen both took the classes together – we were mixed.

One evening the largely female ranks of thrusters and kickers and twisters made room for a stocky little man. You know the kind of build – looks as if he's been dropped off a tall building at some point, heavily compacted, but I found him attractive. Attractive in a very limited, specific and sexist way.

I can only say I felt we were divinely intended for each other. Knowing me as I did, this could only mean that he was some kind of ghastly multiple murderer, or heavily involved with drugs and daytime television, so I avoided him like an acid bath on every possible occasion. Wherever he stationed himself in the workout studio, I would move myself to the furthest possible point. Whenever I overheard him in conversation, I would whistle, or hum, or mutter to screen out his voice, cherishing tiny hopes of appearing contagiously eccentric and unapproachable. In short, whatever he did, I made sure I was doing the antidote. Until the last session.

I let my guard down then, I admit it, and that rip tide got me, the same as ever.

'You've been avoiding me.'

'No.'

'Yes, you have.'

'Yes, I have, then. I have to go now.'

'You're doing it again.'

'Mm hm.'

'I don't mind being avoided, I just wondered why.'

And then I failed completely to keep a grip, was carried away, lost like a gallstone in an acid bath.

'I have my reasons.'

'Yeah?'

'Yes.'

'Oh, well.' One of his feet was making a kind of sketching movement on the floor while he stared down at it idly. It's hard not to find that endearing, not to make a conversational surrender.

'Would you like me to tell you about them?'

'Your reasons?'

'Yeah.'

'I would like that.'

We went for coffee. Which is not a criminal offence. Not necessarily.

Moments were passed in staring at inanimate objects, making little noises and nodding.

'Hmmn.'

'I'm sorry?'

'Oh, just . . .'

'Hmmn.'

Then he opened fire.

'Tell me, have you ever considered that if you find a person particularly noticeable in a way that preys on your mind this might mean that you are, somehow, fundamentally alike? Do you think something inside ourselves occasionally really pushes for us to make children that are going to be more of the same, only doubled, if you see what I mean? Do you think those feelings would be reciprocated?'

He was clearly not the type to beat about bushes, so I didn't either.

'Yes, I don't know, and yes.'

'And were your answers in random, alphabetical or chronological order?'

'Would it matter?'

'Not really. I was only building up to ask you why you've been avoiding me.'

'I like you.'

'That's nice.'

'I find you very attractive.'

'That's nice, too . . . only now I sense a blow being softened.'

'I want to spend more time with you.'

'But . . . ?'

'But I have suicidally appalling taste, always have done.'

'Thanks a lot.'

'You're welcome.'

We smiled at each other, his expression one of trust which was alarming because it probably reflected something very similar of my own. I couldn't help but notice that he had a pleasant face, slightly heavy, even stupid around the mouth, but with bright, clean eyes – comfortable for dipping into.

★　　★　　★

Filled with worrying hopes at our second meeting, I waited for signs of fiction, of information withheld.

'What do you do, though, you haven't told me?'

He shrugged.

'You're unemployed?' I imagined he might be something freelance, like a burglar.

'No. No, I work, but I don't talk about it. There you are, my dark secret. My job.'

'It so happens I don't like secrets.'

'Tell you later. Maybe.'

I was still unhappy, surges of contentment were tempting me to lower my guard. Our relations meanwhile took on a will of their own. One evening I caught myself relaxing in his tidy, average, quiet-man-next-door-we-could-never-have-imagined-doing-something-so-awful kind of flat. I thought we might pass the time by talking.

'Tell me what you do, then.'

'No.'

'Why not?'

'I don't have to.'

'No, you don't have to. You don't have to at all. I just thought you might like to; you might feel a need to volunteer that kind of information.'

'No. I don't think so.'

'This is ridiculous. I mean, we're bound to go to bed together soon – tonight – because we can't do much else, but you're refusing to tell me how you earn your living.'

'I'm not refusing, I'm delaying. And what do you mean, "We can't do much else"? Are you implying I'm boring? You've exhausted all my possibilities?'

'No, I don't mean that, but now you've changed the subject.'

'I know. Because I might want to be seduced a touch; romanced. I might want to know more about you. I'm a sensitive person, you know.'

'A sensitive man – you don't happen to be a vegetarian cannibal, too?' I'll admit I felt slightly ashamed as soon as I'd said that, but only a little. I was annoyed.

'As it happens, I am a man and sensitive, thank you very much. As I shall demonstrate. Stand aside, please.'

This said, he strode to the middle of his living-room floor, inhaled once and took off his clothes, quite simply, as if he were about to take a shower.

'A naked man is much more vulnerable, culturally speaking than a naked woman. Here I am. Vulnerable.'

'Well of course you're vulnerable now, I'm still dressed and you're not.' It occurred to me then he was being rather sneaky. 'You're being rather sneaky.'

'I don't know what you mean. Well, maybe I do. There would, after all be one way to prove the validity of my argument. By equalising the condition of both subjects . . .'

'If I was . . .'

'Mm hm.'

'Sneaky.'

So I undressed too; I wouldn't say angrily but certainly with the air of proving a point. Then I stood, slightly out of breath and really not feeling naked in any way. The locker room had certainly had an effect. I was able to stand and stare at this man (whose name happened to be Ian) and feel perfectly at ease.

'I can't see any difference in status. We're about the same height. You're physically stronger, but, oh look, I can see the whole structure of society lining up behind you in the distance – it appears to be on your side.'

There was something powerfully ludicrous about two naked people, each surrounded by a scatter of clothing, standing with their arms politely folded and engaging in psycho-sexual debate.

'As the man, I feel more at risk.'

'Nonsense.'

'Women are far more resilient . . . you have incredible pain thresholds . . .'

'We need them. Listen, I'm one of the oppressed majority . . . and I've had difficulty adjusting to my breasts . . . I had a bad experience with nipples . . . somewhere in the back of my mind, I still see them as a sign of ill-health and insect attack.'

'What about masturbation. Men get dreadfully guilty about that.'

'We're not even supposed to know how.'

Part of me wanted to continue our discussion, but it was no good, my attention was slipping off our subject. 'Are you cold?'

'Yes. And I think I need a hug. That would make me feel less vulnerable.'

'So at this point I should probably ask if you practise safe sex.'

'Isn't it odd, the way that two separate people can think of the same thing at once? Yes I do.' He smiled, but not unpleasantly.

'Do you happen to have a bed?'

'I left one around here, somewhere.'

'Let's go to it.'

'Let's go to it? You sound like a netball coach.'

'Well, what do you want me to say?'

'I don't know. *Let me take you away from all this?*'

'Let's go to it.'

So we did.

And I even found a moment to reflect on the many unforeseen advantages a cultivation of physical fitness can produce.

Later, I lay with the movement of Ian's breath beside me, proving he was relaxed but still awake. I thought of our two bodies laid out together like the ones on the posters down at the gym. They showed a man with a full, luxurious head of hair, posed like a jazz dancer, rolled hips

46

and open palms and all of him peeled clear down to the muscle and the little bones in his feet. Front and back views. My role-model woman was equipped with another impressive scalp of free, tousled hair and red eyes. Her transparent body was filled with vari-coloured organs, all horribly damaged by the effects of cigarettes and alcohol. They made a lovely couple.

'All right, then.'

'Hm?'

'I'm an embalmer.'

'You're what?'

'I know, it always comes as a nasty surprise. People wonder where I've been. If I've washed my hands.'

'No, you're what? I couldn't hear.' I rolled in to face him.

'I am an embalmer. That's what I do. Sorry. I don't like to tell people straight away because they never take it well. Or they get off on it. You don't know how many women have asked if they could come down and do it where I deal with the bodies.'

'No.'

'Mm. I think it's a power thing. They like to think of the dead being there and listening, not able to stop us, or join in.'

'Maybe they're just glad they're alive.'

'Maybe. You're not into that, are you?' His eyes flinched very slightly.

'What, being alive?'

'Doing it with dead people around. I once did take a woman down there and then couldn't face seeing her again. It's not healthy . . . why are you smiling?'

Of course I was smiling, naturally I was, I could do nothing else. I had a huge, pattering emotion romping along the corridors of my heart and rocking my stomach. I had to smile. 'This is all the truth.'

'Yes, I know. Why would I lie? Spend your time sewing

up the orifices of dead strangers and you'll tend to get straight to the point when you're with someone living. Not that I don't often think where the living will end up. Me, included. Now that's really the truth.'

'No, I mean, you're telling me the truth, you're being honest.'

'Well, relatively.'

'What do you mean, exactly?'

He stroked his forefinger slowly from my shoulder to my elbow and grinned. I tried to worry as much as it seemed necessary I should.

'Don't try to put me off; what do you mean?'

'I mean what I did, just then. You do the same, go on. Feel my skin.'

'What?'

'Feel my skin. Anywhere you like. I trust you.'

I felt.

He smiled.

'There, I'm lying.'

'Look, I'm serious. I know you're lying – you're lying down – '

'Ah, no. I'm extremely serious, too. I'm telling you that what you feel there won't stay. What I feel, that won't stay either. We're nice and fit and healthy now, pretty young and pretty pretty, but it'll go – I've seen it gone. One day I'll be slow suddenly, one day I'll be grey, one day I'll just stop being anything. People think I'm morbid, but I only ever say what I see. And I have to be honest, I can't help it.'

He really was a man, a whole human being, who couldn't help being honest, couldn't even help admitting it.

'You're not morbid, you just have an interest in the truth. Me too.' That big tide was roaring in, the emotional seventh wave. My mind was surfing ahead of me and thinking of having children that would be more of the same as us, only double. An ocean-load of honest little people.

'Ian, you're being as honest as you can be. You are who you are, the age you are, the way you are.'

'For now.'

'That's all we've got.' When I held my breath to watch his face, I knew I loved him: I could hear it – like the pause before sunrise, or the small drumming of clean rain. 'Do you think I could feel your skin again?'

'If you want.'

'I want.'

And for one complete moment, 'I want' was the absolute truth.

MADE OVER, MADE OUT

'You're thinking about her again.'

'How do you know?' Kovacks' voice sounded weird to him. He hated the way it would go sometimes.

'I can tell.'

'How can you tell?' Still no good. Sounds batted around in here like curve-balls, faster or slower than he could expect. 'How can you tell?' There were laws about sound – he'd been brought up to believe he couldn't break them.

'I can always tell. You stop talking, you look at your schedule, but your eyes don't move, so there's no way you're reading it . . . your mouth gets tucked in . . . not a whole lot, but I know the way your mouth is when it's not tucked . . .'

'Not tucked . . .' Kovacks repositioned the bean seedlings and then ran a check on his ability to eat candy in a weightless environment; swimming vaguely after one piece and snapping it in, the way a chocolate-eating fish would. No matter how often he did that, it never pleased him any less. 'You falling in love with me, buddy? I mean, that's a lot of close attention I'm getting . . .'

'Gee, Don, maybe you're right. Take off your glasses for a moment while I think.' Alain bobbed up tentatively and sneaked an eccentricly-orbiting, sugar-coated peanut treat.

'Well, bud, you'll probably find that I don't wear glasses. We accredited test-pilot type of guys don't. And will you quit it with that – stealing a man's M&Ms – that's enough to push a fellow right over the edge.'

'Take it from me, Kovacks, you were born over the

edge. Your mother was lying on it and there you came – born over.'

'Born over.'

'A sad fact.'

Kovacks kicked his locker gently. 'Born over . . . Should be a bumper sticker.'

'Better than *Fly Navy.*' Alain nodded at one of Kovacks' attempts to personalise their numb white decor: a mildly contradictory, adhesive slogan. Like *Swim Dentistry.* He wished he'd never brought the thing, but of course he'd had to – it was part of his being the Navy's good boy.

'*Fly Navy.* Mm hm. You don't like that?' Kovacks manoeuvred left to nudge against Alain's shoulder while they synchronised grins quite harmoniously. 'So what do you know about the Navy, Mr Professor? Hn?'

Alain nudged him back and began to chuckle. Alain could get out of control with those chuckles, if Kovacks didn't watch him, but when they were left alone to each other matters would usually work out fine. They would talk themselves up a non-hostile environment.

'Bud? I'm waiting. Come on now, tell me everything you know. I can take it.'

Kovacks let Alain fold happily over himself, trying to keep a good handle on their positions. Then he nudged him again, 'You're nothing but a walking calculator, right?'

Alain hurried in a breath and managed to gulp out his line. 'That's right; I'm the tin man, you're the bird man.'

'You said it. And a bird man with a greater sense of justice could get all burned up over you. I had to fly my ass blue in the unlikeliest list of slings you could imagine to even have a chance of getting up here. Meanwhile, Alain Sablon; failed golfer – '

'I have a good handicap.'

'You have the hand–eye co-ordination of a deep-sea bass.'

'I hear that's a pretty handy fish.' They were both laughing now, but holding steady.

'Alain Sablon: failed golfer, failed lover – '

'Inadmissible evidence.' Alain punched the air and set himself into a softly inadvertent spin. 'That's an altogether different handicap.'

'I know, I read your file. Failed golfer, failed lover and failed human being . . .'

'But awesomely qualified physicist.'

Alain gave an uncontrolled bow while Kovacks let himself bob and whip a little for the hell of it. He was keeping his M&Ms boxed into a neat formation he could graze through as he felt the need. Alain made a swaying lunge for them now and then, but almost always missed the shot; he really didn't understand the first thing about flight.

'Yeah, that's right. Mr Physicist Alain Sablon spends twenty years polishing one buttock at a time behind a Canadian desk and then walks straight on to the Program. Life is unjust.'

'I don't know . . . sometimes I polished both buttocks at once, that must have been weighed in my favour.' He tapped at Kovacks companionably. 'Listen, that's a lot of ass and buttock references – you trying to tell me something?'

'You trying to ask?' Kovacks slooped in a monster mouthful of candy and then tried not to cough.

'If you'd learned to add up in high school, you could have been here in my place.'

'I like my place better.' Now he sounded sticky as well as weird.

'You could have slid your shiny buttocks right into the space race, no effort at all.' Alain floated gently and tightly in at him. 'What's she like? What do you think about when you think about her, hm?' Alain's words were managing to travel at precisely the pace they should. He sounded quite usual, exempt for the crazy accent – *about* turned into *aboat*; stuff like that.

'Tell me aboat her. What's she like?' Alain scratched his neck, as if he wasn't interested, but only asking to pass the time.

Kovacks knew better, knew Alain, and knew there was something about being up here – the schedules, the terrible turning of light and dark – that meant nobody messed around with time. If he caught a minute, he wouldn't lose it or waste it with questions he didn't care about.

'She's . . .' Kovacks felt an ignition of memory under his breast-bone while, up on the bridge, somebody answered enquiries from a long way away about the testing of units providing auxiliary power. Kovacks liked testing the APUs; the sequence of switches, the snapping down and in, was pretty good fun and looked as if he really knew his stuff, which was neat for the viewers at home.

'Alain, there's nothing to say about her. She's a long way away. That's everything important I could tell you; that's what she's like.'

'No. What is she like?'

Kovacks flipped the final candy to Alain and waited till he'd caught it; first time, too. A clean shot and efficient retrieval, the result of supportive teamwork in the field.

'You've met her – Holly is how Holly looks.' Kovacks knew, he could either tell this story again, the whole way, or shut up now. 'She looks like she'd be . . . enjoyable.' Another sentence and the move was made. 'And she is. She can be.'

Alain shut his eyes to listen. He tended to do that a lot which was probably an indication that he did not come from a combat-training background. Kovacks barely closed his eyes, even to sleep. Alain said this was not caused by combat training, but by raging paranoia. Kovacks was inclined to agree. 'You want the Holly First Night Story, then?'

'Yeah.'

'You know how it makes me . . .'

'You're like that anyway.'

'Okay . . . So. I was training, for the Test Pilot shit – I was already a flier and rolling higher by the day. I was a bird.'

Which was no exaggeration, Kovacks could feel the rip in his muscles right now, the ache that would shimmer in any time that he actually thought of having made it here again, of being in continuous free-fall somewhere thinner than thin air. He was in flight and therefore a happy man.

'I had the instincts of a miracle, could have stepped out on the clouds and just run around. And there I was, aiming every day for a chance at this tub, which handles like a cow on skates. But then again, I'm crazy.'

'You don't say.'

'Anyway, to summarise briefly; I was hot then – in my aviating boyhood – and Holly was hot, too.'

Why didn't that sound real?

'She wanted a flier, any flier at all.'

None of this sounded like his life, like anybody's life. Maybe because he'd told it so many times. More likely, because Kovacks' past was too different from his present to seem possible or true. Kovacks was very familiar with the savageries of change. Now he'd burst up and out to a universe where change was almost the only consistent law and this had come as no surprise.

'Holly then, she was crazy too. I liked that. I enjoyed when she didn't care. She didn't want to know who I was; what kind of man; my favourite leisure activities. Holly just wanted the best in the air and that was me. Top of the top 1%. Me, but only coincidentally. She made me feel so cheap, it was fantastic. *I* was *her* one night stand. You know?'

'We don't get a whole lot of that in Physics.'

'Bullshit. You've been married twice, you told me.'

'I've been divorced twice. That's a different thing.' Alain began smoothing out his sleeping restraint along a lack of gravity. 'Go on.'

'The first night, the very first night, she was dancing all over me – way close enough to feel what that did – and I looked to the back of her eyes and everything inside there was ready to go. She said – '

'Am I mistaken, or is that you?' Alain smiled in a dreamy kind of way and began to incline his feet towards his choice of horizontal.

'Yeah. Yes, she did. And I told her she was not mistaken and that I was taking an indecent interest in her feminine muscle tone and she said she was sincerely sorry we weren't out someplace lonely where we both could really exercise my mind.'

'In the parking lot.' Alain was a truly meticulous man – a consistent eye for the finer points and a memory to match.

'I would have taken her to a motel, but she wanted me there in the parking lot, in the passenger seat of her rather fine automobile. I couldn't believe it.'

In fact, Kovacks doubted it more every day. He could remember his wife precisely in details fast and hard enough to make him bleed, but he couldn't make her believable. Here, over the top of the world, he could feel the minute but constant whip of her attraction and yet not have the slightest faith in whatever they were or whatever they'd been.

'She turned her back to me, like I wasn't there, climbed in, unzipped me open and straddled down. No panties, clear all the way.'

He and Alain had agreed they would always pause there and allow each other room to think. Kovacks usually turned his mind to the instant within an ascent when inertia broke to zero gravity and the sum of himself seemed as it had been always, but now more lovely, more significant.

'Thanks, Don, you may proceed.' Alain nodded respectfully, satisfied with whatever ideas he'd been given by the thought of Kovacks' wife. Good friends could share things – that was reassuringly real.

'Well, I'm up there and quietly losing my mind and officers are walking by with their wives, I can hear voices I recognise and Holly's working me like a trick, but not saying one word. I unfasten the back of her dress – it's the kind with no straps and, after the dancing, I mostly know what I'll get – but she arches her back and sits closer and starts moving tight through the gears and doesn't stop me doing any damn thing that I'd like. I know there's no way that I'll have enough time to do all of the things that I'd like.'

Her breasts hadn't changed. Even after having Max, they were still the small, taut way he liked with a hungry type of nipple that could prickle up his skin; even through cloth, even in a look. And he'd always told her – one suck and he would know her anywhere. That was the kind of talk Holly wouldn't warm to. Not the brand of appreciation she wanted these days. And, of course, his voice would mostly sound weird while they were speaking and that couldn't help.

Weird, like it was today. 'She's pretty much nude to the waist now and if anybody wants to look our way, I'm finished, I am in a world of pain for ever and I do not care. I've got her in both my hands and she is over me like oil and moving like an F-86 and then she whispers, "Look."'

'And you look.'

Kovacks nodded, 'And there's this cute, older couple, arm in arm, walking maybe ten feet from the car. 'My mother and father.' That's all she says and then she comes around me like she's going to yank my brains out down my spine. Then I kind of hit the spot myself. By the time I had my head together, she was walking away. I think I called . . .'

That was the first time his voice had sounded wrong. He'd shouted into the space between the cars where he could see her and the one word he could offer had spiralled and flattened off as if it had never known him and didn't understand what he meant.

'I know I called to her, I said, "Thanks." She didn't turn.'

'Is any of that true?'

'Only everything. I am speaking of the night I truly lost my innocence.' Alain shook his head paternally while Kovacks propelled himself by fingertips into the open airlock and fumbled out the tether he'd use to stop his body drifting in its sleep. Imagine: a grown man dreaming on frictionless air, a loop around his ankle all that kept him from breaking away.

Back home he told Max about that kind of thing, but he could see the kid couldn't entirely accept his Papa's stories. Maybe Holly told him Kovacks lied. Kovacks, of course, did lie, but only to Holly. He would never lie to Max.

'You like it in there, hm?'

'What you say?' Kovacks had forgotten to listen again. Too much perspective could make his hearing slow and, off Earth, perspective was all he got. The seven other people here with him in infinity didn't really give him much protection from being borne over into solitude; into the largest and loveliest loneliness this side of possibility. They couldn't stop the temptation of being dreadfully free.

'I said, you like it there.'

'The airlock? Sure. And somebody has to sleep here. Unless you hadn't noticed, we don't have a whole lot of room.' Kovacks reached for his eyeshade – it was waiting in mid-air where he'd left it.

'But some people might get nervous, being unconscious

so close to a weak point in the ship. You don't ever worry you'll be sucked outside? Or maybe we'll wait till you're sleeping, then close up the hatch, let you out and wave goodbye.'

'As you say, I like it here.'

Kovacks slipped on the eyeshade and enjoyed the tiny buzz of true dark. He could stand most things, but the paintwork here drove him nuts – the type of yellowed white you'd expect to see on especially painful medical equipment or old institutional beds. If NASA went to all the trouble of packing them off with nice shrimp cocktails and pleasantly scented wipes, Kovacks reckoned they could put a little thought into the colour scheme. It would take more than *Fly Navy* or even *Idaho – Famous Potatoes* to do the trick. He should mention that in debriefing.

'Hey, buddy?'

'Yeah?'

'No. Forget it. Get some sleep.'

Kovacks wanted to talk some more, but he could hear Stubbs and Maclehose swinging their way down from topside to catch their own pieces of sleep. When Kovacks spoke to Alain, he didn't like the others around. This had been commented on adversely in one of his assessments, so he'd made an effort to shape up, but now they were out in orbit, he supposed he could pretty much do as he wanted to. Kovacks intended to fully enjoy being secretive. He wouldn't get another mission, he was too old, so he'd decided to behave a little badly, have some fun and remember things one thousand per cent clearly, so he could tell them out properly to Max.

Max was such a guy. Nearly three years old and he already stood like a guy: feet spread apart and his belly out and staring with the start of a pout in his lips, as if things had better be the way they ought to, or he'd have something pretty important and scary to say. He'd particularly strike that pose when he was nude, probably

guessing correctly that his slightly bandy legs and tiny
pecker made him look like a senile general surveying
some particularly sorry battalion of grunts.

'Papa, you're full of shit.'

Max adored saying that. He was smart, he knew it
would get a reaction. If Kovacks was on his own, he'd
laugh until his head swam and Max would join right on
in, wriggling across the floor like a tickled pup. If Holly
was there, Kovacks would still laugh, but she'd bawl him
out for poisoning Max's brain, or similar, when Kovacks
had never done any such thing and had – in fact – been
surprised as hell the first time Max pulled that one out of
the hat.

Kovacks guessed that once Max hit nine or ten, he'd
be hustling for a loan of his Papa's car, so he could cruise
out and do all the guy kind of things. He was some kid
and deserved a lot of freedom. Kovacks had often told
him, 'You know when I'm up there, when I'm not
on Earth? Just before we leave the whole damn thing,
this sheet of angel-coloured light hazes down around us
and then falls behind. And you know what that is? It's
a halo. No shit. This planet has a halo, I guarantee, which
means nobody here can ever do anything wrong. So if
it feels right, do it. Okay? Whatever you need to – it'll
be fine.'

Max would listen, on the edge of a frown, maybe on
the edge of understanding and Kovacks would get sick in
his stomach because children were so easy to bend out of
shape. You said one thing and they took it up all wrong.
Or you corrupted them on purpose, this being such an
incredibly easy thing to do. The poisoning of the innocents,
you couldn't help it.

'You're full of shit, Papa. Shit. Shit. Shit.'

Smart kid.

Kovacks opened his eyes inside the shade and smelt
space. Eventually, any kind of darkness started to smell

of space; that was to say, of a compound of sweat, confinement, chemically treated fabrics and the sweet suck of forever. Flopping his body up on to nowhere until it was comfortable, Kovacks felt himself held, hammocked by his undiluted freedom from physical normalities. It touched him entire, in one big grasp: small of his back, soles of his feet, exactly around his thighs, all the more and less important places where Holly might go when he was home. Might go again, or maybe not.

Earth-bound, he and Holly came together, heavy as a lock. Kovacks sometimes thought his bones would burst. His domestic arrangements exerted unusual pressures and span out fields of influence that could make him confused or disorientated at any time.

'Kovacks.'

Alain's whisper was almost stunning and plunged him into a piking dive. Kovacks allowed himself to be steadied by familiar hands. He'd been drifting to sleep there, untethered and unprepared.

'Kovacks. You okay?'

Kovacks pushed up his eyeshade and let in a mild scream of light. 'Yeah. Apart from the cardiac arrest, I'm jim dandy. Anything I can help you with?'

'Keep your voice down – don't want company, do we?'

'No. No visitors – I haven't a thing to wear.' He swung into the perpendicular and shook his head awake. 'What's up? Sick again?'

Kovacks settled into the tight little thrill of being illicitly awake. The last time he'd known that, he'd been creaking his way to Holly's room in her parents' house to perform soundless, breathless, pre-marital, grievous bodily sex. As if anyone inside that house had expected him not to; they'd been watching him walk straight into the lock and waiting to turn the key.

Time before that, he'd been one of two bad boys in

a bad place and together, planning to do bad things. Happy days.

Alain huddled in for Kovacks, but didn't speak.

'What's the matter, bud?'

'I'm fine. Those Synergine shots do the trick. I haven't felt nauseous all day.'

Kovacks noticed how Alain's body had turned tentative – the whole shape of him was readied to handle discovery, to apologise, to explain itself transparent, if this should prove to be required.

'Good. Glad you're feeling fine.' He wasn't going to ask again, if Alain had something to say, he could choose his own pace.

'Were you ever sick, Don? The first time?'

'Yeah, I was sick. Sick I never got to see Skylab and ended up jammed inside this coffee can. Man, if I'd got in that place, I'd have looped the loop until they shot me down. You got *room* there, you could *do* things. But no, I've never been sick of space – space wants me, so it's never made me sick. I've got good ears, they'll keep me calm and balanced anywhere – life excepted.'

'I always thought you were well-balanced, no matter what everyone said . . .' Alain made a soft type of smile and watched him, quiet.

'Okay. So what do you want? There's no use proposing again, I told you, I'm already spoken for.' Alain put on the look that meant Kovacks should get with the programme and shape up. 'Alain, what?'

At least Kovacks' voice sounded normal when he kept it quiet and low. This was the way his life seemed to be – for no planned reason normality would settle in, keeping him nicely anxious for the next time it sprang aside.

'I wanted to ask you . . .'

'Yeah.'

Alain sighed. Kovacks had never heard him do that

before and was disturbed. Sighing was unhappy. He didn't like his friends to be unhappy and Alain was his friend.

'Tell me. I can take it.'

'Be serious, Don. Listen to me.'

'I am being serious – why d'you think I'm fooling around this way? Not because I'm having fun. Now, come on, you're giving me cabin fever – standing there like you're viewing the body, for Christ's sakes . . .'

'Kovacks, do you believe in this?'

'Believe?'

This was the question you were not allowed to ask. Not even Kovacks allowed it to creep in his head. He knew it would show too clearly if he did and he was over the edge already, after all.

'Do you believe we should be up here? Do you believe we solve any problems beyond the ones that we make for ourselves by being here?' Alain shut down the distance between his mouth and Kovacks' ear so that his final sentence tickled as it went in. 'Do you seriously believe that we advance the cause of humanity by ripping ourselves out of the atmosphere with a cargo of vegetable seedlings and spy satellites?'

'I can't answer that. You know I can't answer that. I can't even think that I know the answer to that.'

'Kovacks, I've seen you. You didn't come for the reasons they gave us. I won't believe you did.'

'Then don't.' Kovacks wished that all the windows weren't up aloft. He had a powerful idea this conversation would only really be bearable, if he could look out while it happened and think his way into space.

'Why did you come? Kovacks? You can let me know that much.'

'I came to fly, bud, you know that. I came to be a famous astronaut; I came to save a drowning marriage; I came to impress my son and please my wife; I came because I thought it would help my country

65

to seem strong in the eyes of the world and preserve peace. Which is a crock of shit – I came to fly. This is the most that anyone can fly. I can step out through that airlock, I can strap on the MMU and I can jet myself away, be completely separate from everything on or of the world.'

'You didn't want to come back did you? Yesterday. You burned away further than you were meant to. You weren't going to come back.'

'I never said that.'

'You didn't have to, I knew.'

Kovacks remembered the thin conversation they'd stretched between each other yesterday afternoon. Kovacks had ghosted the Manned Manoeuvring Unit off into an absence of horizons and – yes, indeed – mislaid any reason for coming home.

Turning his back on the shuttle – safety lines, schedules, commands – he'd become a true satellite. As agreed, he'd narrated his way towards the dream blue-and-white meniscus that hung above him, the monstrous drop of Earth. Beginning the fatal, burning fall that would bring him home, he'd run out of words. His helmet was filled with the smooth press of his breath and, in his feet, he could already sense the empty ice that separated planets, the gap that was filled by physics and prayer and his body in his suit.

Alain's voice had fuzzed and crackled round him while Kovacks lifted his arms and brought his hands together to cup and then obscure the whole of anything he'd ever known. Nothing about him felt different without it.

Beyond that point, he couldn't remember his thoughts. Kovacks knew he'd turned, as instructed, but had then let himself drift. He'd left the Earth behind him and he was on his way to passing the shuttle, before dying of suffocation, or of beauty, whichever came first.

Alain had called him in; hooked him out of the sky so he'd be safe. Not that Kovacks had intended to mention that his life had ever been at risk.

'Okay. I got lost. I forgot where I was going. You talked me down. Thanks.'

'You knew where you were going – it wasn't anywhere you could be.'

'Okay. Enough. Thanks. I've said thanks.'

Kovacks patted Alain's shoulder and Alain patted him back. Beyond the airlock, Maclehose and Stubbs were breathing in the regulated, regulation way, properly asleep.

'Kovacks?'

'Yeah?'

'I don't believe in it. I do not believe in it. In why they send us. But I do believe in being here.'

'Okay.'

'I'm sorry to say these things, you know?'

Kovacks shrugged. In a couple of years he'd be saying them himself. He'd be telling Max how the Program was started with the help of Nazi rocket scientists and how Kennedy had made it happen because it was a way to beat the Russians at something, at anything. Kovacks was flying a reusable shuttle where the only reusable item was the john. He was inside the universe of statistics that strangers had built to be neater and better funded than the real one where they lived; the real universe of predictable speeds and explosive gases where a whole crew could fireball to vapour in the void between hope and massaged mathematics.

Kovacks had spent his share of time, smiling at school kids and reporters and mentioning science and research but knew he had only ever been sent here because of past and present and future wars. And all he'd ever found over Earth was peace.

Alain seemed ready to swim back to bed, but Kovacks caught him gently before he could.

'You're not going now. You know I can't sleep if I'm suffering from doubt – it's my combat training, you've upset my chain of command.'

'Like you ever had one.'

'Okay, they don't command me, but when they tell me things I try to agree. I'm a good boy so they'll send me up here, where I learn what they'll never know. Nobody knows the world like we do and nobody loves it like we can. Only we can see it small enough to love it properly: whole.

'Then we have to come down and it doesn't matter where we're going home to, it's always hard to be back. Max can smell it off me: how I need to be someplace else. He gets glad when I first pick him up and hold him, but then he cries.'

'You're terrific with him.'

'I'm lousy.'

'No, you think you're lousy, so you're good.'

'I wish that was dumb enough to be true. Alain?'

'Mm hm.'

'They fool everyone to get us out here. But then we fool them. We never come home the way they made us, we're never the same.'

Alain looked happy, way down in his eyes. 'And that is absolutely dumb enough to be true. I'm going to get some sleep.'

'Yeah. Better keep to the schedule.'

'The way that good boys ought to do.'

Kovacks watched Alain's face and felt how great they were together and hoped they were going to be friends for a long time after the mission because he would need to bring something back with him from the way he'd been in flight. In addition, a man with a combat training could occasionally have the desire to be comradely.

'Go on and get out, before people talk. You know how gossip wounds me.'

Alain cast off backwards quite neatly and allowed himself to recede.

'What do you need to be so private for – you going to whack off in there, or what?'

'I'll give it some thought.'

'You're crazy.' Alain smiled. 'Good night, Kovacks. Take care.'

'I'll give it some thought.'

Lying back inside his eyeshade and with his tether satisfactorily in place, Kovacks gave it some and then more than some thought. Turning an endless corner up over the spin of the world, he carefully pictured Holly in exactly the right kind of jeans. He let his mind's eye cruise her, line-dancing in Houston, the way a properly socialising NASA wife should do. She loved that stuff: stepping and bending into those slightly uneasy poses that would let him watch every angle of her, tensed. Other guys would look at her, too, when inertia slapped a move on through her tits, or she offered up a hip buck, an ass roll, a seam snug on the line to the warm and the wet of her. He saw them, seeing her. Then she'd walk off the floor with a high-voltage smile and leave the room hard. She knew how to show folks a good time.

He span his thought of her slowly: lifting it, parting it, making it show him enough. Kovacks only ever wanted enough. Naturally, this was a changeable amount, although the variables upon which it depended were not unpredictable. Here, where he was safe in motion and light, only a stroke or two of bad-boy thinking, brought him up half alive.

But when he braced himself steady and let his hand in for a touch at the anxious gristle, the usual bully and coax, it wasn't right. The sweat and acid taste of Holly began to grit through his teeth and he remembered the balance of her fingers fixing him down. He wouldn't be able to manage, if she came any closer than this.

Drifting on to his side, Kovacks stared at the dark of the eyeshade and tried to concentrate. He recalled the magical haul in his blood from lift-off to escape. He repeated the figures that made the velocity to guarantee escape. He summoned up the pale and rosy lightening fields that bloomed above Africa and he oversaw slow deltas of poison, smoking and snaking into oceans built with marble from the mansions of God. Kovacks imagined his body, caught in the heat of a climb and flowering into force and released dimensions and unutterable flight.

Kovacks was a good and attentive friend to himself. He did what he wanted in exactly the place he'd always wanted to and in contravention of so many rules; it was enough to make a grown man come.

Kovacks brushed off his eyeshade and watched himself stream forward into the lack of gravity. He was like blood into water, or strange milk; unfurling and then pooling in perfectly spherical drops, just as the laws of physics said he must.

As his own constellation of personal liquid progressed, Kovacks untethered and matched its pace, watching it merge and separate. Finally, he patted it into a unified halt and then tenderly drank his evidence.

THE ADMINISTRATION OF
JUSTICE

For Jack Vettriano

Not long after I met her, I gave away all of my clothes. Coming home from our first proper evening with nobody there but ourselves, I knew that I just wouldn't do as I was.

That night I got undressed with the lights off and climbed into bed in the snug, slow way I was used to, so that I would be comfortable; but I could not be at ease. Although we had hardly been intimate – had barely touched – my skin and sheets, my pillows and my brain smelt of her. The whole mattress was roaring beneath me with the rhythm of her walk and I couldn't sleep. So at some point between my lying down and morning I realised that I could never wear my old clothes again. Everything around me was changing and waiting for me to do the same.

I respected my decision when I woke, but in a gradual way. Forgiving myself for a necessary piece of backsliding. I put on a familiar pullover and corduroys I had been fond of, before filling two black plastic bags with dull, soft handfuls of my past – other pullovers, other corduroys, tired shirts, sad ties, five pairs of blue socks and seven pairs of grey. My final inventory was unimpressive. For some reason I had imagined there might have been more, an unexpected waistcoat, a forgotten set of overalls, but the finished catalogue was only predictable and slightly sad.

On my way back from the Cancer Research shop where I left my plastic sacks, I bought a pair of jeans and a sweatshirt, a pack of assorted and colourful underpants and some short, red socks.

Home again, I removed the last of my old self, folded it into a carrier bag, re-dressed in my new self and went out to pay a call on Save The Children. I had found there are far more charity shops than I could ever manage to have clothes.

For the next month or so Cancer Research showcased various items from my wardrobe in their window. I became used to walking past a tailor's dummy, unmistakably wearing matching selections from me. Often I didn't intend to look, but my eye would be coaxed aside as if it had been caught by an unexpected mirror and there would be my headless, dumpy ghost, relentlessly modelling how I had been. I would try to align my reflection with whichever shabby assembly stood between the record collection and the not-for-sale chest of drawers and be pleased when my present didn't quite fit over my past. Nevertheless, I came to hate the window and the fact that it changed so slowly, that no one was buying my clothes.

In this way I began to uncover and recognise my daily habits of hate, the sly distaste that could overwhelm me as I bathed in the evening, that could slip through the naked space between my towel and my pyjamas and cover my skin like salt. Years of careful loathing slowly showed themselves, like rings in a severed tree.

I also found that whatever I make, whatever I touch repeatedly, or in any way deeply, will become a measure of my contentment. A bed, a pot of tea, a garden – or just a little sentence – almost anything will do. If I am its maker, its owner, then somewhere underneath it will be the stain of how I am. Happy bread tastes happy and sad bread does not. My clothes in the window could not help but show the way I stood inside them. I had made them ashamed of me.

You can look at the words on this paper and, because they are the ones I am used to choosing, they will show you the shape of me. I am here to be read in the way you might read the impression of my weight in a bed after a still night, a restless night, a night not alone.

Now, of course, I give her my words and she gives me hers back. Some of them are exactly the same – less of a conversation and more a swap – but because we touch them when we speak, we can look among our sentences and see each other.

I can see the way she is bored at the cafe and wants to be at home with her own work, not out late with somebody else's. I can see she is, now and again, afraid about money and serious illness but not about death. I can see the way her tongue will always be hot enough to shock. I can also see her laugh. She has an enormous, disgraceful, music-hall laugh.

Waiting in the cafe for my soup, I knew where she was by her laugh. I had come in because the place seemed accommodating when viewed from the street and advertised cheap meals on an orderly blackboard by the door. Inside, the atmosphere was jovial, with low, sensible music and nice chairs and, even so, her laughing exploded improperly through all the air of relaxation, making it seem quite inadequate.

I eased in between the other tables and knew that I wanted soft bread and smooth soup and a cup of warm water and I wanted her to bring them to me. I wanted her near me. I specifically ignored any approaches from the other staff, staring off as if I were profoundly distracted, or hunching over the menu with my eyes half closed by concentration. The second time she passed my table, I caught her arm. She tells me she knew I would do this which is odd because I did not.

'You're ready now, are you?' That looks sharp on the page, but she didn't say it sharply.

'Yes, yes I am. I would like some soft bread and some smooth soup, or clear soup, if you have any, and a cup of warm water.'

'Really?'

'Yes.'

'What's the matter?'

'I have . . . I *had* a wisdom tooth and now I don't. Not any more.'

'Oh, nasty. Today?'

'Yesterday.'

'The day after's always the worst. The smoothest soup is leek and potato and I'll cut the crusts off your bread.'

I think she did, too. This would not normally be part of a waitress's duties, but I do think that she cut off my crusts. Perhaps to eat them herself, she likes crusts. For whatever reason, I had the immediate benefit of her personal care and attention. Not sympathy, attention, something I could accept.

The following day, I brought her my tooth. I had scoured away any traces of my blood the night before. It was respectable.

'God, it's like a parsnip.'

I felt proud.

'It must be terribly sore.'

I nodded, light-headed with painkillers and with unkilled pain and with letting her hand hold my hand, holding my tooth. The fierce, sucking ache in my mouth fluttered.

I watched her move away to bring me the smoothest soup of the day and felt something like a little stone, dropping the length of my spine. Except that my spine escaped untouched. This little stone fell from under my mind, through my heart and stomach and then down further again. My skeleton was not involved, this was all flesh. The blood banged suddenly in my jaw and for a moment I closed my eyes and let my entire self be a fierce, sucking ache until I became too frightened to continue.

I kept my overcoats. Overcoats are furniture, not clothing, and both the jackets I have were my father's, not mine to give away. Luckily, these were things she liked. Their heaviness, oldness, made her want to stroke and hold them. I intended that she should want to stroke and hold everything I might wear, but for several days I lacked the courage to ask her what she most liked. I was in danger of buying items at random and unwittingly offending her, driving her off. But despite my reservations, necessity soon forced me to purchase a shirt in which I might go to work. Even the smallest shops offered an unreasonable depth of choice. I was lost. In despair I chose the colour closest to no colour at all, white.

And she loves white. I am completely unable to tell you with nothing but words how deeply she appreciates white.

I was safe to be terribly happy then. Simply and immediately happy. The best possible shirt I could wear for her would be white and I was wearing it. Since then I have been able to look down at her warm hand gently set against the cool of my shirt-sleeve and to know how infallible her judgement in these matters can be. We are perfect together when I suit her. Absolutely right. Now I save and buy the finest shirts I can for her, good seams, reliable collars, the thickest, brightest cloth with a tight, snapping shine and that wonderful, luminous roll of folds from shoulder to wrist. It is all quite magical. She takes care of me now, advises, sees I have turned out well.

At first it terrified me when she said she was a painter. I considered how she must have trained her visual sense and then immediately felt that sense rake itself down hard over me. She let her eyes into mine, held me there, and explained how she could watch any one of her cafe customers and then sketch them back through to the skin. Her nudes were never the result of direct observation, she hadn't needed that in years. I shivered when she blinked.

And when she finally showed me her canvasses – the private, finished images of her imagination and skill, stacked quietly in her flat – I wanted to press my forehead very hard into her hands and have her hold it, I wanted to sing something funny and tuneful, I wanted to lie down and roll on her floor because I was so near to so much of her. Then she introduced me to her paintings of naked strangers and I had to lean for a while against her doorframe while my whole brain was shuffled and cut and shuffled right through with jealousy. I couldn't move until the feeling stopped. Within a minute she had dealt me out and back again and all I wanted was to stay being back again, never to reproach or hate her because of something harmless but disturbing that she might do. Also I felt the pain of her imagination imagining me, adding the sum of my inadequacies.

To see if she would let me, I kissed her and instantly wondered how this was possible, what this meant, if this was her plan or mine. Before I left that evening, she kissed me.

I went home and cried. Or more strictly speaking, I cried on the steps outside her building and then went home and cried again.

Because I saw how terrible it all is. Nature will not let us close, you see, not close enough. Time and space both constantly tick and rush between us and we can only overcome them by concerning ourselves with each other. I must be with her, and I cannot be her maker, could not dare or wish to be her owner, so I am her lover. I love her. That is what I am for. And when I love her, I touch her. Repeatedly and deeply, I put myself in her arms. I kiss her eyes shut so that I can be with her and nothing but, none of my awkwardness or stupidities in the way. In addition, she touches me.

But I do not know the rules for lovers. I am not sure if it will be possible for me to touch her this much and not begin to change her for the worse. Because she makes me utterly contented in my mind and heart, I hope she cannot also be a sign of my contentment or its lack. I think perhaps

I am a sign of hers. Except that I'm not so good sometimes, I let things down, I'm not quite the way that either of us would like.

'You worry too much.'

'I try not to.'

'Maybe you try too hard.'

'I know. That's one of the things I worry about.'

Burrowed down in the hollow of my bed, both of us in our bed, and we are talking. On the night stand is our beautiful clutter of watches and house keys and change, her earrings and my lucky Spanish coin which I picked out of the ice on a frozen road one New Year's Eve without being hit by even a single car. Lucky for me.

While the contents of our pockets wait for us to claim them I close my hold around the astonishing scoop and flex and blood-heat of her back and feel her chuckle.

'You worry about that, do you?'

'Oh yes, I worry continually – and that's a great worry, too.'

Which is the same joke we made before, but with different words and we like it anyway because we always make it and it's ours and funny and true. I wait, spooned against her, while she starts to laugh and am quite sure that I will worry for as long as I know her. She is my finest thing, you see, and I want to do her justice.

I want to be passionate for her, imaginative and free, but I don't know how. I want to love her enough for me to feel it and believe in it and still be nothing but gentle and I never do know the right way. There are evenings when I can only look at her. No. No, a little more than that.

I stand above her with my weight as evenly balanced as I can judge, a slight bias towards the toes, and I tuck back my head so the base of my skull rests snug against my neck. I make my expression soft. 'Relax,' I think, 'Feel young and happy.' So I do.

She thinks I'm silly – all this preparation, complication,

delay. I tell her there are times when I have to be formal. With her permission, although I need to touch her more than I need to breathe, I wait and do almost nothing instead. I anticipate her. I offer her the appetite she deserves.

My eyes close and I watch the after-image of her whole skin, here in the dark with me. I shut my eyelids very gently, they don't make a sound. In that respect, I am as silent as light, or as one of the pictures she's made of me. She'll even paint ugly old me, make me part of her work because I have individuality which is far better than handsomeness.

I pause.

When I begin to raise my arms, the rustle of cotton from my shirt is patient and dry and somehow quite correct.

From this position, I find it simple to lean my face forward, slowly and down. There is a thin sweat around my mouth which my movement through the air makes chill.

From here, I am almost with her. In the purely vertical sense we must be, at most, three feet apart. I lick my lips. Once. So I can taste her.

Soon I will lie with her and try to be my best. For now, I stand where she can see me while I think that for all I have left of my life she has made me unfinished when I was so sure I was done. There is no adequate repayment I can offer her for this. I worry and I do what I can.

A Short Conversation Concerning the Rain in America

Love would have been something else. Something more. More lovely or maybe more ugly. More convincing, anyway. Definitely more convincing. Given time, even a very good lie will thin down to nothing any kind of sane person would ever take seriously. The thing had been a lie and not love.

A jogger dodged by her, squinting against the sunlight and the cold in very much the same quite unattractive way Chris imagined she must be squinting herself. Apparently there were always joggers here. Round and round the Sankt Jorgens Sø and the Peblinge Sø and the two halves of the Sortedams Sø – the four flat, slatey and almost perfectly rectangular lakes: a limitless chain of jogs. Feet almost silent on the sandy path, breath held up before them in stern and healthy clouds they circuited from the bright side to the shaded and back, until a satisfaction had been reached. It was hardly her place to consider if their conduct was constructive or not.

Instead, Chris was studying the lakes. She didn't like them. They were offensively man-made, viciously concreted against every innocent roll of water and the softly squabbling ducks. Still, in a way, they did have an innocence about them – the lakes, not the ducks. It hardly made sense to think of a duck being anything but innocent. The lakes were encouragingly up-front about themselves. Nothing was hidden by landscape, under green confectionery, none of their process had been tucked away. If all that could be made here was over-wide canal troughs then that was that – what you saw was what you got. Her surroundings could not be thought of as anything other than plain speaking.

This seemed to bring out a corresponding need for directness on her part. For a moment she undoubtedly wanted to walk up to one of the benches set out by the path. She wanted to tear at the planks, pull them off and break them, throw them to the road or to the water or to wherever the fuck they would go. She would then also shout extremely loudly, something internationally obscene, like – appropriately enough – the word 'fuck'.

Everyone understood that, it didn't matter where you went. Chris was glad to have been brought up with such free access to what might casually be described as a World Language. Should she scream 'fuck' right now, centuries of bloody Empire and grinding economic dominance – albeit hugely faded – would rush to her aid along with the all-pervading influence of American cinema.

And for that one moment, only that moment, she really did almost shout, thrash about, throw things. Instead, of course, she stood and watched the dark of ducks reappear and disappear over the blinding showers of sun that even very minor movements of the lake could catch alight.

'Did he do that thing, tell me, did he do that thing where he was so angry he couldn't speak? He would just turn up angry and you'd have to make him tea and not disturb him, even though he was sitting in your house and interrupting your life and, let's face it, not being what you'd call sociable?'

'Yes.'

'Or so sad he couldn't speak, or so mad he couldn't speak. It was all about not speaking. I thought about that afterwards. I think he preferred not to speak – in case he gave himself away.'

'Yes.'

'I'm sorry, is this upsetting you?' Dorothy leaned forward

to tap ash from her cigarette. She was barely smoking. Now and again she would pick up the cigarette from under its thread of vapours, tap it, set it back to lie. She might just as well have been knitting, or dealing cards, for all the nicotine she was absorbing. Perhaps she was being careful of her lungs. 'This doesn't bother you? Talking about it.'

'I. No. Not exactly.' There was nothing Chris could say. All of this was so somehow long ago, so unlikely. Besides, it was clear that Dorothy assumed Chris would be strong, so strength would have to be what she displayed.

'But do tell me to shut up if I go on. I can remember how odd it was to work through the dates – you know, finding out with someone if we shared him, how many of us overlapped. Discovering he'd kept us each as one in a stable of possible rides and then calculating the longest-serving mount. I have to say, I'm not really interested now. We can talk about other things, after all. I'm sure you and I have more than him in common. Generally, I find that's true.'

'What do you mean? You've met the others?'

'There are definitely things we have in common, you know?' Dorothy was drifting into a theory – one built up out of facts only she understood.

'Other ones have come here?'

'Oh, no. You're the only one that turned up personally, but I've had phone calls.'

'I'm sorry.'

'Why be sorry? I find us all so interesting. Not when we talk about him, naturally – that never changes at all. He meets a woman, lies to her, fucks her. Maybe in a different order, but that's it. Meet, fuck, lie or meet, lie, fuck. Sounds like a Korean President – Meet Fuck Lie.' She hesitated for a wave or two of cigarette and a thin smile. 'It all sounds a bit hideous when I put it like that. But I can't say I'm not very thoroughly used to him by now – to his behaviour. I mean, he's been nothing if not consistent through the years.' Dorothy stubbed out her stub. 'What

I enjoy now is a good chat – about how *our* lives are. We all seem to do well. After him. Our false start. Only one ever called who was still with him.'

'Yes?'

'Upset. She'd found my number and made up stories, invented irrelevant dreadful truths and everything was so completely out of date. I'm his ex- ex- ex- ex- ex- ex- and then some, for goodness' sake. I wanted to put her right, but I didn't know what to say – so as not to make it worse. That's the only time I've felt like calling him. Giving him the piece of my mind he never took.'

'Was she in love?'

'Oh, probably.'

Love had not been the best thing to mention, perhaps. The word opened a peculiar space in their air which it could not be in any way useful to investigate. Chris decided to turn their course slightly aside.

'I suppose . . . I mean *we* don't look like each other. Do you think? Do *they*? Do we? Ever?'

Dorothy smiled, lit another Marlboro and allowed herself to sip a narrow trace of smoke. '*That's* not it. I don't think he was too specific about looks, exteriors. Unless they were his own. No, I have come to believe that we were all the same inside.'

'Inside.'

Chris felt herself begin to frown, even to blush. The comforting fog of noise around them ebbed lightly back and Dorothy carefully made herself look patient.

'Oh no, not like that. At least, I really wouldn't know. I suppose – you don't mind me saying – I suppose he said yours was the tightest he'd ever known. Did he? Tight. That's what he liked. Tight. After a while, I discovered I was thinking that way, too. I had reduced myself to a ring of muscle.'

'Did he buy you that book?'

'With the exercises? Oh, yes. Still, nothing's wasted;

another one of us told me you can use the same drill to prevent any risk of late onset incontinence. Not uncommon in women of my age. You have to laugh.'

'Yes.'

'No. I mean that. You have to laugh. Eventually. You must.'

'I laugh a great deal. I have always had a remarkable sense of humour.'

Chris stirred the chocolate powder down into her cappuccino and tried to appear essentially humorous while another rising band of unattended smoke swung across her breathing space. Behind them both, a dry, American voice continued to speak.

'The solar plexus is yellow, it's the emotional centre. You see, this card is the sun and it's yellow, it's golden. This is where everything moves from – it stays still and everything moves from it. Like a wheel.'

'What is he talking about, I can't see?'

Dorothy didn't have to look. 'Oh, that's his pitch. I don't know if he fucks them afterwards or maybe he just needs the company.'

'I'm sorry, that doesn't explain . . .'

'He does Tarot here. It takes about an hour – he buys lots of coffee – nobody minds. A different person each time. As far as I know. I don't stop by every day. It's nice to hear English sometimes; don't you find that, even American English? Danish – Danish isn't a language, it's a speech impediment.'

This was embarrassing. It genuinely was. Chris couldn't be comfortable. This woman, this Dorothy, was being publicly insulting to the public in a public place and the American voice was drip, drip, dripping away in sensible tones. Talking nonsense, every word.

'This is all of life, the three experiences, everything. The spinning wheel of life lets the important things be important and the unimportant things be unimportant.

You just dance on the spokes. It's safe to dance on the spokes. Spoke. Spoke person. Spokesperson. Are you a communicator? I think it's important you should speak. That's what this is saying to me.'

The three experiences. Three.

Chris had known more than three. Even *she'd* had more than three. No matter what she took to be his meaning; in any sphere, she'd had more than three experiences, quite indisputably. She tried to ask a question without sounding stupidly hurt.

'Do you hate him?'

'Hate him? There's no reason to. I don't think he even asks them for money; it's a game they're playing.'

'No. Him.'

Dorothy patted at Chris's hand, her touch was surprisingly, almost unhealthily warm and moist. 'Oh, *him*. I don't think so. For a while I did, but what's the point? I'm hardly going to search him out and then hack him to death; even just shoot him painlessly – why else would I need to hate?'

'But while he was there?'

'And I was there? Oh surely, I hated and loved him at least enough to kill.'

Dorothy had said that the way a song might, the way a greetings card might, the way that he might almost certainly have done himself: as if an absolute lack of sincerity was essential if one wished to convey a hidden truth. The medium betrayed the message, but it was really the thought that counted and the thought had been of you.

'Thinking of you.' What a vague, pathetic, noncommital phrase that was. He'd always offered it up like some kind of gift which now made it deeply irritating to recall. She wished she had asked him, even one time, 'Thinking in what way? Could there be an adverb with that please? Thinking fondly, thinking badly, thinking quite randomly of me, or of the money you owe me, or me in the context of disappearing wetland habitats, or of me providing what you'll have for breakfast this weekend, or me in comparison to the girl you're going to screw tonight? I mean could you, for once, be something even approaching precise? How exactly *are* you *thinking of me*?' That would have been a liberating outburst, Chris supposed.

Fortunately, she now enjoyed all of the liberty she could wish. She rarely felt the need to speak loudly, never mind to burst out. She had freedom. Enough for two. And nobody called any more to tell her about their thinking or where they were. That was his other favourite trick.

'Hello, I'm in Birmingham now.'

'Hi, I'm in Bury . . . Machynlleth . . . London.' She had no way to know if he'd been lying. He could have been anywhere. Once, he'd said he was ringing from Boston. Boston, America. He had also asked about her weather, possibly to prevent the expansion of what was already an uncomfortable and no doubt expensive trans-atlantic pause.

'Oh, it's raining. Started at lunch-time, I think.'

'We had rain yesterday, it was heading east.'

'It must be yours, then. Here.'

'Yes.' He'd liked to be the source of everything. 'Yes, you're having American rain.'

The idea of American rain had been rather lovely at the time. She had even walked out to the paper shop, so she could let herself be under clouds that could have darkened the night across Ireland and an ocean, that could have muffled sunset above a man of her acquaintance and the city of Boston, Massachusetts.

'I had to get away eventually.'

She wasn't sure when Dorothy had started speaking and wondered briefly if she'd missed something of impor-tance.

'I knew he'd been all over Britain, one way or another, so I didn't want to be there any more. But my father used to work in Copenhagen – we lived here for a while, so it was very slightly like coming home. And there was no need to learn Danish. Nobody does.'

'They are very friendly, yes.'

'That's one word for it. Now here's a thing. Do you happen to remember any of his solos – his virtuoso efforts?'

'What?'

'When he first confides in us and there are all those stories about his Granny being crazy and standing in their back yard naked, calling the family names. About how sorry we should be for him, how understanding? Um . . . there was one where his mother had a ruptured ulcer and there was blood all over the bathroom and he'd been there on his own and not known what to do. That one. He never actually told it to me – I heard it later. Convincing details, hm?'

'That wasn't his.'

'Who knows? he was such a sad, old fabricator.'

'No. That wasn't his story . . . I didn't realise. He stole it.'

'Like I say – '

'You can't say: you don't know. He stole it from me, from my mother.'

'Oh – '

'My mother started bleeding in the middle of one night. There was nothing I could do. The ambulance – it took some time. You know? It took time. Did his mother die in the story? Did her heart give out somewhere they never could really pinpoint on the drive, so he couldn't even say where she died – except that it wasn't in hospital and wasn't at home. Did he say he never got to see her again and that this mattered a great deal.'

'Well, I'm not sure if – '

'Did he say that?'

The American voice stopped talking.

'What did he say?'

'Something very like the way you tell it. I am sor – '

'Don't be.'

'But it can't matter any more. Trust me. He doesn't matter any more. The man is too pathetic. Who would even think of doing that? He's – '

'I know exactly what he is, thank you.' Chris inhaled preparatively. 'Thank you very much and now will you either smoke that cigarette or stub it out because all the time I've been here, you've been lighting those things and leaving them so that I get all the smoke. I don't smoke. I've never smoked. I will not ever want to fucking smoke and you are making me. Don't you ever think about the other human beings out here? Keep that fucking stuff in your own fucking lungs or keep it the fuck away from me.'

'Well, thanks for the advice, dear, I'm sure.'

'Oh, fuck off.'

Obviously, there were very few things Chris could really do after that. All of them involved leaving, so she did; clattering, almost stumbling into the choking cold that fell straight down out of the clear, early night.

This morning she had moved through a tiny period of calm just beyond her sleep. Then the dark in her mind had snapped on again and she could find no way to forget the sensation of burglary in her brain, the new pain of an unanticipated theft.

Sitting up in the chill, hotel bed she thought, for example, of passions expressed, of casual movements and of each particular network of betrayal. Fearing the sadness of her own company within a closed language, a country and a city she barely knew, she had breakfasted quickly and set out for an extremely extensive walk.

Now and again the almost-familiarity of a post-box or a cash dispenser would distract her. She would think of home and hurt. Then an altogether foreign and pleasant building, an expression of needless courtesy from a cyclist in the street, could make her ridiculously happy that she had come. At some points she felt quite considerably content and at other times she could only recall how she missed the American rain.

THE SNOWBIRD

THE SNOWGIRL

They were fascinated. It wasn't his fault, their fault, anyone's fault. No one to shout at and no one to blame. There was just some quality about it that tugged their imaginations away from anything else he could offer – the Snowbird and firemen, Santa Claus and earthquakes – they each of them failed completely to be of interest.

'How about I read you something?'

'No. Tell us what you did today.'

'I could tell you about the Snowbird that comes in the night and shines like glass, like glass full of rainbows in the dark, all of himself. He makes the frost on the windows out of snow glass. I could tell you about . . . that.'

'Tell us what you did with the boxes. Were you in the boxes today?'

'The love boxes.' Sarah, getting it wrong on purpose which she could sometimes like to do.

'They're glove boxes. Glove. And I did what I did with them yesterday, all over again today. Nothing special. They're never special.'

'Please.'

'Go on, Dad.'

'No, you go on now. If you can't be sensible then I'll get cross. And it's too late. You should be asleep.'

'Oh, Dad.'

'You always say we should be sleeping when you don't want to talk.' She might have been noting her temperature, or the time. This is the way that my Father is, the way he is naturally made.

'Why can't you just be good. Why can't you just for

once be good. Every time, when you're back from your mother it's like this. I mean, what are you trying to tell me? Do you want to stay with her? Is that what you want? You can tell me?' That wasn't a question, why did it come out like a question? He was losing the grip on his inflection. 'Well, tell me. If it is.'

Without warning, his emotions splintered and he lowered his head to massage his eyes, knowing they might well be unnecessarily wet. The sisters looked up at him the way they generally did, neither embarrassed nor alarmed. And patient, that's what they were, unutterably patient. Amanda and Sarah staring, with their sympathetic, clear, sad eyes, as if they were women hiding in behind girls' faces. Because he had never been anything better than a child in his life they were growing to be his sisters, not his daughters. They were pushing aside time so that he wouldn't be lonely, so that he could talk to them. Rely on them.

No, that was only his thinking. He felt guilty because they mattered to him and therefore made him encounter his failings as if each were a permanent, almost infectious disfigurement. This couldn't be helped but he had to remember that he was no worse than many fathers and not truly guilty at heart. His daughters both made him uncomfortable at heart. No more than that.

'Daddy, do you have a headache?'

'Sssh. Yes he's got one.'

'Don't talk about me as if I'm not here!'

They blinked, almost flinched while he shouted. They were such flowers really, it made him breathless inside to think of the damage he might do them and not know. He mustn't forget that he was still bigger than they were, louder and more frightening. He must be nourishing. With them, their mother would be catty, competitive, female and his duty must lie in offering everything else. They knew about simple baking, internal combustion and electricity because he wanted their knowledge to grow outwith the limitations of sexual stereotype. He wished he could show them a way to be feminine, but this obviously wasn't possible in any genuine sense. And they were in fact quite feminine all by themselves, more so every day, in a soft, unhysterical way that would probably make their mother ill.

Sometimes he loved them unreasonably well for simple things like that, little denials of half their genes. He dabbed their heads with his fingertips, kissed his hands and dabbed again.

'I'm sorry for shouting. That was wrong. Yes, my head hurts.'

'Will I get you some water with pills in?' Amanda diving into practicalities with a smooth, calm nod.

She was wasted on her generation – should have been a refugee, evacuee, the smile to keep your spirits up while adrift in the open boat. He often wondered how she would manage to rest here contented in such unchallenging surroundings and saw her grown up and protesting and debating and migrating and dispensing courage overseas. She had almost a lifetime to live, only a little taste gone from its start, and already she loved it all: had such a magnificent, frightening appetite. Every morning she ate up the most savage papers, conquered the news of misery, acquiescence and dissent, then trotted happily off to school, full up.

'How many has he had already. Of the pills.'

'No, ask him.'

'How many pills have you had already, Dad. To make sure you're not over dose.'

'Overdosed. That's the word, he told us, you remember.'

They watched his mouth, ready to understand. He had made them like this, too understanding, too intense. Sarah was holding Amanda's hand and they sat, perfectly still, as if they had been cut from paper and then folded open into two little children of equal solemnity.

'I haven't had any today, but I will do now. Two, please.'

'All right.'

It was Sarah's turn to bring him a glass, carefully half full and carried in both her hands like a present or a dove, its water still fizzing slightly with relief of the appropriate dose.

'Mind the water, Dad, it's nearly freezing. Outside is making the pipes go frosty, will they burst?'

'No, I don't think so.' He swallowed his first mouthful trying not to show the flicker of pain at his nervous tooth.

'Is it too cold? Amanda could put in some hot. From the kettle, not the tap.' Amanda had told her about the dangers of lead in the pipes and boiling kettles. Sarah trusted Amanda. More than she trusted him? Differently, just differently.

'No, it's not too cold. It's fine.' Say thank you always, so that they will. 'Thank you.'

'It's our pleasure.'

He watched them nod and move to the stairs. They would get themselves ready for bed now, brushing their teeth together – Amanda behind Sarah because she was tallest, both of them spitting neatly when necessary and then cleaning the bowl. They would wash thoroughly, leaving each other alone for the private things and having their own odd organisations for who went first. Sometimes, up there, they would laugh. He had no idea why.

When they needed to be tucked in, they would call him.

The telephone rang and his hand jerked in response, slewing water out of the glass and down his shirt. That would be their mother.

'Yes, they're fine. Just getting ready for bed.'

Except they would be listening now, getting ready but collecting every word, not forgetting the pauses.

'It was time for them to go to bed, that's why they're going to bed. If you want to speak to them, they can still come down. I didn't know you were going to ring.

'No, I couldn't have guessed.

'Will I call them –

'I'll call – '

Now she will talk about your job which means about money and her house which means about money and the swarms of bad habits she imagines you have fallen into without her, which means about money which you spend unwisely. She will suggest without ever saying that you are lying about, even now, smoking smokes and drinking drinks and eating foreign foods in your morally weakened state as a person divorced from her. You must surely be letting your children look at wicked comics and wickeder television without even intervening to point out what a poisonous kind of sump it is and mentioning that you would push your foot right through it if this wouldn't cause a potentially hazardous explosion.

But the home and money stuff is not a threat – he mainly wishes she would not talk about his job because of how this makes him feel. His job does not give him good ground to stand on – she can score points without even knowing why the weakness she finds is there.

'Of course I'm getting them presents. It's Christmas. I've got them presents . . .

'You can buy them whatever you like . . .

'Me? Nothing special. I'm not good at thinking – they tell me. Just useful things, clothes, that's what they asked for. And a stuffed dog, puppy kind of thing. Sarah wanted a penny whistle, Christ knows where you get them.'

Trying to keep it bottled, the way her voice made him feel. He shouldn't be annoyed because she would like that. He shouldn't be annoyed because the girls wouldn't. He felt squeezed between them.

'I know, I know that. You can still buy her piano lessons.

I don't think a whistle will stop her playing the piano, I think she's musical. You can't carry a piano about, can you? Maybe that's why . . .

'Look, I don't mind. Ask them, they know more than me.'

Now she'll pull something. Every Christmas, she tries something. More often than that, but particularly at Christmas. Why do people do that? Families, everyone tearing each other apart just at the thought of being together, never mind what they get up to on the actual bloody day. Why at Christmas?

'If you wanted them to put up the decorations, they could have done it tonight . . .

'What do you mean? How not ready could they be?'

She wasn't going to have them again, take them away. Tomorrow lunch-time, their school would give them up to him for the whole of the holiday – the three of them on holiday at once which was difficult, a whole year's miracle, to arrange – and she wouldn't get them again, not until Boxing Day. She'd had them at Christmas last year and now it was his turn.

Not that it mattered. None of it mattered, all of this stuff just descended into incredible pettiness, but it only took one person in any pair to get petty and then you would both have to be petty or you would lose – the cunt would wipe her shoes on your face, in your mouth. Bad word. Shouldn't think cunt. Their mother, that's what she was. Their mother. Bad mother. But their mother.

'Daddy?'

Were they calling down to save him? Were they? Yes, because they were lovely girls. His girls. Their own girls.

'I'm on the phone to your mother. Hold on a minute. Is it an emergency?'

'Just that we're going to sleep.'

'We're in bed, we're not asleep yet.' Amanda, she liked to correct, get one over on big sister. You could sneak her into talking that way, if she was having a sulk, just say something inaccurate and she couldn't resist pulling you up. No getting away from reality with her around. Very like her mother.

'I'll be up any minute. Look, I have to go. I thought we had this all agreed –

'Well –

'Well – '

He really would shout, if he couldn't push his way in here. It was always more difficult, breaking her flow when you couldn't see her. And she knew it.

'IwillhavetogonowbecausetheyareshoutingmebutIwill callyouagaintomorrowifthatsallrightfinegoodbyethen.' Not leaving a toe-hold to kick her way in. Petty. But she started it. Yes she did, yes she did, yes she did.

'Daddy?'

'On my way. Feeling much better now. No headache. Thanks for the pills. On my way.'

They'll know. They'll look at the way you're walking, the closed smile on your face and they'll know it didn't go too well. People should be able to suspend what they do while their children grow past them and get safe away. Why give two girls such a terrible idea of what a relationship could be? Maybe they wouldn't even enjoy Christmas, would associate it with arguments and turn to other religions in later life, how could you predict?

He would wash his hands and face before he saw them, give himself a good all-over scrub and pretend he was checking they'd left the bathroom tidy.

'I'll take you for your shoes tomorrow, if you'd like that.'

'You could wait until afterwards and then there would be sales.'

Amanda saying it and meaning it, but not seeing Sarah's eyes. She still wanted presents on the proper day. Then

Boxing Day ones from her mother, that part must be quite nice, really.

Why the hell did their mother want them to go over and decorate her house? She surely wouldn't want all that nonsense for the sake of one day and then just have it hanging round. He couldn't imagine anyone wanting to decorate for only themselves. She would go into a depression and end up phoning the girls, crying, making those acid promises. Leaving him the threats.

'What are you thinking about, Dad?'

'Oh, bits and bobs. What do you want for Christmas dinner?'

'Well . . .' very cautious, 'Mum said she was getting us turkey so maybe we should have beef.'

'Or pork is nice.'

What a good idea – makes you wonder who put it there. So she was having the fucking turkey. It didn't matter. He didn't like turkey – missing it only had an effect because it was some kind of peculiar victory. Probably, she was over there, right now, keeping score, making her winning advantage secure.

'Whichever you want. We could have beans on toast.'

'No.' Sarah could not imagine Christmas with beans on toast, it was too horrible to joke about.

'All right, we'll decide tomorrow when we're out and order ourselves a nice cow or a pig.'

'Or both.'

Yes, but there was no need to overdo it. He had the feeling Amanda would be vegetarian by next year, she had that kind of mind.

'And now you can tell us about the glove boxes. You promised.' Sarah, soft as yoghurt and single-minded as an ICBM.

'Oh, no. I didn't promise at all.'

'Tell us.'

'And then we'll go to sleep.'

So admit defeat because it has been a long day and the days will get even longer before everything of this is over and the new year has arrived and is already dull.

'I worked in the glove boxes today – '

'In the Citadek?'

'In the Citadel. I worked with the glove boxes and with the big black gloves so that none of the bad stuff would get out. Sort of like the glass box with those rats they had on television.'

'OH. You haven't got rats, have you.'

'No, we don't have rats.'

'Good.'

'Come on, we've got an early start in the morning, lots to do. And I want a nice wash before I go to bed.'

'You like nice washes, don't you?'

'Yes, I do.'

You can say that because it's true.

You can say that because you would love now to be scrubbed down, hosed down, until there is nothing to see of yourself, nothing to feel of yourself. You would love to be washed away.

You can say that because another container spilled today and filled the Citadel with something you can only imagine as very fine glass needles, flying and burrowing. You have heard things about the glove boxes, their safety, the invisible sparks they let slip to sink under your skin and burn through the codes that make you yourself. You could be changing all the time in ways too small for you to feel, impossible for you to see, only poorly translated into a colour change in your indicator badge, a decontamination or two. But how can they clean away something that has made itself a part of you and is waiting to tell you its time.

You don't know what you bring them back from the Citadel, a little more each day. The weightless sightless something you could be breathing into your former wife, pressing into the hands of your properly registered childminder, stepping into the pile of your carpet, hugging into the hearts of your daughters' bones.

You should be apart from them, kept away in case of accident. Unless the accident has already happened in their air or their water. They maybe have eaten their death in spite of you, or walked through it on the way to school. You live too close to the Citadel here. At night it shines and you do not meet its eye and you wish it had never been thought of.

Diseases can be triggered psychologically, you know that, which is why you must, most of the time, not think. You wash yourself too often. You don't want to hurt anyone.

'We like them, too.'

'Sorry?'

'We like nice washes.'

Their skin has an almost glowing pallor about it, a blueish, Celtic fragility they have from their mother who could never and probably still cannot go out in the sun. They are snow children, happy and safe in winter. You wish it would snow for them this Christmas because they would like that and anywhere will look better in snow, even the Citadel. Although that is always snowed-over somehow, hard to look at and really see, difficult to contemplate. You imagine it sometimes like a black umbrella opening inside your head and then turn away from it again.

'That's good. Girls, how do you like being at your mother's? Is it all right?'

'All right.' Sarah speaking quite clearly, although she is almost asleep. She has the nicest voice of the whole family. You dream of her sometimes becoming a singer, an actress, newsreader, preacher – someone to change your mind.

'It's nice to be back home, though.'

'Much nicer.'

'Well, I'm glad you like it here.'

Tuck them in and leave them alone. Do not ask them questions they will not understand. Do not make them understand. Do not make them frightened just because you are afraid.

'Go on then, Dad.'

'Mmh?'

'Your wash.'

'Yes. You sleep tight, then. Kisses on the heads and sleep tight. Call me, if you want something. Anything important. Night, night.'

And go and run the water in the dark, think of it mouthing and nudging up, settling round you, licking where you think. Open your eyes. Close them. No change.

BREAKING SUGAR

'This bread tastes sweet.'

'Mn?'

'This bread, it tastes sweet.'

'No, I don't think so. Do you think so?'

'Of course I think so. I wouldn't mention it if I didn't.'

Nick bit again, chewed warily. She watched him, also wary, but differently so.

'Sweet?'

'Sweet.'

'Probably brushed against something at the baker's – you know.'

'Brushed? It was the same last time.'

'No, it was brown last time.'

'But it was still sweet.'

'Really? No, not sweet, surely.'

'Yes. The bottom edge. Definitely. Sweet.'

'I'll look into it.'

'Look into it?'

'With the baker.'

She couldn't tell him. He wouldn't understand.

He would fail to see her point. Nick was a clever man and she couldn't doubt that he was good, but they did have to keep their differences, here and there. She no longer saw any purpose in openly rehearsing their odd little shades of thinking and ideas because she would end up having to differ about them and differing was no fun.

What was more, differing simply involved you in saying out loud what you already knew you believed in. Your opposite number did the same. You both, quite inevitably, reinforced each other into deeper lines of difference.

Being experienced with Nick's mind, she could say it was a nice one but also that it clearly wasn't hers – not even close.

Except, of course, on the point of Mr Haskard: there they had been perfectly agreed. He was the right man for them. They were both very lucky in Mr Haskard, very fortunate and blessed.

In the matter of Mr Haskard's skin, which was pale and dry like a powdered bandage or perhaps more like an expensive tablecloth, they were fortunate. Nick's mother had a similar complexion which had once made her greatly sought after, quite apart from her many other, more spiritual, charms. Her glistening lips and the plush interior of her mouth – casually glimpsed – seemed hypnotically moist and intriguing – in comparison, for example, to her dusty chin. Whilst set against her arid cheeks and forehead her eyes were a pure liquefaction of lapping thought, brimming at every available hour of the night and day.

So Nick liked Mr Haskard.

In the matter of Mr Haskard's sociable habits of life which were charming, small and unintrusive, they were blessed. She would watch the corner of his mouth peaceably sucking his pencil's end as he studied his quality broadsheet's crossword and remember all her catalogue of relatives who had not ever left their newspapers properly folded after use and who had not been wise or honest in their responses to even the simplest of crossed words. She had always wanted to be on amicable terms with a man who could unravel puzzles and find delight in harmless, indoor games. Mr Haskard did not chew gum, cough nervously, practise a musical instrument or make immoderate use of alcohol, boot polish, toilet paper, coffee or boiled sweets.

Mr Haskard's beard, she and Nick had both agreed, was glorious. Thick and plump at the mouth; succulent, waggish and probably ticklish in a soft, fine, animal way, it was eminently touchable. Although they didn't dream of touching it, naturally. They only watched and grew used to the modesty of his half-concealed smiles; the sudden, red laughter; the possibilities of hidden bite.

They loved to know that Mr Haskard lived above them slightly like a quiet household god: slim and undemanding; up in the two connecting rooms they were happy he should rent. He patronised the launderette, rather than disturb their washing machine, left the kitchen truly cleaner than he'd found it, and she had never once feared that in the bathroom he might let himself drip astray.

And if she liked Mr Haskard better than Nick could, this was purely because she saw much more of him. Nick's life was increasingly full of lectures and night classes and intensive seminar weekends, while she stayed largely at home, not giving lectures or night classes or even considering seminars. The possibility had always existed, in a theoretical way, that they might both work. They might even have been capable of both holding posts at the same university, but their approaches had been too differing, as had their results. She had slowly found herself unable to relish her teaching or its success. Her life was now the house and its lodger and her research. When her private studies were complete, she intended to write a book. A good, exhaustive, independent book. Nick did not know of these private intentions because they would cause him to differ with her again.

Mr Haskard was in no way cowed by the intellectual atmosphere of his new home. She became oddly used to sitting with him by the window and sharing conversations during which he would offer up the proofs of his own learning.

'Your dress fastens at the back.'

'Uh, yes it does. Nick bought it for me.'

His left forefinger cradled his moustache and concentration winked behind his eyes. He swallowed, then held his own hands, patient and soft.

'Now I might well advise against that.'

'I beg your pardon.'

'Against backward fastening. There are three reasons.'

'Really.'

'Yes. In the first place all popular means of restraint for lunatics tend to fasten and buckle at the back. This is a bad association. In the second place, most clothing designed specifically for the dead, is opened, for post-mortem convenience of dressing, at the back. This is a bad association. In the third place, backward fastening disempowers the wearer. Like an invalid or a child, one may not always be able to dress oneself unaided. One becomes dependent.'

'Bad association?'

'Indubitably.'

'I can see you've given this some thought.'

'Some thought, yes. But I intend no offence. The dress is extremely flattering: offering, as it does, little or no distraction between the motion of your form and an observing eye. I do hope it is also comfortable.'

'Quite. Thank you.'

He perused her kindly, as if she were a well-phrased headline or a foreign stamp.

Nick had conceded that all Mr Haskard's rent money should be hers, to spend as she wished. This was not as good as earning her own money in the course of pursuing a satisfactory career, but it wasn't entirely without its rewards. Mr Haskard always settled promptly in advance with a fold of notes he passed from his hand to hers as if he were returning a happy loan. She never felt like his landlord – or landlady – more like a rediscovered friend.

'Another calendar month, then. Thank you.'

'Thank you, Mr Haskard. And, ah, Mr Haskard?'

'Yes.'

'Do you like it here?'

'Of course.'

'You could pay quarterly, if you wanted to. You have been so reliable.'

'Oh, no. No, thank you.'

'To pay every month has something temporary about it, even untrusting. And frankly, I'm surprised you don't consider a mortgage – your job . . . I mean to say, are we going to lose you, Mr Haskard?'

'Well. I don't think so. Not for a while. To explain myself, I am something of a freelance. Systems analysts of my calibre – if I might be permitted to say so – are in constant demand. Mobility is an asset. And I also disapprove of mortgages and the blights of private ownership.'

'I see. Thank you for answering so comprehensively.'

Curiously, the demands Mr Haskard mentioned meant that she saw a good deal of him during the day. Often, while she was sleeping beside Nick, Mr Haskard's cellular telephone would quietly call him away to pad invisibly down the stairs and out across the city, its dark, geometrical streets and narrow lights. Tight up under her dreams he would search and correct the programs that ran for ever and nowhere within silicon labyrinths. He understood and tasted their atoms' electric shake, admonished the ignorance of their languages, loved and scolded like a father, noted each trace of disease.

Perhaps as she stirred her mid-morning tea, she would hear the open and shut of his door, the bath starting in to fill, the toilet flush. Perhaps she was glad to be aware of his company and to wait for his stepping into her kitchen, his face still slightly softened and coloured with washing and sleep.

'Furniture should be taken outside as often as possible.'

That morning Mr Haskard had unveiled an especially alarming lack of health within a banking company's patterns of thought and he was in fine spirits. There was almost a growl in his voice, a small wicked note that could make her wonder whether he lifted out all the diseases he found or simply changed their shape and then left them behind to switch and oscillate as signs of his passing.

'You have extremely suitable chairs here; they should be in the sun.'

A young summer was blazing, its sunlight pleasantly bitter against the skin, and Mr Haskard pattered along the hallway at her side with a surprising lack of physical reserve.

Within minutes, at his suggestion, she caught herself lifting her kitchen chairs and table out onto the grass at the back of the house. She and Nick had bought the house for its garden – the kind of lazy, unruly expanse that made her imagine English country lunch parties and more money and security than one generation would ever be likely to amass. In fact, their garden wasn't so terribly big as all that, but had enough size to encourage imagination and to accommodate – she now discovered – a considerable range of furnishing.

Mr Haskard loped over the grass, positioning waste-paper baskets, table lamps, a random selection of ornaments. Her belongings looked tired and silly in the sun, too formal and too dull.

'Now you understand.' She discovered he had been reading her face, the disappointment. 'All of these things, they are really no protection, not in the face of nature. In this country, our surroundings are, currently, gentle; we can imagine they are tamed and patient. But when we take our indoors out of doors we see how dead and insubstantial our achievements and defences are.'

'Yes, Mr Haskard, I suppose we do.' She sat down on one of her transplanted chairs and felt it sink into the grass.

'Would you like some pear?'

Mr Haskard had picked out a likely fruit from the bowl near his feet and was cutting it with a little pocket knife.

'Thank you.'

In her mouth, the soft wedge of pear was sweet with a tiny shiver of salt where his thumb must have rested against its skin.

The sun dipped late and slowly for them, burning along the chair-backs and sparking out from the group of cut-glass cream jugs Mr Haskard had set on the table. Before dark, and before Nick returned, they knew without telling each other that everything should be back where it used to be: warmer and scented with grass and the open air, but back where it used to be.

She walked behind Mr Haskard as he picked up the bread-bin from close by the hedge. Their shadows darted ahead of them, narrow and the colour of wet earth rather than of darkness.

'Look.' Her voice stopped him, held him absolutely, until he could execute a turn to face back at her. Startled by the obedience of his expression, she repeated herself, 'Look.'

'Oh, yes. Our shadows.'

'But look at them.'

He did so, quietly, neatly, with one hand smoothing at his beard. 'Tell me.'

'Well.' She wanted to be clear for him, to match his patterns of expression and then join him inside them. Generally, she had noticed his sentences felt as comfortable as her own within her mind. 'Well, I see myself there, pulled along through time to something I can't know. I see how strange and flexible I can be. A little bit of sun can tip me out in the grass like paint.' He had, she noted, half-closed his eyes to listen. Her voice would be alone with him in the dark. 'This makes it very clear how small I am and how tiny any risk I take could ever be. Therefore, how easy.'

He nodded, appreciating her point, and considered the parallel progression of the two shapes they cast on the lawn. 'I see time.' He began walking towards the house, stopped and without looking back said, 'I always do see time. And I think that I would rather walk this way, with my back turned on the sun, and see time laid down at my feet, so that I can understand what I mean. So I have myself in perspective. I like that. Thank you.'

Having given them courteous notice, Mr Haskard would leave them alone for a matter of days every two or three months. In their different ways, they felt his absence, but were surprised at how great an influence he could be even when he was gone.

At these times, she and Nick talked together a little more than they might have done and perhaps, in addition, they genuinely listened to whole sections of what each one said to the other. Nick would come home sharp, rather than spinning out the time around night classes and ultimately returning, sodden with the smell of cigarettes, gin and sweat. He had occasionally given her cause to doubt him. But not now.

'Come on.'

'Not here.'

'Why not. He's away, come on. We used to do it out of the bedroom all the time.'

This was a lie, but an attractive one. She still shook her head, smiling, shrugging out of his arms.

'Why not?'

She backed through the doorway and into the hall, keeping her focus on his eyes, imagining the tilt of his emotions, his likely response. 'Not here, upstairs.'

'Ach.'

'No, right upstairs.'

She watched Nick thinking, beginning to smile.

Mr Haskard's rooms were easily opened – she had the

spare key. They crept through his dustless, orderly study, vaguely aware of the books he'd added, the small coloured pictures he'd hung on his walls. She forced on, pushed back the door to his bedroom, plain and peaceful.

For no reason she could imagine, she sat up on Mr Haskard's naked dressing table and waited for Nick to look at her.

The table was built at an oddly convenient height. Her dress, Nick discovered, fastened and unfastened completely with a number of tiny buttons at the front.

They easily accomplished the necessary act and allowed a degree of unusual passion to overcome them both. She welcomed Nick into her arms and self, closing her eyes and inhaling the brusque, warm scent of Mr Haskard which was, quite naturally, all that filled his rooms.

For some considerable time, she continued her intimate life in much this way. Whenever Mr Haskard left, she found she would take advantage of his living space; would cautiously enjoy his unwitting accommodation.

Nick always remembered to open a window and thoroughly dissipate their tell-tale ghosts of perspiration and she checked they removed any items they might have brought with them and then left to lie.

Whenever Mr Haskard was at home, she continued to enjoy the pleasure of his company and to think – now and then – of her uncovered skin against his door-frame, his wallpaper, his carpet, his dressing table, his wardrobe and his desk.

'Might I ask you something, Mr Haskard?'

'Yes.'

'Where do you go to? When you go.'

'I'm afraid I don't understand.'

'When you leave us; your trips away. If you don't mind my asking. It's really no concern of mine, naturally.'

'Ah. Where do I go – that's easy: I go to apologise.'

'I'm sorry?'

'No. I am sorry. That's why I go. Will I show you? Yes. I think I will.'

He motioned her further along the hallway, smiled and ascended the stairs at a trot. She followed. His door was unlocked, needed only a gentle turn of his wrist, a light push.

'Come in. I was a little fast for you there, I think.'

'No, no.'

'But you're out of breath.'

'Then maybe you were faster than I thought.'

'You should exercise.'

'I've been taking more lately.'

'Good, good. We all have to, don't we. Please. Come in.'

She moved inside with him, noting the unfamiliar signs of his occupancy.

'I don't mean to disturb you.'

His lamp was set to shine at a soft angle and his cardigan draped easily over a chair. His desk was studiously cluttered with papers and a partly folded map. She felt a stranger here, breathing in the strong new presence of fresh laundry and shaving lotion and warm, unfamiliar skin.

'You're working – I don't want to take up your time.'

'You don't. Any more than I want you to. And no one can work all the time. Come here now.'

His hand extended smoothly, heavily towards her and she stepped to meet it, to feel the calm pressure of his fingers, the tug in. When she was standing beside him, he released her again and spoke.

'This is where I go.'

Because she was looking at his face, she did not at first understand him.

'Here. This is where I go.'

He nodded to the pictures on his wall, made a neat smile.

Photographs. Regular, rectangular commonplace photographs of uneven fields and hillsides, strangely insubstantial buildings. Each of his images had a certain emptiness, as if he had arrived too late to catch the heart of it.

'This is only a selection. I travel extensively.'

'But there's nothing here.'

'I suppose not – not any more – but that's why I go. There, the tower you're looking at, is in York. Built to replace the wooden one, burnt around the city's Jews. Here: torture and execution of Welsh resisters to English occupation. Here: a supremely avoidable mining disaster. Here: murders from the Bloody Assizes. People remember these things, the names and the places can be found out.'

'Why?'

'This one is near the place where I was born: the pool where Witchfinder General Matthew Hopkins was thrown, bound hand and foot. He floated, so they burned him as a witch, like the hundreds he'd condemned. A lovely place. I do go back there, but not as often as I'd like. No time.'

'Why are you doing this?'

'Because I know what these places were; I know what happened. I can't be sure how I began to, but now I do know and I disagree. As deeply as I can remember, I disagree, so I drive where I have to and I speak to what people I can and then we all know. I also take photographs and pray.'

'Does it do any good?'

'Yes. I make myself content. I hope I may go on to Africa, India, North and South America. There are so many places and so many times, naturally increasing, and no one has ever regretted them formally. I can see I may well be busy until I die. I cannot live in an evil present with any comfort, I constantly feel the harm banked up around me. Perhaps I shall never leave this island. There is so much here to take into account. And perhaps we should go downstairs now. It's such a lovely day, I would hate to miss all of the sun.'

She watched him take a chair out into the garden and sit; gently, slowly rolling his shirt-sleeves up on his thin arms, and she thought how strange it was that all the harm and death he must have in his head didn't show. He was only ever peaceful.

The next time she embraced Nick up in Mr Haskard's rooms, she found her eyes ticking aside to the photographs lined near the bed. She considered for a moment the drive he was making that morning, away from her house – the square, where a peaceful crowd was fired on – Glencoe, full of politics and death – two forts of armed occupation – then Inverness and Culloden and more of the ache and the darkness of old blood. Mr Haskard had outlined his route. He had also talked of the beauty he hoped to encounter in the available countryside.

'What's wrong?'

Nick could be remarkably alert, even as he held her, even as he seemed to lose himself in the thought and the reality of her moving reflection in another man's looking-glass.

'Oh, I was thinking of Mr Haskard, how long he would be away.'

'Really.'

Although her answer had been almost true it seemed to displease Nick. He seemed to have misinterpreted her sense, to have given her a different meaning.

'We don't have to bother with him now.'

'No. Of course.'

'This is our house.'

'His room.'

'Oh yes, and his bed.'

'No. Nick.'

'We gave him a double bed – the poor old bastard doesn't need it. Why not?'

'It's . . . It would cause problems.'

'We can deal with them.'

She washed and dried Mr Haskard's sheets, re-made his bed, replaced his folded pyjamas under the pillow where they would be safe. He must have another set for when he travelled. Unless he slept naked while he was away from them.

When she held her hands up to her face they smelt of cotton and of night and of her certainty that she would never say what she had done, even though Mr Haskard might well be able to guess.

Nick left to teach his evening class and stayed out late – lost in a discussion too interesting to curtail.

She only realised she had not been waiting for Nick's return when he had settled himself coolly to her left and her restlessness remained.

Three hours later the front door snapped and sighed open. Mr Haskard was home. She lifted herself fully awake and listened for the fast, light movement on the stairs below, beside and then above her, the gentle setting down of a travelling bag. Mr Haskard creaked softly across her ceiling, became silence and almost allowed her to sleep before his descent began again. She could only think he had noticed their intrusion and abandoned his rooms.

The kitchen door was closed when she reached it; a big, numb dark swung out to meet her as she moved inside. She must, after all, have miscalculated, misheard. Mr Haskard must really be sleeping upstairs as usual – only her guilt could have made her think otherwise.

'Do close the door.'

She span left and felt her hand bark suddenly against wood.

'I am sorry. I imagined you knew I was here.'

'Mr Haskard?'

'Certainly not an intruder. You didn't think I was?'

'No.'

'Good.' He didn't whisper, his words made one low, even tone. In the absolute blackness, his sound was almost solid. 'If you step forward and very slightly right, you'll come to a chair. When you sit I will be beside you. Mind the table.'

'It's so dark.'

'Yes, I've drawn the blinds and the curtains. It has to be dark.'

'For your photographs?'

'Oh, no. I haven't the slightest interest in their manu-facture. This is something else. Watch.'

She listened as Mr Haskard's hands made a gentle disturbance near her, then felt a minute shudder through the air. Then she heard a soft, sudden impact, saw a splash of violet light. Another stroke fell, more light.

'What are you doing?'

'Breaking sugar.'

'No, what are you doing?'

'Breaking sugar, I said. Here – that's it, that's the hammer. Now –' Something slid towards her. 'This is your bread-board, feel it?'

'Oh.'

'Yes, and that's the sugar and there's a cube I haven't crushed.'

'But –'

'Shhh. Check where it is and then move your hand. Hit it. Hit it hard.'

She released a faint line of purple sparks where the hammer struck some scattered fragments.

'No, remember where it is. Now.'

The tiny explosion flared for a moment and then bleached the dark against her eye.

'I've always loved to do this, since I was a boy. I would

look at people stirring their tea and think I knew a secret
– that sugar was more than sweet.'

'It's not the sugar, it's the crystal. The structure. If you
crush a crystal, you get light.'

'Which makes it even better. A law – under the most
extreme pressures, there will be unexpected light. And no
one can ignore the laws of nature.'

'Mr Haskard, I think you should know – '

'I know.' His fingers found her hand, pressed it calmly
and lifted away. 'I do know and I quite understand.' The
small push and heat of his words fell against her cheek.
She reached into the numb dark and let herself explore
the change from the soft hair by his ears to the harshness
of whiskers grown over the skin and muscle of his cheek.
When he swallowed, the muscle moved. There was a larger
motion when Mr Haskard spoke. 'That's really quite all
right. I know.'

She heard herself exhale in one long, live moment and
swayed with a lift of weight from under her heart. The
matter was very simple now and plain; she and Mr Haskard
would break their sugar together and make their sugar dust.
It would sweetly coat the floor, the table-top, their hands
and clothing, even rise against their faces and flavour their
lips. This would be only a small inconvenience, water-
soluble and easily removed. A morning after sugar need
never differ from a morning after undiluted sleep. They
would have no reason to leave involuntary evidence.

'I happen to have some more sugar here, would you
like to go on?'

She heard Mr Haskard carefully breathing like a large,
close cat and knew she would be quite able to scrub their
bread-board and to wash any possible imprint of sweetness
away. She also knew she never would.

FAR GONE

He could feel himself gladly abandoning sanity.

'This is not our fault.'

'Well it's not *my* fault; if it's not *your* fault then whose fault can it be?'

'You have a separate ticket.'

Something was trickling from his hairline, and then creeping down the left side of his face. He guessed this would either be sweat, or cerebral-spinal fluid escaping the dreadful conditions at large in his skull.

'I know I have a separate ticket; it's a separate ticket for a flight that I will miss because your aeroplane won't get me to New York in time to catch it. And this is *my* fault?'

'This is your fault. You missed our flight.'

'I missed your flight because the flight that got me here – the flight which is not on a separate ticket, the flight which is on the same ticket as your flight – *that flight was late.*'

'This is not our fault.'

He examined the ticket girl, perhaps trying to find if she was really, truly different from him in a fundamental way. Was she less human than him and incapable of fellow-feeling? Or more human than him and possessed of such a massive, spiritual perspective that individual ruined lives were meaningless to her?

He felt instinctively that she was set apart from him and his species to such a catastrophic degree that he should be able to kill her now and abandon her body and be charged with nothing more grave than littering. He also knew this feeling was not helping his communication skills. If he hoped to win her over, to charm her, he would have to find some detail about her that he could like and which could moderate his temper, no matter how mildly.

She was wearing purple lipstick so her mouth would match her uniform. That was rather sweet, or rather sad – depending on what degree of corporate control this implied could be exerted on her body. Now that he looked, all of the ticket staff had co-ordinated lips. Their grasp of transportation systems would barely help them get across the street, but their cosmetics were absolutely organised.

She brushed at her forehead, as if his attention was beginning to leave a stain. 'You are going to America.'

'No. Obviously, I am *not* going to America.'

That stumped her. She almost frowned. 'But you *are* going to America.' She flapped his dead and separate tickets with authority.

He had to admit defeat. 'I am *trying* to go to America.'

'You have a Green Form?'

'What?' She'd got him there, right under his guard.

'You have a Green Form?'

'Yes, I have a Green Form. *I* am organised. *I* know what I'm doing. *I have everything I need.*' He tried to glare at her accusingly, but managed something which felt much more close to a vehement squint.

'I can see your Green Form?'

Not content with marooning him here for sport, she was now implying that he'd lied, that he didn't have a Green Form, or that he'd lost it, or that he was in some way unreliable. He considered berating her, but found he couldn't muster the will for a good berating. Someone would end up crying and it would probably be him.

He passed over his form which was suddenly dog-eared and so could not be flourished as effectively as he'd wished. 'You are making me mentally ill. My doctors will sue you.' He grinned in a way which he could almost guarantee was not remotely menacing.

'Thank you.'

She made him wait.

'I may have a nervous breakdown at any time.'

She passed him back his embittered sheaf of documents and waylaid him with an upsettingly human smile. 'Thank you.'

'No. Thank *you*.' He fankled at the strap on his bag, 'Thank you so much.' and attempted to break through the bleary queue behind him, 'So *very* much indeed . . . Oh, yes.' He was mumbling to himself now and hugging his hold-all, 'Oh, yes.' reduced to a maddened traveller after three hours apart from his home, 'Oh, yes.'

The tranquillity of his surroundings didn't help: the softly rolling trolleys, the contented security guards, the silence which spread unflappably about him while he flapped. And one of his shoes was squeaking. It had never made a sound before, on any surface, but now it was whining at every step: a tiny pedal protest in the face of something; everything; life. He was coming apart.

Before he could find the departure lounge, he limped past a cafe, a casino, a cafe, a bar, a cafe, a restaurant, and he knew that he was hungry but wouldn't eat. This was Holland. In Holland, they used Dutch money. He didn't have any Dutch money. He didn't even have any British money, not any more. He had dollars, American dollars, and he wasn't going to change them for anything else. They might be forcing him to stay here for six unnecessary hours, but they couldn't make him buy their currency. They couldn't make him buy their anything. He could not be forced to contribute to this airport's economy. Even if some of the places took dollars, even then, he was determined he would not co-operate.

And inside his inside pocket, as he walked, was the minor resistance, the thin-paper rustle of a sealed aerogramme which he should have posted. Instead, he was posting himself. Air Mail. Air Male. Oh, yes.

The idea of his arriving in America unannounced swam

through him like a saucy ghost, fingering his hopes and tendons as it went. He would manage this; he would be later than he'd hoped but he would manage and finally get there, where he wanted, where he needed to be.

The lounge whispered consolingly around him while other passengers meandered by with food they could eat and drinks they could drink and duty-free treats for their loved ones, he didn't doubt. He read an abandoned magazine which featured an item on 'Dentists To The Stars' which was not unamusing, but included a list of the tiny items found caught in celebrities' teeth: fragments of wine glass, carpet fibres, human hair.

The mention of human hair disturbed him. He imagined successful, desirable mouths, sexually active mouths gaping under orthodontic hands and surrendering signs of satisfaction – brown, brown, blonde – wedged back in molar notches or tucked beside incisors. Evidence of dirty goings on. Nicholson, Newman, Baldwin, Cage: they'd slope themselves down in their dental chum's chairs, furred up with libidinous encounters, part their lips under the spotlight, and then glisten with absolute oral complacency.

He wished every one of them septic gums.

And then stared at his ankles, in lieu of better things. Blue socks. Plain but with a light pattern in the knit; were they the correct kind of thing, he wondered? He hadn't thought his personal presentation through this morning, not properly, not with his trip being so impromptu, so fast. All his clothes were clean on and ironed and matching and everything, but perhaps blue was not for the best and – now he thought of it – he was currently something of an exercise in blue. He knew this would bring out the blueness in his eyes which could seem a shifty, soupy verdigris if he was tired and he *was* tired and would be more tired before he arrived. Unfortunately, a pale blue, like his pullover, would drain out the colour from his skin and leave him looking recently exhumed. A bright-eyed cadaver – this was not the particular dash he'd intended to cut.

He should examine himself somewhere private; check.

No. He should just sit. *Fearing* the worst was always much better than actually *knowing* the worst. The rest of his journey would be appalling, if he was certain of being ugly all the way. He would simply have to slap himself about the face before he met her, get some blood into the flesh. Before he met her.

Adrenalin noosed round his stomach and stubbed out something acrid in between each of his ribs. He closed his eyes and inclined his head the way he might to resist an especially moving piece of music. A terribly distinct and entirely fictitious image began to besiege him. He saw himself wearing his best blue/black coat – the one that he'd brought with him. He stood in it on a porch he had never seen but which, nonetheless, was aromatic with old wood and snow-melt and pockets of gentle but hyper-chilled air. His breath festooned around him magnificently while he shifted his weight and made little boot thumps on the planking. Deep in the house she was possibly wiping her hands clean from baking, or putting down a book. He couldn't quite decide which to imagine, so he looked at both. Then she was, very definitely, walking to answer his knock at her door, coming to welcome the whole of his body inside.

He would let her unwrap him. He would let her sample each of their contrasts in temperature, the good ones: his cold hair, her warm neck, the sly refrigeration of his hands, the heat of her shiver as she licks at his ice-water lips and then the open ache and simmer of his mouth.

The way she would prise at him was almost hypnotising. He throbbed with the idea of it, throbbed altogether too much. As a kind of counter-balance, he tried to think of Malcolm Rifkind and of televised fishing matches and still throbbed. He pictured penetrating Nancy Reagan roughly from behind and felt a devil-may-care tweak of perspiration before a body calm began to spread in him like glue. He thought of spontaneously combusting and leaving only a pristine foot in one good, blue sock and one good, black boot – along with a thoroughly unpleasant, greasy residue – and found he was slipping back to normal, just about.

Normal for a man who'd been trapped in Amsterdam entirely against his will. Normal for a man on the way to Ithaca, America, when he should have been on his way to Uddingston and an overdue progress report. Normal for a man, cleared out of Scotland and cleared out of his mind.

It was lovely being out of his mind, very roomy. Now he could go anywhere he liked.

Which, in three hours, would be his designated departure gate. Looking like the dead, mad passenger he almost was, he would set off along the moving walkways, nearer and nearer to take-off and at every fifteenth, squeaking step, he had decided he would hold his breath and imagine her nipples, firming out under his tongue. That thought would strike him, scratch him, draw blood up under his skin, but he wouldn't mind because it would also keep him very much warmer and very much saner than he might otherwise seem to be.

Fresh start. He flat-footed down the dirty bridge carpet and into the belly of the plane, lickety-spit, a jolly man. The tight air, packed with claustrophobia and vertigo and aviation fuel reek, barged into his lungs like electrified water and meant he smiled at every single flight attendant, every fellow-traveller, every overhead luggage locker and every empty seat. He was ready to go and able to go and happily inside a vehicle which intended to fly to New York and which was filled solely with people who wanted to fly to New York: people exactly like him. This was grand. Oh, yes.

Over there, it was just after lunchtime. He wondered what she'd eaten and if it was nice.

Soon they would begin to move and then taxi. He anticipated their gallop along the runway, inertia clawing gently at his bones, and their first, unlikely leap into a climb where they would join the condition of feathers and gases and occasionally hearts – absolutely airborne.

He could have phoned her. Finding out her number and calling would have been no problem, but had seemed like the wrong thing to do. She'd always liked his little surprises and general impetuosity. Her face on the porch when she saw him would show that lovely, familiar blend of confusion, wonder, charmed irritation, modesty and shock. Pleasure, as well. Above all, he'd give her pleasure – like before.

'My headphones.'

'Yes?'

'They don't work.'

The discrete howl of the engines beyond them dislocated everything but consonants from their words. The attendant leant in over him, anxious for his meaning and touched his shoulder with her fingertips.

'D-n't w-k?'

'Ah. No. Can't hear with them.'

'Right channel?'

'No right channel to have. No sound.'

'Oh dear. I am not a technician.'

'Don't worry, I am not either, but it doesn't make me sad.' In fact, he felt extraordinarily happy. Caffeine was racing under his breath and his second small but free bottle of wine had started to round the edges on life very pleasantly.

'You have tried . . .'

She leaned and glanced enquiringly across him to the other free seats at his side and left him awash with the scent of what he guessed must be her face-powder and possibly also the gravy unique to airborne catering.

'I have plugged myself in the whole length of the row. I can't hear.'

'You can't hear?' He craned up and watched her become suddenly worried, which was kind of her.

'The sounds that I should. I can *hear*. But not in the headphones. This is all too difficult isn't it?' He giggled.

'Sorry?'

'It's all too much.'

'I will send a technician.'

'No. It's fine. I don't want to hear. Hearing is not important any more.'

'I will send someone.'

'No. No, thank you. Don't. Thank you.'

He nodded reassuringly as she trollied away. Deprived of sound, he had no way to watch the movie or listen to the radio, and really this was very good because it meant he would be bored and go to sleep. The more rest he could manage now, the better for later on. He should drink a great deal – but probably less alcohol, although they did keep on offering it to him, it was hardly his fault if he drank it; he should keep himself correctly hydrated and he should snooze.

Cabin fever was already attacking his legs which he longed to really stretch out comfortably in a way that he couldn't, or cross in a way that he couldn't, or run up and down on in a way that he couldn't. Across the aisle a couple were sprawled out on each other stickily.

The woman, who was dozing with her mouth ajar, had odd teeth, slightly misaligned. She would lisp, probably, or dribble. The man he couldn't see so well – except for a scalp like waxed paper and one pasty arm. Not an attractive pair: more like hideous, but in complementary ways. He had noted, lately, that hideous people seemed to get lucky especially often. They were constantly pawing each other in public places while quite presentable people only drifted, unattached.

He should sleep. He should fold back the armrests, gather the pointless little airline pillows into a mound for his head and try not to let his feet extend across the path of any passing refreshment wagons while he was unconscious. One could never enjoy being woken by the shock of accidental amputation.

Hugging his arms in under his armpits, bending his knees almost foetally, trying for comfort, he panicked slowly at some turn in flight: a minor pitch of wing-tips as the whole, great parcel of them nosed across Greenland at five hundred miles an hour and far below freezing. The impossibility of his position occasionally crept up and scared him.

Unless he allowed her to fumble out into his mind and work her way round to the dimmer corners, the shame-faced places in his thinking, and bewilder him with need. Oh, she was nice. All those letters she'd written since he'd left – how they were – how she said things – she was racy, always had been, wouldn't change.

The way she smoked, for instance, was outrageous – not as if she liked smoking particularly, but as if she did very much like doing something else. Puckering and sucking till his thigh muscles clenched and screamed in to the bone. Which was not a thing to think of here and now, although of course it was too late to stop, and the feel of her hair spilling over, light and tickling on his stomach, of her kissing him in from his hip, savaged through him so that he had to kick and turn beneath his plastic-scented airline blanket. Something metal in a seat back stabbed him in the spine as he went. At least that gave him a good excuse to groan.

Consciousness dipped and jerked against him and then blurred away again while his mouth forgot him, responded to kisses that were not there, coughed back to life and the taste of tired sweat. Her last letter, he'd understood it at a time like this, when he'd been lying on his sofa and almost dreaming and almost not. He had suddenly known absolutely what she meant.

Henry and I are as happy as we could ever expect to be
as we could ever expect to be

It was so plaintive, such a cry for help, he couldn't think why he hadn't realised before. He'd read through her other letters then, every one, and all the signs were there, distinct.

Mrs Spano. That's me now. No more Bonnie Youmans, only Bonnie Spano. It feels weird. Maybe I shouldn't of picked a Spano, what do you think?

He knew what he thought very well and so did she.

Henry and I took a ride out to Buttermilk Falls, we had a great time.

Because she'd been there before that with him; they'd been there together, in amongst the turning leaves, and he'd wished he had a camera and their time had been more than great. Unbelievable was the word for that time: the best. He couldn't ignore the significance of her writing about Buttermilk Falls.

She wanted him to come and get her. She didn't want to stay with Henry. It was obvious.

He'd have to find a bigger flat, of course, the place he'd got now was no good. They'd have immigration problems and then her divorce and both of them might argue a little because of the strain but mainly the whole ordeal would draw them together and make them quite sure their decision had been right. He would admit that he'd been wrong to leave her without really understanding how he felt and she would already have told him, goodness knew how many times, that Henry had been a mistake and caused only by her being on the rebound after him.

Although Henry would have fucked her, because this was the kind of thing that husbands did, it wouldn't count. Bonnie would have submitted out of duty, or maybe loneliness, but Henry wouldn't do it right, there was no way that he could. There was no way to imagine Henry dipping into her with that achy, jazzy rhythm she'd remember or mouthing at her neck, her armpits, breasts – there was no way to see him doing that, anytime he wanted, home suddenly for lunch and a jumping session, horny round the evening kitchen, loose in a bed with her naked. There was no way to picture that.

He rolled again and caught another jab at his back. He groaned obediently.

Bastard Spano. Lucky bastard Spano. But not for long.

Because flight time was passing and real time was folding in back on itself, and when his body had reached the small hours of the morning he could set his watch to match the late evening of America, Eastern Time. When the plane landed, he might even applaud. Not in the way that more sheltered Southern Europeans did – celebrating their deliverance from high-altitude death – but in the way that a man might if he had come to claim a bride. Someone else's bride, granted, but that would soon be sorted out.

He would climb down the thin metal steps from the aeroplane in that classic, star-crossed, B-movie way and he would breathe, really breathe, because this would be the one time he could tell what America smelled of, before he got used to it. He would harbour its sweetness in his mouth, ignore the bitter tang of machinery and pick out the long whip of energy and space. At least, that's how he remembered it smelling – of a good and sweet and somewhat stimulating space. Which had been just precisely the scent of Bonnie Youmans.

And to get out and at Bonnie Youmans, all he had to do was queue. This would normally have made him impatient, tetchy, grim, but for America he tried to be a good boy, a nice boy. Oh, yes. Because he was utterly certain that, right now, he was tired enough for anyone to do anything they could possibly imagine, all over his helpless body for hours on end. They could take him away, strip-search him, violate him horribly and he would not produce one syllable of complaint, although he might whimper a little if they did something involving electric shocks. He attempted to walk, rather than shuffle, under the sore, bile-coloured lighting of JFK Terminal Something-or-Other, and did not look directly at any uniformed personnel for fear of being picked out for pistol-whipping or the unanaesthetised insertion of genital bolts.

It could be that paranoia had set in. He was most certainly unfit to be thinking, whimsical with exhaustion – if that was the right word, probably not – and, as a result, his thinking was most certainly unfit.

In fact, he was subjected to only the smallest cruelties. Having queued to get off the plane, he then queued to have his bag checked, his declarations of moral good-standing accepted and his passport stamped. He did what he was told to, now suddenly fearful of the past night's damage to his back; the pains of a night which had not happened here, not yet. Then finally he limped, eyes forward, across the magic line into a new, unopened, E Pluribus Unum, United States type of night.

'McGhee. No, ah, sorry, McFee. My name is McFee. Sorry. Tired.'

He booked himself a motel room near the airport, the other airport, not La Guardia, the other one, Newark. Yes. Had to get there next. If he turned his head, an ominous pressure burst open at kidney height. He shouldn't turn his head.

'One person. Ticket for one person and one bag. McFee. No. McGhee. No, that's right, actually. McFee.'

Every batter of the bus convinced him he would be paralysed when he got off. Or rather, when he found he was unable to get off. Then he would have to signal that his relatives would sue the company. There was only the problem of getting relatives – he would have to make some. His and Bonnie's children, he'd teach them all how to sue.

Leaning against his window meant that only half his spine seemed dreadfully endangered. Perhaps this would mean he could get himself about, after some practice, with a kind of dragging hop.

Except he would be all right, really; he would survive because Bonnie would need him healthy and, from what he remembered, fit. He tried to remember what he remembered, to find a grubby something he could focus on to keep him hearty through the journey. Her back – hugging up against her back and letting his prick give a little knock between her thighs and the tuck of her arse. That, he could remember, every inch.

If he got to the hotel alive, he could have a wank. He'd look forward to that.

'McFee.' He didn't die in the queue at Reception.

'Room for McFee?' A bath and a wank.

'McFee?' Just a wank. 'Good. That's fine. Terrific. Good. Thanks.'

He fell asleep on top of his bed, not watching Jay Leno.

Then woke from a dream of frost across forests, of milk and bottle-blue streams and the sun caught pink along iced brush and birches: the image of the country that Bonnie must see every day. She loved it, he knew. It would be the only reason she had stayed.

Outside, snow was treacling down through fog, and dawn was struggling to break.

He dealt with his hard-on under the shower: imagining her skin, her kiss, her everywhere in a kind of gasping blur that brought things to an end far too abruptly. That would do for now, though; there'd be more and better later on.

'Mr McFee?'

'McFee, right. Checking out. There's a way I can get to the airport?'

'Why certainly, yes.'

Which was quite beautifully true. He fragmented a couple of vertebrae in another suicidal minibus and scrambled out at Newark Airport to claim his seat on the very first possible Ithaca flight. Minor weather-related delays were in the offing, but cancellations were highly unlikely. All was well. He'd get his ascent above pine woods and soft hills and pastel houses built like beehives and love.

He decided not to telephone her now. He should get to his gate and be ready. Besides, at this time in the morning, good old Spano might still be at home. In this precise moment, it was possible he was lying next to Bonnie, waking, touching her, because married people often slept together and did these things, even if only one of them wanted to. The slick idea of Spano's fingers plumbing Bonnie made him nauseous.

He could phone and then say nothing; that would stop any carrying on, but might arouse suspicion and also prevent his arrival from being the nicest possible surprise. God, she'd be so pleased to see him. She'd smile in her eyes first and then her face and he would hold her if she started crying, which was quite likely, because she would know that, from then on, she was saved.

Lack of breakfast was making him giddy and his middle back was aching like a weal, but he was boiling with joyfulness because he was breathing round a secret which had finally turned hot. Nobody knew what he'd do – that he would stroll out from Ithaca airport and catch a cab to Dryden, 41 Rochester Street, and within an hour, maybe forty-five minutes, he'd be lapping at Bonnie Spano till his whole mouth needed shaving, have no doubts.

He found he was hugging his hold-all again, overcome by want. Both his arms were beginning to shiver although he knew that everything was fine now and that today his ending would be happy. Oh, yes.

THE CUPID STUNT

She'd told Peter the X-ray story without even meaning to, which was nothing if not an encouraging sign for their possibly mutual future.

'A man at a party?'

'Yes.'

'Remarkable.'

Usually, a conversation would need to be steered conscientiously towards even breaking the ice with a modestly surgical sentence, or the most glancing mention of human flesh. More general medical topics would quite often make a good start, a kind of permission to proceed, and then she'd bring in the X-rays and hope little thoughts of anatomy would ensue. It was her favourite story and rarely failed.

'I was twelve and I think my parents were having a party. This man, he walked right up the stairs to where I was standing and gave me a handful of X-rays. To keep.'

'Were they his own?'

Which had been a very good question: a point no one had raised with her before. Peter had really helped her tell him what she wanted to. He'd been keen and interested, focused. Asking for it.

'His own? Well, I suppose so. I mean, they probably *belonged* to him, but, yes, they could well have been *of* him, too. He didn't tell me. I only remember him shaking my hand and then he went away.'

'You didn't know him?'

'No. He might have been a friend of my parents, but maybe not. He could have been a randomly gate-crashing radiologist. Happens all the time.'

Peter had then smiled in a way that must have been slightly audible, or tangible, because it had made her look at him directly and join him in a grin. A small one, exploratory, but more than enough to stumble her straight across that hi-hat feeling: *pt-tssch*.

When the comic hits the punch line, when the tune beats to a stop, when you touch the touch that's a good touch, one that licks the brink – that's all the same thing, that's the hi-hat. *Pt-tssch*. A tremble of snare-drum that bumps through to a cymbal; one strong clatter, in under the line of your waist, and you know that the moment is reeling by nicely and may well deliver the goods at any time. The hi-hat makes you want to reach for something, for someone, and then hold on. Because of it, your skin develops a hard, instinctive thirst.

'What did you do?'

She'd looked at Peter's hands. They were okay, shapely, she'd been able to think of them touching her without hesitation or doubts. She had clearly foreseen him touching her.

Breath. Check the breath.

'What did you do? With his X-rays? You can't stop now . . . not when I want to know.'

Peter had been breathing all evening – obviously – but she hadn't caught a scent in his breath. No problem there, then. Anyone could have an off day, orally, but he'd been fine. He'd offered no trace of that strange, plaque-and-sinus-haunted aroma that some men's mouths produced and that anyone could tell would be permanent, congenital, a source of shame and ostracism for whatever kind of children they might make.

'I did what you're meant to with X-rays, I looked at them. I took them up to my bedroom and I looked.'

'Ten years old . . .'

'Twelve.'

'Still precocious, all the same.'

The skin beneath Peter's eyes had been, in the standard way, quite soft and thin and had moved very slightly and almost delicately when he blinked. The effect of his blinking had not been standard. She had found it very pleasantly uncommonplace.

'I was an old twelve. In a hurry. You know.'

Peter had blinked again and that time it had been intentional, she'd felt sure: a conscious effort to be attractive, because he'd known that with his eyes shut he looked good.

Watching his eyelids flitter and rise to show a green-grey attention, she'd let the rest of the X-ray story nuzzle in. There was no need for her to be forward when an anecdote could lead the way. A description of those wide and peculiarly flexible medical transparencies of a welcoming sea-water blue could, for example, make anyone pause to consider the wonders of science for a twelve-year-old and the later wonders of a body's discovery.

Mention images more specifically, and easy imaginations would see the lovely, milky ghosts of bones. She had avoided any reference to the pain or illness that would, most likely, have demanded X-ray penetrations and plates. This had meant Peter could simply appreciate the structure of all that was currently supporting both of them. That was something they'd already had in common – an interior skeleton.

A further nudge of intimacy had tickled in, as soon as she had catalogued the even closer details of deeper-than-skin photography. She'd gently described the display of bright lace and smoke cages that held a smirr of tender organs meant for inspiration, inhalation, procreation, sex. No one could imagine physicality for long without a hint of sex.

Most signs being favourable, her standard discourse would have finished with her favourite, the pelvic plate; its sacrum and lower vertebrae afloat with teasing curves. There'd be nowhere to go after that but far wrong, which was always nice.

The X-rays were a great encouragement towards a touch of what was always nice. They enabled any individual to cultivate the view that bodies were like landscape and textbooks and art: made for close understanding and looking and thumbing through. They'd introduced a type of fascination that blinked up from holographic snapshots of personal interior design and that one special, faded glimpse – like muslin under water – of a buttock. A stranger's buttock and a private trace of thigh.

That first evening, left alone with the X-rays and no more than twelve years old, she had tried and then failed to decipher all the tiny tugs of interest even translucent limbs could cause. She had hoped Peter might feel a retrospective sympathy for her lot.

And he did, indeed, prove pleasantly obliging. Peter had started laughing about nothing in particular before she ever mentioned the buttocks, or the pelvic plate, and they had then giggled between each other, exhalations disorganised, gestures inclined to be smaller or greater than they had meant, until they'd stuttered down into an ache of silence. They both breathed, both blinked and faced their decisions for each other: both in favour of going on.

Leaving the bar, she'd felt wonderfully, sickeningly tense. Their arms had slowly counter-crossed, guessing at the form of bones and backs in passing, and had snibbed them in together, hip to hip. The night had been quiet and not cold.

They'd lasted five months. Her lucky number, five.

Still adrift in the doze of one dim early morning, she had stretched in a small way and turned to her side.

'Peter?'

She had thought of the rasp and slip of him, the consolation of his hands, the meat and the frame of something which could often approach love and which certainly compensated for the petty irritations of the day, the temper and the fragments of unease.

'Peter?'

Five months.

Like the X-rays, he had taught her what men could be made of: things that felt good and left neatly before dawn.

Friends had been kind and invited her inside their homes so that she would meet other men, ones composed of more reliable elements. She was welcomed into flats and houses choked full with the husbandly, wifely comforts, including useful kitchen utensils, muffled children and bleakly smiling photographs. These benefits of marriage did not attract her. She wanted to touch and to be a touch. *Pt-tssch*.

Trying her best to seem resilient and consoled, she had met with many of the kindly offered men. She had talked to them about dental and medical matters, but each one had been unable to board her trains of thought. Rather, strangers had doggedly told her about their asthma and their mother's legs and whined about recurrent golfing injuries without a twitch of sensuality and she'd known what their skin would feel like and decided it could be forgone.

Slowly, the spaces between her fingers and under her palms had begun to shiver and pine. She had sought out the vague rub of crowds and public places and had accepted advice which suggested that physical pleasure without the hi-hat could be drummed up quite easily. For instance, she had only to pay and she could be completely re-modelled, at the level of her superficial dermatology. That would unmistakably be a kind of touch. The plucking and buffing and waxing involved could peel her raw and ready for any available sensation and dib, dib, dib, she would be prepared.

But instead, she had let herself be slipped into a Dead Sea tank – a small, expensive container of the liquid made by adding water to whatever was left of the Dead when you took out the Sea. Her unnatural buoyancy had been alarming, but the salts had burned her enviably smooth for the nothing and no one she'd grown used to smoothing against. Her clothes had stopped fitting, but this didn't matter, because she didn't like them any more and because she had decided to be a different shape. A type of hunger had begun to inform her movements. Her body had inclined indiscreetly while she talked and she had held hands too intensely in a shake. Every morning she had washed and dressed a middle-aged reminder of why she was mildly but continually sad.

And at nightfall, if she hadn't made herself very sternly pre-occupied, a longing would have prised her, pawed through her, fiddled with her lungs, until she had wanted to run off and leave herself, winking and ogling at the corner of an unfamiliar street; to walk out without her whole body; to just leave it staring from a jammed revolving door while she slipped away. Her body had been too demanding, too arbitrarily quiet and then too imaginatively, too viciously alert.

She had known there was no solution, no wholesale amputation that could be performed. Once exhaustion had made her desperate enough, she had simply abandoned her hope into the hands of a temporary, symptomatic cure. She had decided she would pay a man to touch her and be satisfied that way.

Hourly rate. No funny business. A genuine and ethical, if not medical masseur.

She liked him in a sort of way; probably because he did his job well and felt studiously good. He maintained a constant contact so she could close her eyes and tread the water across somewhere soft which her thinking hardly reached. Relaxation drifted by to unbutton what was tight.

While she breathed in a regular manner, he was careful, used his fingertips in mapping from her ankle to her knee, and his every application of neat force set a sparkle of something near pain coursing in beside her muscle, edging her bones. Their agreement seemed to be that he would steer her to the point where she could break from her body, like bread torn part from part.

Nothing but thorough, he opened her joints, ran through the fear and anger tucked up in the meat of her back, tapped out the panic in her neck. After the third or fourth session, she was familiar with the slow jabs of his elbow, his knee, his thumb, and the beneficial violence he would escalate across her until she might even make a little noise so that he would pause and his touch would rest against her, an inquisitive weight.

Whatever he did, whatever fierce care he applied, he kept his touch precisely neutral and controlled. His pressure on her buttocks was unerotically exact. He sited work above, or below, but never at her breasts. Although he would palpate her stomach, there was never a suggestion he might cross the bikini line and no leap of excitement leaped when he bent her legs and pressed his abdomen forward against the resistance of her feet. She felt him breathing and slightly warm along her instep, that was all. He knelt and stepped and reached himself comprehensively about her, but never transgressed an erogenous zone.

Sometimes she went to him after she finished work, rushing through a yellow evening to reach her appointment in time, and the rain would make smudges of shadow run down his Japanese-style blinds and she would lie on the white of his mattress and be warmed uncomplicatedly. They would have chatted briefly about the current flexibility of her frame and the frequency with which – on average – she opened her bowels. Next she would have lain herself down to be ready for him, aware that, in a certain way, he knew her rather better than anyone else would even wish to. Then he would stretch and fold her at his will, nudging the edge of discomfort, before he let her be again. After a good, strong session, she could go home and be quite sure that her bed was no longer spring-loaded and she could rest herself against it, her body's needs and distresses already massaged into sleep.

Her friends told her she looked terrific. They assumed

she also felt that way. They guessed she was now with somebody new, touching and being touched and that everything was splendid. *Pt-tssch*.

She did not tell them they were wrong. She did not disillusion them, because being disillusioned was a most unpleasant thing. She did not tell them that looking terrific was no help.

Pt.

But she still goes to the room with the Japanese-style blinds and the mattress covered over by a clean, white sheet. She lies on her back with her arms un-tensed and heavy at her sides and hears him breathe. She listens to the tiny disturbances of cloth and the call of brushed skin and she feels him touch her body as if it were a clean and healthy and touchable thing.

Although she has thought she might like to, she cannot imagine him being another man. He does not feel like Peter, or anyone else whose body she has known. His hands are unmistakable and conscientious, giving her absolutely what she pays for, no less, no more.

She eyes his ceiling and knows all the ways he is moving and all of the different forces he will use. Occasionally he swallows, brushes his forehead, or parts his lips and she makes a point of hearing him. If he ever releases a tremor of recollection, a drag of absence, sewing through her veins, he does so by pure accident. He doesn't mean anything by it and she doesn't take it personally.

Because this is only her rehearsal, this is only her little reminder of the very minimum of how it would be, how it *will* be, when she's this close and closer to anyone again. This is how she keeps in touch.

She is making do by arranging something which is better than nothing, because nothing is no good at all. She knows that, she understands. She isn't stupid.

Original Bliss

For Robin Robertson

Mrs Brindle lay on her living-room floor, watching her ceiling billow and blink with the cold, cold colours and the shadows of British Broadcast light. A presumably educative conversation washed across her and she was much too tired to sleep or listen, but that was okay, that was really quite all right.

'What about the etiquette of masturbation? Because everything runs to rules, you know, even the bad old sin of Onan. So what are the rules in this case? About whom may we masturbate?

'Someone we have only ever seen and never met?

'Quite common, almost a norm – we feel we are offending no one, we superimpose a personality on a picture, in as far as our dreadful needs must when that particular devil drives, and that's that.'

Harold Wilson's baby, friend to the lonely, the Open University.

'How about a casual acquaintance? Someone with whom we have never been intimate and with whom we never will? Someone our attentions would only ever shock?

'Actually, that's much more rare. We imagine their, shall we say disgust, and find it inhibits us. We steer our thoughts another way.'

Mrs Brindle rolled onto her stomach, noticing vaguely how stiffened and tender her muscles had grown. Women of her age were not intended to rest on floors. Beside her head, the moving picture of a man with too much hair, grinned clear across the screen. Video recorders were catching his every detail in who could tell how many homes where students and other interested parties were now sensibly unconscious in their beds, their learning postponed to coincide with convenience. Mrs Brindle didn't care about education, she cared about company. She was here and almost watching, almost listening, because she could not be asleep. Other people studied at their leisure and worked towards degrees, Mrs Brindle avoided the presence of night.

'On the other hand, we are highly likely to make imaginary use,' the voice was soft, jovially clandestine, deep in the way that speech heard under water might be, 'Of someone with whom we intend to be intimate.'

She tried to concentrate.

'The closer the two of us get, the more acceptable our fantasies become, until they grow up into facts and instead of the dreams that kept us company, we have memories – to say nothing of a real live partner with whom we may have decided to be in love.

'And here is where we reach my point, because this is all one huge demonstration of how the mind affects reality and reality affects the mind. I indulge in a spot of libidinous mental cartooning and what happens? A very demonstrable physical result. Not to mention a monumental slew of moral and emotional dilemmas, all of which may very well feed back to those realities I first drew upon to stimulate my mind, and around and around and around we go and where we'll stop, we do not know.

'That around and around is what I mean by Cybernetics. Don't believe a soul who tells you different – particularly if they're engineers. *This* is Cybernetics – literally, it means nothing more than steering. The way I steer me, the way you steer you. From the inside. Our interior lives have seismic effects on our exterior world. We have to wake up and think about that if we want to be really alive.'

Something about the man was becoming persistent. Mrs Brindle felt herself approach the slope of a black-out, the final acceleration into nowhere she needed to worry about, a well of extinguished responsibilities. It seemed not unlikely that his voice might follow her in.

She counted herself down the list of things still undone through her own deliberate fault: breakfast not prepared for, low milk not replaced, her surrender to the pointlessness inherent in ironing socks.

Dawn was up before her, but still not entirely established, just a touch delicate. The television was dark and dumb in the corner. She must have remembered to turn it off. Her left hip throbbed alive, commemorating another night spent bearing her weight against a less than forgiving carpet. Not for the first time, she pushed herself up to her knees with thoughts of how much more convenient she might find a padded cell. The idea didn't crack a smile, not this morning.

Furious, humid rain was banging at the windows. Its noise must have roused her. She relished downpours, their atmosphere of release. Stepping gently through to the kitchen, she knew this particular pleasure came mainly from the air pressure falls that could accompany lavish rain. The harmless impacts of water on glass were among the small, domesticated sounds that Mrs Brindle loved. Like the first whispers from a kettle when it clears its throat before a boil, they made her feel at home and peaceful in ways that many other things did not.

She steeped real coffee in the miniature cafetière that held exactly enough for one and tried not to remember the space in her morning routine. Mrs Brindle tried not to think, 'This is when you would have prayed. This is when you would have started your day by knowing the shape of your life.'

While she sat and waited for the time when she could set the bacon to the grill, Mrs Brindle remembered the programme she'd slept with last night. It had been about steering. A long-boned man who spoke about steering and wanking. That didn't seem exactly likely, now she thought, but the man who'd spoken seemed too coherent and unfamiliar and just too *tall* to be someone her imagination had simply conjured up and slipped inside her sleep. She hadn't exactly dreamed about him, but something of him had been constantly there, like the ticking of a clock, leaked in from another room.

Having completed her coffee, she worked her way through yesterday's paper and considered she might even try to find out his name.

'Edward E. Gluck. Edward E. Gluck. Edward E. Gluck. You hear that? I have a wonderfully rhythmical name. My mother gave it me. She played semi-professional oboe when she was young and I think this meant that she always approached things as if they were some kind of score: arguments, gas bills, christenings; anything. I could be wrong on this, but I like to believe it anyway, you know?'

Radio Two, Mrs Brindle's favourite; it didn't pretend to be better than it was. She was mixing a batter for Yorkshire pudding, properly in advance so that it would settle and mature and make something which would taste well and be sympathetic with gravy. She was nowhere near the time for gravy yet.

As Edward E. Gluck repeated and repeated his own name, she recognised his voice. On the television, he had sounded just the same – he made very ordinary words seem dark and close. Now, beneath his enthusiasm, she could hear a harder type of consistent energy, unidentifiable, but engaging. She put the batter bowl into the fridge and sat to concentrate on Gluck.

'She was a lady, my mother. A remarkable woman. On the night I'm referring to, I was maybe four years old and unable to sleep because freight trains ran close by the back of our flat almost continuously. And I was restless because my parents had separated not long before and I'd been moved from my home and money was tight and sleeping seemed too much like dropping my guard. Anything could have happened while I was out.

'Now I remember this clearly. I'm sitting up, right inside the dark with the blankets neat in to my waist and the rest of me cold. I'm concentrating. But there's no way to know what I'm concentrating *on* – I only know I've *been* thinking when my mother opens up my door. She snaps me back from a place in my mind that is smooth and big and nowhere I've been before. I've liked it. I want to go there again, to the place that's only thoughts and me thinking them.

'Mother, she sat by my bed. I can still picture her beautiful shape and know she smelt all powdery and breakable and sweet. She waited with me for the next of the trains to pass. She made me listen to the carriages – *listen* to them, not just hear.

'And they were saying my name. All of them, all of the time, for all of their journeys, were saying my name. *Edward E. Gluck, Edward E. Gluck, Edward E. Gluck.* Every train on every railway in the world can't help saying my name.

'That night, my mother taught me two things I have never forgotten since. That she loved me enough to offer me her time. And that my fundamental egomania will always cheer me up. I indulge it as often as I can.'

Gluck talked a great deal about himself – he put his inside on his outside with a kind of clinical delight. Mrs Brindle rolled cubes of pork in egg yolk and then salt and black pepper and flour and listened to someone with ridiculous personal confidence and a small but happy laugh. Whatever his life was doing, he seemed to understand it perfectly, because that was his job, his Cybernetics. Within the few minutes of his talk, he ricocheted from essential freedom to creative individuality and his new collection of accessible and entertaining essays which dealt with these and many other subjects. Available in larger bookshops now.

Mrs Brindle knew about bookshops. For a while she

had thought they might help her. Publishers were, after all, always bringing out books intended as guides to life and all-purpose inspirations. She had scoured an exhaustive number of first- and second-hand suppliers without finding a single volume of any use. She had also discovered since, that the fungi which thrived upon elderly books – even of the self-improving type – could cause hallucinations and psychosis and were, in short, a genuine threat to mental health. This did not surprise her.

The amount of time and hope she must have wasted in that particular search for enlightenment threatened to make her feel discontented now, so she decided to focus her mind on Gluck. She would like to read Gluck. This would do no more harm or good than the reading of anything else and would allow someone entertaining inside her head.

Her previous experiences had taught her that she could reach the closest sizeable bookshop, buy herself a book, and be home again in time to preserve the success of her evening meal. So she left the kitchen and then entirely abandoned the house with the radio still singing and murmuring to itself behind the locked front door.

She hadn't forgotten where to go. Through the side entrance and downstairs for RELIGION, SELF-HELP and PSY-CHOLOGY. Those three sections always seemed to cling together, perhaps for mutual support. She was familiar with many of the titles they still displayed. She was equally familiar with sidling across the broad face of SELF-HELP in the hope that she would appear to be very much on the way to somewhere else – perhaps towards HELPING OTHERS, or GENERAL FICTION – and not a person in need of assistance from any source. SELF-HELP was, in itself, an unhelpful title – Mrs Brindle was unable to help herself, that was why she had bought so many books and found them so unsatisfactory. Their titles winked out at her now like the business cards of cheerful, alphabetical frauds.

Today, as always, there were no sections assigned to FEAR OF DYING, or ABSOLUTE LOSS. This was presumably due to a lack of demand. Or else the low spending power of readers overly obsessed with The Beyond.

Gluck's essays were piled on a table to one side of PSYCHOLOGY – twenty or so copies of a cream-coloured hardback with the author's name and title marked in hard, red type. She could also make out the cream image of a cleanly opened skull, still cradling the hemispheres of a brain, very slightly embossed. Lifting one copy, she ran her forefinger quietly over the curves and edges of the paper skull. It felt good. She allowed herself a pause. Finally, she split the fresh pages, smelt the bitterness of new print and gave the opening a skim.

For many decades an unholy alliance of neurophysiologists and engineers has sought to produce mechanical imitations of the human brain. In a few limited areas, they have succeeded. One might wonder why they persist in their attempts, when two sexually compatible and fertile human beings can develop the real McCoy and the perfect system for its support in a matter of months and at relatively little cost.

On the back of the dust-jacket there was a grainy photograph of Gluck – unsmiling and against a background of dramatic cloud. She could only see his head and shoulders, so it was impossible to tell if he was standing on a roof, or a cliff-top, or, indeed, the upper deck of an empty bus. Something about the light on his face suggested he had taken up a stance in front of a very large window. Perhaps he could afford a house where such things were available.

Meanwhile computerised technology has become increasingly sophisticated. We have witnessed the irresistible rise of successive generations of machines which add one to one to one, at ever more stupefying speeds. The computer has simultaneously come to represent, not an imitation of the human mind, but an emotionless goal to which it might, one day, aspire.

Half a dozen stops on the underground and she would be walking back home and no one need ever know she had run away. The book was a small thing, it could be put in a great many places. Not hidden, only put in a place that was safe.

Tunnel lights and stations roared and arched around her while she held *Gluck — The New Cybernetics* gently and privately against her coat. The firmness of the book's construction was reassuring and that was pleasant in itself; she shouldn't build up expectations for its contents. She should just occupy a little of her time with Professor Gluck's writing and maybe not actually understand a word, but that wouldn't matter. A dose of mild confusion would be nice, it wouldn't hurt. And she would be reading someone who really did know the mind: his own and other people's. He understood things and she could be there in his book while he was understanding.

As the train shivered and shook her, Mrs Brindle recalled how much she had once looked for that, for understanding. She'd never wanted spirit guides, or dietary healing, aura manipulation, or the chance to be woken up sexually. She'd never wished to be a qualified stranger's second guess. She had never sought the temporary comfort of childhood hymns, of absolution, or even of very lovely Mysteries. Mrs Brindle had only wanted someone who understood, a person who would tell her what was wrong and how to right it.

Somewhere in our science the original and the template have become confused. The limited, mechanical model is now used to analyse and find fault with the shamefully underexplored, biochemical original. The computer's admirable ability to store information and its rather more plodding efforts to draw conclusions from available facts are held up as the pinnacle of possible intelligence. Lack of flexibility and, above all, lack of emotional content in the storage and retrieval of information are regarded as essential. Already, in certain spheres, Reality and the hideously impoverished Virtual Reality are held to be completely interchangeable.

Political and social theories pursued on the basis of Numerical rather than Completed Facts, cannot be influenced by human joys or human pains. Is, for example, a death only a negative number in our combat readiness or population totals? Or is it a major intellectual and emotional loss? How will our species prosper if we treat ourselves, according to Numerical Facts, as no more than arithmetic? Humanity, its potential and inherent strengths as expressed in the human brain, are being systematically erased.

The New Cybernetics represent an effort to reverse this erasure. The following essays deal with its applications in the treatment of disease, information technology, the development of personality, learning and — more speculatively — in the fields of history, philosophy and ethics.

That night she re-ironed the collars and cuffs on fourteen shirts and then sat on the carpet with a black-and-white movie splaying out across the shadows of the room while she read Gluck.

At first she was afraid. She didn't want him to tell out every part of Mrs Brindle into emptiness. Some things, she hoped, could never be wholly explained: how she laughed, the way she peeled oranges like her mother, what made her upset. She didn't want to learn that all of her was only atoms joining other atoms and cells joining cells and charges balancing up and down a wiring system that happened to bleed. Otherwise, all she'd have left of herself would be a type of biochemical legerdemain. She was afraid that Gluck might have the power to slip her apart and break her in the space left between nothing and nothing more.

But Gluck reassured. He wound her slowly through the glistening darkness she began to imagine was her mind. He personally assured her that she was *the miracle which makes itself.*

This was a start, a nice thing to know, but rather lonely. Before, Something Else had made her and looked upon her and seen that she was good.

Somewhere within her ten thousand million cells of thinking, she remembered when loneliness had been only an easily remedied misunderstanding of nature, because there had always been Something Else there, just out of reach. He had, at times, been more or less revealed, but had been always, absolutely, perpetually *there*: God. Her God. Infinitely accessible and a comfort in her flesh, He'd been her best kind of love. He'd willingly been a companion, a parent, a friend and He'd given her something she discovered other people rarely had: an utterly confident soul. Because Mrs Brindle had never known an unanswered prayer. For decades, she had knelt and closed her eyes and then felt her head turn in to lean against the hot Heart of it all. The Heart had given round her, given her everything, lifted her, rocked her, drawn off unease and left her beautiful. Mrs Brindle had been beautiful with faultless regularity.

Now she was no more than a bundle of preoccupations. She avoided the onset of despair with motiveless shopping and cleaning, improving her grasp of good cuisine and abandoning any trust in Self-Help books.

She had been told that her life in its current form represented normality. Existence in the real world was both repetitive and meaningless; these facts were absolute, no one could change them. Ecstasy was neither usual nor useful because of its tendency to distract, or even to produce dependency. Her original bliss had meant she was unbalanced, but now she had the chance to be steady and properly well.

Mrs Brindle tried to seem contented in her suddenly normal life and to be adaptable for her new world, no matter how hard and cold this made every part of every thing she touched. She allowed herself to betray what she had lost by ceasing to long for it. But when her betrayal became too unbearable and she began to believe she was fatally alone, she tried to pray again.

At first her efforts felt like respectably articulated thought. No more than that. She found she had lost the power of reaching out. Now and again she could force up what felt like a shout, but then know it had fallen back against her face. Finally the phrases she attempted dwindled until they were only a background mumbling mashed in with the timeless times she had asked for help.

So Mrs Brindle withdrew for consolation into the patterns of her day. She sought out small fulfilments actively. There were check-out assistants to be smiled for, chance encounters with cultivated or random flowers and overheard melodies to appreciate and, every week, she would do her utmost to find at least one new and stimulating, low-cost recipe. It was all bloody and bloody and then more bloody again, but faultlessly polite and inoffensive and there were no other bloody options she could take, but in her case, the path of least resistance was the one that she most wanted to resist.

Now another bloody year was grinding its away into June with hardly a protest or a sign of life.

Mrs Brindle encouraged habit to initiate and regulate her movements in the absence of her interest and will. Friday morning's habit was the recipe trawl: twice round the local newsagents with a fall-back position provided by the library.

On the third Friday of June Mrs Brindle found what she needed at only her second high-street stop. A belligerently cheerful magazine winked out at her, shamelessly covered with posing and pouting fruit flans: almond paste, cherries, apricots, vanilla cream and appropriate liqueurs; each of their possible elements boded well. She could explore a good dessert theme for weeks. This would be today's encouraging victory of the positive.

When she saw the article; the magazine's other article, the article which was not about transformative accessories, or any kind of flan, she was standing by her sink, holding a new cup of tea and half-looking out at signs of neglect in the window box. Somewhere beneath her breastbone she felt the warmth, not of surprise, but of familiarity and she may even have smiled down at the photograph of the prominent and fast becoming really rather fashionable Professor Edward E. Gluck. A small article mentioned his theories, his controversial Process and its undeniable results and she knew about these things already and in much more detail from his book. She was able to cast a knowing eye across the journalistic summary of his ideas and find it wanting. They didn't understand him the way she did.

Equally, they knew something she did not. They were able to point out that Gluck would soon attend a meeting of high-powered minds in Germany. Professor Gluck would be resident in Stuttgart for at least the week that ran from one plainly given date in July up to another.

It seemed right that Mrs Brindle should know where Gluck would be for the whole of one summer week. It seemed right that she should think of Gluck and Stuttgart and be happy and happiness is a considerable thing, a person should never underestimate what a person might do for it. Foreign travel might be seen as no more than a necessary inconvenience along the way. No matter how much justification and expenditure a trip – perhaps to Germany – would demand, it might seem possible, reasonable, worth it.

Having read Gluck as thoroughly as she could, Mrs Brindle knew about obsession, its causes and signs. She was well equipped to consider whether she was currently obsessing over Gluck.

Certainly she was close to his mind, which might cause her to assume other kinds of proximity. Obsessive behaviour would read almost any meaning into even the most random collision of objects and incidents. Chance could be mistaken for Providence. Fortunately, her Self-Help reading meant that she knew her thinking very well and could be sure she was a person most unlikely to obsess. She had never intended to seek out Gluck, she had simply kept turning on through her life and finding he was there.

'Were you ever happy? Tell me, were you ever truly happy, that you can recall? The right-now, red-flesh and bone-marrow variety of happy – yards and yards of it? Hm?'

He had a tan. Professor Gluck was standing and talking like a real live person, right over there and with a tan.

And there was so much of him. Every shift of his shoulders, every weight change at his hips, gave her three dimensions of unnerving reality. She had guessed he was photogenic, that he made conscious efforts to shine, but she had not anticipated how very well-presented he might actually be.

'Happy so there's nothing to do except smile and smile and smile and then again, well, you could always smile.'

Professor Gluck smiled luminously down about himself, as if to demonstrate. His little audience seemed to flinch gently, perhaps distressed by so much personality, all at once.

'Oh, the first time or two, you'll try to cough it up and maybe you'll shake your head about it, but in the end you'll just have to grit your teeth and grin it out. This is an inescapable thing you're dealing with. If you want to be happy – for example – it is highly likely that you will. The Process works. Naturally one can't infallibly predict the minutiae of its results, but speaking very strictly from my own experience I can say you may end up so contented you frighten strangers. Hold that thought. Now . . .' He paused and looked directly across to fix on Mrs Brindle and she realised how completely she must appear to be out of her place. With only one glance he could tell who she was – the crazy woman who had written to him and said she would be on her way. 'I am about to be late for an appointment. Thank you all.'

The circle around him found its hands shaken and its shoulders patted aside as Gluck sleeked his way precisely to meet her. His attention withdrawn, the group shuffled and broke away.

'Mrs um, Brindle?'

Something in her letter had persuaded him to meet her, which was good because it had taken her weeks to write. Her problem now would be that she couldn't make herself that clear again; not out loud where he could hear her. She was also too nervous to breathe. The uneasiness under her skin made her hands twitch while she tried not to gulp for air. She wanted to start this all over again at another, better time when she could feel more ready and less like a recently landed and naturally aquatic form of life.

Gluck's voice was unmistakable, dipping now and then into an octave below the norm, and holding that constant dry rumble beneath the rhythm of the words, his personal melody. 'Mrs Brindle. I am right?' His face waited, appraising.

He was said to be quite a singer. She had done her research. God, it was not fair or reasonable that she should be this afraid.

'Mrs Brindle?'

'Yes, yes, you're right. Professor Gluck.'

'My favourite sentence. "You're right, Professor Gluck." Well done. There's a table over by the wall where no one will bother us and I have asked for coffee, although it may well never come. Are you staying here?'

She felt herself propelled by something very like his will, or the sheer force of his words, or maybe just his hand, lightly settled at her back. She made a kind of answer without thinking, while her throat panicked tight. 'Me? No. No, I'm not.'

'Wise choice – I think this is the worst hotel I've never paid for.' He nodded in passing at a young man with a briefcase, flapped his hand to a couple by the door, then inclined his head very slightly towards hers. 'We may have to make a run for the last few yards, I feel the pack is closing fast.' His mouth barely avoided a smile. 'Oh, don't mind me, Mrs Brindle – I've had to be charming all morning and it never agrees with me.'

She didn't know if she minded him or not. She wasn't sure about the charming part, either, but he was undoubtedly something, a very great deal of something that was definitely Gluck. She walked on as carefully as she could, her awareness of his shape beside her threatening to distract her so much that she would fall. His hand continued to propel her with a useful and disinterested force.

Safely installed in their corner, Gluck lounged one leg out over the armrest of his chair, allowing it to be clear that he was both remarkably long-limbed and indisputably at ease with his surroundings. He seemed delighted that he might be adding creases to a suit, already expensively distressed. Now and then he spired his fingers, or bit his brown thumbs with his white incisors while he watched and grinned and watched, his interest held flawlessly at shoulder height. Once he had seen his fill beyond her, he angled round again to catch Mrs Brindle whole and finish with one slow blink dropping down over eyes the colour of blue milk.

'Now we shall get to know each other, shan't we? But do relax first, it will save so much time.'

She had already eased herself back in her seat and now tried not to move her arms in case they proved unreliable.

Her limbs felt slightly less anxious now, but also strangely insubstantial. Still, it did seem she could trust both her hands not to shake. That was good, she could build on that. She just wished she didn't know she was pale and that there were obvious shadows around her eyes. Red was prickling on her cheeks and nose after yesterday's unaccustomed sun and she felt visibly sticky, despite the extremely efficient air conditioning at work on every side. Her physical condition should have been irrelevant – Gluck would hardly be concerned with how she looked – but she did wish she could have seemed slightly less hideous, for the sake of her pride. A person was unlikely to enjoy asking favours from a position of grotesque inferiority.

'Tchick, tchick, fffop. Zippo.' Gluck winked at her and indicated a bullish man in his shirt sleeves who was straining at a fresh cigar. 'Zippo lighters, they always sound the same. When I was younger, I wanted to smoke, just so I could use one.' The white of his eyes blared a little too loudly over his grin.

'You never considered pyromania? Better for your health.'

He sat round to stare at her squarely, his face shining briefly with a peculiar kind of appetite. 'That's certainly true, certainly true. Remind me of what I can do for you, Mrs Brindle. Now that we're really speaking.'

She liked that she could sometimes change how people thought of her, just by saying out some little surprise. This didn't work in crowds because quite often no one heard her – she seemed often to be an inaudible person – but undoubtedly the good professor was now offering her a further chance to shine. He was trying to work her out, hoping to uncover just exactly who she was. She came very close to admitting she knew how he felt.

Gluck leaned in. 'Don't be alarmed, by the way, if we never get our coffee. They used to send it over with a very attractive young waitress – now she no longer comes and I often get nothing. You're in bad company with me, I do admit that, but I also wonder what precisely I did wrong. It is a shame, she was a nice girl.'

She knew he was watching for a reaction, to check which offence she would take, and she tried to maintain a correct indifference. He drove on with his stare, unconvinced, and then exhaled into a kind of shrug. 'Ah, well. I don't have your letter here with me . . . but . . . might I say first of all how impressed I am that you should have travelled so far. I do hope your journey will be adequately rewarded.'

'I needed a holiday.'

'And this is almost as good a location as any. Quite true. Do talk to me, Mrs Brindle, I'm beginning to feel alone.' Gluck pulled away, his eyes leaving first, cooling, their light closing down.

'You know about the brain. You . . . when you write – '

'I know about me, thank you. Tell me about you and your problem and I don't intend to rush you, but I must be in the Conference Room by 2.25 at the latest. You're attending the lectures?'

'Yes, I am.'

'All of them?'

'Yes. Most of them, at least. Some aren't open to the public.'

'So it isn't only my work that interests you?'

'Your work interests me the most. That's why I'm here. Please, if your time is so limited . . .'

She gathered a stiff breath and forced out something she hoped might be what she believed she thought, or hoped she thought, or hoped *he* thought, or just something *someone* might have thought at some time when they were trying to make sense of something. 'Religious experience, spiritual feelings . . . do you know if it's only chemistry . . . electrical spasms. Can you tell if . . . ? Is it likely . . . anything . . . from descriptions. Do you know *that* process? Possibly it never occurred to you – why should it . . . I mean . . .' She tried not to sigh. 'I have a problem.'

'Obviously. One you currently seem quite unable to describe. Have you had a religious experience?'

'No, at least that's – '

'Would you like a religious experience?' He failed to hide the glint of a smirk.

'Spiritual.'

'You would like a spiritual experience, or you would like a definition of a spiritual experience?'

'Either.'

'I think you might be a little more specific about your requests – it's the only way to get what you want.'

'I'm sorry.' But she didn't feel sorry. Humiliated, that's what she felt.

'I certainly can't give you a spiritual experience.'

Gluck's eyes were enjoying her unease, raising an unpleasant shine. He had decided to treat her as an interlude, a joke, and she wanted to be angry about that, but there was no room in her mind now to do anything but listen for what he might say. She was too hungry for any trace of help to be dignified. Their gazes crossed and locked and broke. Gluck's voice almost disappeared in a resonant rumble. 'As far as definitions go . . . I could give you a roomful – chemistry, electricity, extremity, psychosis, psychotropics, trauma . . . If that all seems distressingly un-supernatural then you must simply remember that an answer is only true until it's been discredited. I don't work in a field of absolutes. Even a Completed Fact isn't really complete, it's just our current best attempt – a healthy admission of constant defeat. Sometimes a definition is no more than a convincingly detailed guess. Or are we talking about God? Faith? About which I know little or nothing.'

'I'm sorry, I'm wasting your time. But there was something about your work, your understanding . . . there was a quality about it, perhaps not the theories themselves, but perhaps *in* the theories . . .'

The foyer, she knew, was quietly noting their every exchange: gestures, pauses, glances. She was using up time they wanted, wasting away the moments they could spend near their favourite: hoping for a trophy, a token, a moment of recognised intimacy; anxious to figure, even badly, in one of his famous anecdotes. If Gluck himself registered their attention, he was keeping it tightly at bay.

'A quality. A spiritual quality in my theories? Hhum, well, that's natural – any genuine exploration will touch the boundaries of our experience, will press forward into what is unknown and possibly unknowable and there we will experience humility. Humility is, I believe, something somewhat on the spiritual side.'

'You're humble? Even when you say you're an ego-maniac?'

He licked away a sudden grin. 'Remember when you quote from interviews, that they are very often works of fiction and should be treated as such. But yes, I am possessed of a considerable ego. I use the word in a strictly un-Freudian sense, no need to drag *him* in. But I still experience humility. I personally can be completely in awe of myself – humbled. I am, after all, working at the forefront of a field I single-handedly created. Good trick if you can do it.' She watched as his face paused, relaxed, betrayed that it was frighteningly tired. 'Mrs Brindle, the size of the work and the beauty of it – not my part in it, the work itself – that is something humbling.' He stopped again and might almost have sighed while he swept back a droop of his over-long hair. 'I'm not helping you, am I? I can tell.'

'What do you mean?'

'I mean, you are now frowning far more than when we first met and looking truly distressed. And we've had no coffee – I couldn't even offer you that. I have failed and,

I'll be perfectly honest with you, I am no longer used to failing.'

'No, I suppose not.' She tried not to sound impatient. 'Look, I didn't mean to . . . I think it's being here, this bloody foyer and all the people. I'm too tired now. And this heat is killing me. It was so hard to arrange a meeting and the hotel people here wasted so much time and I thought . . . I know you're leaving tomorrow and . . . Do you think I could speak to you? . . . later?' She dwindled to a quizzical whine and felt stupidly close to crying.

Gluck's head dipped forward, his voice emerging in a low, solid growl, unpleasantly patient. 'Mrs Brindle, as we speak, I am being considered for a Nobel Prize. Again. My lectures this week are relayed from the theatre to a hall that will barely accommodate my audience overspill. I have only recently declined the offer of an interview with a major – if mildly sleazy – gentleman's magazine. To be blunt, there are quite a few people, besides yourself, who would like to speak to me.'

With her head lowered, he wouldn't notice that her eyes were closed, sealing in any sign of unsuitable emotion. 'I quite understand. As I said, I came for a holiday. Thank you for . . . for your time.'

He was standing over her, frowning her down, almost before she could reach for her bag.

'Mrs Brindle, don't be so impulsive. You really are a one for that, aren't you? All the way to Stuttgart with no guarantees . . . of any kind. No stopping you, is there, hn? It would be impossible for me to talk to *everyone*. That's what the lectures are for. But outside the lectures, I choose who I *like*.'

His face cleared into a portrait of benevolence and she tried not to think of what he might mean and who he might like and how she might like to reach up and shake him by the shoulders so that Gluck could understand she was relying on what he could do to set her right.

He slowly sat and faced her and Mrs Brindle thought she could see a change: a large, cool stillness in his eyes. Inside the mechanism, the metal, oil and cordite Gluck exercised each day – a little to butter his toast with, a little to light the world – he had decided about her.

'Could you tell me my position, Professor. I have to say, I think I'll miss your lecture. I'm sorry, but I need to sleep. I haven't been sleeping.'

Gluck hunched his shoulders and pocketed his hands. This seemed to be a sign of real concentration, if not actual doubt.

'Professor? Your audience is waiting.'

'Mm?'

'I don't think there's one person in this foyer who isn't watching us.'

'No. There is one, if you check, by the windows. Her name is Frink . . . no, Frisch and she doesn't like me for reasons which are quite unscientific. I think we might be kind and summarise them as disappointment.' Gluck took care to appear both modest and bemused. 'She hasn't looked at me once all week which is some trick. Takes a lot of arranging. Anyway, what I was thinking was: there's an Italian place opposite the cathedral which you can't miss. Even when you're tired.' A note in his voice cleared and his eyes dodged away. 'You do, I beg your pardon, look tired. Go and get untired and . . . the best time would be about seven. Tonight. I'll be early, so you needn't bother. You look the early type. Is that all right.' One straight glance, as if he was fixing her now for later use. 'Mrs Brindle?'

'Well. Yes. My hotel is . . . I'm not far from there.'

'Fine.' He was already standing, coughing, changing himself into something public. 'That's fine then. We can shake hands now. Oh, and don't tell anyone.' He smiled oddly. 'If you don't want my audience, that is. Now, what looks like *goodbye forever*? Oh yes, I know.' He pressed her hand lightly between both of his, the touch warm but dry.

Although she was almost accustomed to something of his scent, his sudden approach left her breathing a pleasant mixture of soap, fabric, lotion. He smelt clean and mild and probably expensive with only the faintest undertaste of sweat. 'And what about a Germanic bow?'

'I don't – '

'Customs of the country.'

'You have . . . too much hair. I mean, I mean, I didn't mean to . . . mean anything. It would flop. That's all.' She scrambled to smile intelligently while sounding entirely inane. Gluck remained unreadable.

'Well, in that case, I'll just have to leave. Seven o'clock. Ta ta.'

He turned away and moved through the foyer with a kind of studied grace, head and slightly tensed shoulders above the general height.

In her hotel room, Mrs Brindle went to bed. There she lay perfectly still and listened to American Forces Radio while it happily sang the praises of the wily Confederate J. G. Rains who invented fine bombs and lovely torpedoes and that all-time family favourite, the anti-personnel device – *another first for the American Civil War*. She listened to AP Network News. She listened to the excellent prospects awaiting in the US Postal Service for all those choosing to leave the Military. Finally she listened to the daytime murmur of the hotel surrounding her and the super-heated, orderly silence of Stuttgart beyond. She couldn't sleep for the ache of listening, her ears wouldn't fill.

The bath was clean and deep, if slightly too short to lie down in. The complimentary foaming body gel was not unpleasant; nor, for all it could matter, was the complimentary sewing kit. The towels were in good condition, neither overly soft nor harsh.

Clean carpet.

Bedsheet fresh and white.

She settled back beneath the quilt.

This wasn't going to work.

Mrs Brindle's skin, even under the covers, felt impossibly naked – the touch of herself, alone with herself, the brush of her arm on her stomach, of her legs against her legs, tugged her awake. There was something unnatural about her. She felt her limbs cold. The sky that raked between the flimsy curtains was screaming with heat above ninety degrees and her room seemed hardly cooler, but she knew she had a shiver in her blood and whenever she lay down it showed.

The Konigsplatz was bending under the sun while a courteous electronic billboard noted the doggedly blistering temperature in degrees Celsius. She sat downwind of a fountain, trying to concentrate on its regular drifts of spray and the heat that lifted each droplet back up from her skin, almost before it fell. She was still tired and perhaps Gluck had only been joking, perhaps he wouldn't come. It would only be reasonable for him not to come – she was not famous and he was.

Mrs Brindle knew she was wearing the wrong things, lifeless things, their colours insubstantial in the merciless light. A scrabble of panic touched her and faded again, leaving an airless tension in her chest. Gluck was making her frightened already, even though he wouldn't come. She would go to the restaurant and wait for him stupidly until she was too embarrassed not to go away.

Or he would come and then she would be too stupid with fear to make any sense and she would waste all the time she was going to get with him.

But that wouldn't happen, because he wouldn't come.

Beyond the flying water were parapets and cliffs of concrete. The whole city was boxed and canyoned in searing concrete and palely mountainous heat. British bombing had left only tiny islands of the past to stand: a church here, a municipal building there. The evidence of violence didn't disturb her, only the lack of a tangible past. She felt she had been lost in one vast, white amnesia.

'Amnesia?' Gluck's really very large hands killed another breadstick. The table that filled the space between them seemed strangely insufficient. Gluck was of a size to be invasive, effortlessly. 'You're only abroad, Mrs Brindle. That's not so bad, people do it all the time – it's called going on holiday.'

'Well, I know that.' She failed to sound anything other than abrupt.

'But even so?'

'But, even so, I didn't expect that when I left my country, everything else would leave me. I mean, if the people and the buildings are different – the churches – then I seem to stop believing in anything. I don't even believe in me.'

'You are very tired, remember.'

'Professor, it really isn't because I'm tired.' He might be an expert on most things, but he wasn't an expert on her. 'This started years ago, in Scotland, and now it's finished here. I am a person who has no faith. I'm over. That's that.' Mrs Brindle was the only expert on Mrs Brindle that she knew. As a field of study she was more than specialised.

Gluck softly shook his head and rubbed at his fringe with one hand. A little shower of stubble fell to the tablecloth. For a moment, she couldn't think why and then she noticed. 'You've cut your hair.'

'Yes. About five hours ago. I've just spent most of one of them with you.' He was trying to seem aggrieved and managing very well.

'All right. I didn't pay attention. I'm sorry. But I came here to talk to you seriously and I've now stared at three different courses that I couldn't eat because I have no appetite and because . . . because, to be honest, I'm nervous – '

'You don't say.'

She thought of giving him a cold look, but then couldn't. He smiled gently and then she couldn't look at him at all. 'Yes, okay. I know that you know that. But all that we've done for one hour is discuss all the people you don't like at the conference and your favourite type of car and *nothing*. Now you want to discuss your hair?'

'I had it cut.'

'I know you had it cut, that's why it's shorter.'

'You didn't like the way it was, so I had it cut.'

This made no sense. Gluck sat, his head seeming slightly larger, more plainly capable of holding all that thinking and more obviously grey. She wanted to be extremely angry with him, but nothing was coming out right and Gluck was being oddly tentative, tense. She could think of nothing to say but the truth.

'Professor, I don't know what's going on here.'

'Nothing too out of the way, I assure you. I wanted to do something that would be pleasing, make you relax. Something like that.' He coughed his way into a mumble. 'Obviously I haven't been successful. But that's what I was trying to do. Small talk. And that kind of thing. I don't do it very often – work too much.' Another, more forceful clearing of the throat. 'Actually, it's the same with my hair. I usually cut it at home in my mirror to save time. The way it is doesn't bother me – I don't have to look at it, after all. So I get it damp, sellotape it down around my face – to keep it even – cut it a bit. Suits me. Suited me.'

'That's nonsense.' Still, it was drawing her in, however nonsensically.

'No it's not.' Gluck registered a mild degree of hurt. 'That's how I do it. And I liked it long because I knew I was going grey, as you can see; or white. I thought of trimming back my sideburns where they're white.' He turned his head to show her and rasp at one with his thumb. 'But that could go on forever; I'd end up with a kind of bridle path cut over the top of my head and I wouldn't like that. I am vain.'

He might have been stating his nationality, rather than a character defect. Gluck's vanity was part of Gluck and therefore could not be a fault.

'Professor, you don't need to talk to me, or to make me relax.' A moment of irritation or alarm seemed to shadow across his eyes, but she continued anyway. 'I don't relax any more. I don't expect to. Just tell me, can you help?'

He tapped at his glass and watched the red surface of the wine sway and settle. 'I don't know.'

She'd tried to be prepared in case he gave a sore answer, but what he said still hurt. Within the plainness of it, there was nowhere to fix a hope. He seemed to understand she needed more and went on.

'I would *like* to know. And to help. Very much. I feel for you. But I do not know. And now it's time for us to leave.' He patted his jacket to find his wallet out and looked about him for their waiter; Edward E. Gluck, someone used to restaurants and being served.

Mrs Brindle studied her dessert fork and tried to understand that this was all the time she would be given, finished and over with. She would have to go back to the dark in her hotel room and the night that was already waiting for her outside. Gluck had made her used to the pressure of his mind, his presence. It wasn't fair that he should make her so alone now and so fast.

'No – '

'Mrs Brindle?'

She fumbled towards what she could tell him, now that she'd started to speak, and a broad, familiar sadness smeared all her words away. Why bother?

But to make him understand – only to try and make him understand – she lifted one of his hands – brown, healthy, heavy, warm – and pressed his fingers to the open face of her wrist. Her pulse overwhelmed itself while he held it, running dark and high with only her skin between him and her fear.

Gluck winced, but kept his hold. 'What's the matter? What's wrong?' His voice smaller, close. 'Mrs Brindle?'

'That's the way it is. You feel that?' His face said that he did. 'I'm scared. That's what's wrong. That's what's always wrong. I'm scared.'

He smoothed his grip forward to cup her hand, whole inside his, and keep it as if she might be pulled away suddenly, against both their wills.

'Mrs Brindle, there's no reason to be scared. Nothing will happen to you. We're leaving because I'm taking you somewhere else – a place where I'll be able to think and you can be distracted. Nothing bad will happen. Do you understand that.'

'Of course not.'

'Listen.' The waiter hovered, courteously embarrassed by the way they were clutched together. 'You say you've lost everything. Well then, how much worse can it get?'

Gluck passed over his credit card, while setting his focus firmly on her face. The waiter stalked away. 'We are here now, in this moment, and nothing is anything other than it should be. We are both equipped with minds to perceive and alter all possible worlds – we will be fine.'

She wouldn't have thought Gluck would be good at reassurance, but as he led her away to a taxi she felt something approaching safe. Mrs Brindle did not wish to feel safe because of Gluck the man – she found that intellectually alarming – she would have preferred to find comfort in his thinking, his advice. Then again, any help should be appreciated and if she was feeling relief, it was her feeling so she would have it and like it, no matter who or what was responsible.

Gluck sat away from her in the back seat of the car, folded uneasily into the possible space. 'This won't be a long journey. So we needn't talk. Unless you would like to. What do you think?'

Mrs Brindle would have preferred not to think. Thinking at night was unsafe.

He reached over and found her wrist faultlessly, no doubt in the evaluation of his touch. 'You're not so frightened now.'

It wasn't as if he was actually *holding* her hand. If he'd been *holding* her hand, she would have told him to stop. This was taking her pulse which was different, scientific. Still, she felt the uneasy snag of something: a cautionary chill tugging her back.

Gluck continued, touching, talking, 'Not that I can tell anything except that your heart's going slower. I'm glad I'm not that kind of doctor.' He released her back to herself.

'You don't like touching people?'

'Oh, I don't think that would be true, no. I just would have been no good – diagnosing and all that. So tell me how you are and then I won't have to guess.' The bars and splashes of light from the windows made him seem to advance and retreat arbitrarily. 'Mrs Brindle?'

'It doesn't go away, the feeling, it only goes to sleep, so I can't. That's how I think about it. As soon as I'm not doing something, as soon as it gets dark, the thing wakes up and gets me. It always knows where I am.'

'But what is the thing that wakes up?'

'Did anyone you cared about ever leave you?'

'Yes.' He answered immediately, as if she had a perfect right to know. 'My mother. She died while I was in America studying. I was twenty-two. We'd never been more than a few hours apart until that autumn. Not to bore you; she had looked after me before her divorce. My father didn't . . . I was too tall for him to like me. I stood out, annoyed him, made him want to knock me down. And she saved me. Always. When they separated she worked very hard and was very ashamed of herself so that I could be very educated and she could be very proud of me – from a suitable distance, of course.

'Blood clot on the brain. Killed her.'

'I'm sorry.' That sounded completely inadequate, even though it was true.

'Sorry? Oh, yes, so was I, but people adjust. Who did you lose?'

'God.'

'Not a person?' He didn't understand.

But she might make him. 'More than a person. Someone that was Everything, *in* everything. There wasn't a piece of the world that I could touch and not find Him inside it. All created things – I could see, I could smell that they'd *been* created. I could taste where He'd touched. He was that size of love. Can you imagine what might happen if a love so large simply left you for no reason you ever knew. One morning, you're looking through the window and you can't make any sense of the sky. It's like dying. Except it can't be, because dying ends up being what you want, but haven't got.'

That was such a melodramatic thing to say, she hoped he could tell it was only a fact now and something she was used to – not some kind of female, hysterical threat.

Instead of making any comment, he reached for where her hand rested on the seat and pushed his knuckles against hers with a light, slightly varying pressure that could not cause offence. They were driven on together quietly.

'Mrs Brindle?' She had been letting her fingers relax against his so that their contact would not mean more than it should inadvertently. 'Mrs Brindle, I would rather not keep on calling you Mrs Brindle. I would be quite happy to be Edward. Would you be happy to be something else? Something other than Mrs Brindle?'

'Helen.'

'Is that your name?'

'No, I just made it up. Of course it's my name. Helen. I've always been Helen.'

'Not always Mrs Brindle, though?'

'My maiden name was Howard. Helen Howard. Too many H's, really, for one person.'

'So there was a Mr Brindle?'

'There still is.'

'Oh.'

Helen realised she hadn't thought to mention Mr Brindle before, because she hadn't thought of him, not for several days. She had forgotten him and never felt the difference. Astonishing. 'He's at home. Didn't want to come. But, yes, he is at home.'

'Why doesn't he . . .'

'Why doesn't he what?'

Gluck rubbed at the back of her hand and drew away, aligning his balance with a turn in the road. He set his fingers near his mouth and she realised without intending to that he was breathing in the scent of her skin from his hand while he thought of whatever it was that he couldn't quite say.

'What? Why doesn't he what?'

'It's none of my business.'

'That doesn't matter.'

'Well . . . I don't mean to presume, but I'm surprised he doesn't help you with this . . . your problem. Does he try? Does he know you're so upset?'

'Not all the time. There's no reason why he should. Not if I don't want him to. He's, um . . . he works, he's busy, and he's not, I don't know . . . religious. He didn't like it when I was. But the way I am – my problem – isn't his fault. This isn't his fault.' She did think she was being accurate to say that – she wasn't defending him.

'Still, maybe it would be better if you were more alike.' Gluck coughed, rubbed his neck.

'Maybe. But we're not. There's no point in thinking otherwise.'

Inside the car, around them, Helen was sure she could

smell or feel a trace of Mr Brindle: something at the edge of acrid and much too familiar.

'That's a shame.'

'No, it's not.' Helen knew she shouldn't let Gluck know this. 'That's not a shame. I'll tell you what's a shame . . . But it'll sound stupid.'

'I'm sure not.'

'It is stupid. It's the most stupid thing I've ever known, but it's how I feel, it's how I've always felt.

'I can't stand his hair. Not the hair on his head – all his hair. He has so much hair. It doesn't stop. From the back of his skull and right the way down on his neck it stays thick, in fact it gets thicker and then it curls up into wool, black wool. I can feel it under his shirt, springy, as if he was already wearing something else. When he sweats, it stays with him. I imagine it running and sticking on him and then he doesn't seem clean. I don't think Mr Brindle is clean. When he showers, the water kind of combs the hair out flat, but then it looks worse; like fur. Animals have fur. People don't have fur. Well, do they?'

'I . . . some men . . . I don't . . . have fur. Only the usual. Not that it's . . . relevant. Not fur, no.'

'It makes me panic sometimes when he wants to touch me.' Edward had turned to his window, away from her. 'I don't mind that, though. The first time I ever had . . . had a sexual . . . I mean, fear seems to be good for me, for that kind of thing. It can make you more aware – because of the adrenalin, I suppose. I'm sorry, this has nothing to do with anything.' Her breathing felt light-headed, strange.

'I would have thought it was to do with you.'

'Yes, but if I was working correctly I wouldn't mind about him. He would be my husband and that would be all right.'

'I see. I think I see. We're here, by the way.'

Helen realised the car had stopped.

*   *   *

As they walked into what appeared to be an ageing warehouse, Edward moved around her, near but never touching,
opening doors and clearing a path through the orderly
crowd inside. He was keeping her insulated. She couldn't
tell who was in need of protection and who was being
dangerous, but began to step tight in beside Gluck, as if she
might indeed be incorrectly wired in some way and pose a
potential risk.

The tiny auditorium filled and manoeuvred beyond her
while she let herself be eased in ahead of Gluck. Somewhere
a smoke machine began to spit and bluster enthusiastically.

'Now.' Edward sidled close between the rows of seats
and put himself next to her. She was reminded again that
public spaces seemed never to be designed for men of his
proportions.

'What is this?'

'Nothing at the moment,' Gluck smiled quickly, then
stopped himself. 'But it *will* be modern dance. It always
helps me think. I have no idea why and not the vaguest
desire to find out. I go with the flow and watch. After I
met you, I booked the seats.'

'Modern dance.'

'It's just what we need now, trust me. They're from
Finland, apparently.'

'Finnish modern dance.'

'It'll be a distraction. And it really will help my mind to
clear. I use it a lot. How are you feeling? Be specific.'

'I —' She took a moment to check. 'All right. I feel
all right.'

'Good. You see, people *don't* feel bad constantly. Not
always. They simply don't bother to monitor how they
are with any accuracy. When we're un-selfconscious, we
actually get relief. But we don't notice or remember,
because it happens when we're not being conscious of
ourselves.'

A heavy chord of electronic sound beat up through

their long bones and their chairs and jarred at the gathering smoke.

Edward inclined towards her knowledgeably, 'Ah, that'll be us starting, then. The music is usually a clue.' He fed his legs forward under the seat ahead of him and let his chin slump to his chest. Helen watched while a huddle of slender young women circled each other out from the wings and stood. They shuddered as a mass. Then stood. The smoke banked and thickened round them. A man in the front row began to cough.

For thirty-eight minutes, Helen was aware of the movement in Edward's breath and careful not to answer the rhythm of pressure where their shoulders couldn't help but meet as they sat. Synthesised music shuddered her ribs, or screamed in her teeth and the seven women twitched towards and away from each other across the stage. The obscuring influence of the smoke became a blessing, albeit mixed. Helen couldn't tell if Edward was enjoying this. She only knew he was trying not to choke on the chemical mist.

Green lights arced through the fog as one and then another and then all of the dancers tugged at the lengths of muslin which had been keeping them more or less wrapped. The cue for their closing blackout was apparently the unveiling of the final pair of breasts. Helen felt a crawl in the skin beside her jaw. She didn't mind the nudity, it was hardly offensive. She minded that half-naked women were happening now, while Edward was here. They made her position seem odd.

'Come on now, interval.' Edward sneezed, 'Excuse me. That smoke.' and then grinned.

Helen waited, surrounded by closed German conversation, while Edward slipped his way back from the bar. Naturally, his height gave him a clear view across the room to her. He was trying to catch her eye, but she couldn't let him.

'There you are.'

She gripped the damp of the glass, avoiding his hand. 'Thanks. So this is the interval, then.'

'Yes. But another two sections to go . . .' He laughed suddenly, as if someone had shoved the sound through him. His head tilted back and to the side and he unsteadied his feet in a kind of private confusion that seemed peculiarly young. 'Oh, I am sorry. You can't stand it, can you?'

'Well –'

'Of course, you can't. Because it was total crap: so bad it was almost hypnotic. That's what I love about bad dance, it's utterly, utterly meaningless and wonderful to think against.' He was checking her face to see how upset she was, trying to say what she would agree with, trying too hard. 'And there we had a perfect example. Not one redeeming feature. Bad music, bad dancing and, Jesus Christ, bad smoke.'

'But on interesting themes.'

'Hm?' She'd made him puzzled. She'd made him stop.

'Themes – constipation and electrocution. That's what it looked like, anyway.' He bent into another sudden yelp. She'd made him laugh. She liked him laughing. 'From Finland? Seven dancers?'

'Mm.' He wiped his eyes.

'You know what that would make them?' The last word came out as a squawk, but she couldn't laugh yet because that would stop her speaking.

'What?'

'The Seven Deadly Finns.'

Edward wheezed and then whimpered while he shook his head and she couldn't help doing much the same. He patted her shoulder and buckled again. The other dance connoisseurs edged away from them, unimpressed.

Edward took a long moment to lean on her arm. 'That's dreadful. That is the worst thing I've heard in years. Oh God, I can't breathe.' He smothered a giggle. 'Can I take it we won't be going inside for instalments two and three.'

'Not unless you want me to swallow my own arms in despair.'

'Dear me, no. And maybe they'd make us look at more breasts. That was too many breasts.'

Her answer was overly fast, 'Only the usual number.'

'What, two each? Yes, but fourteen, all together and with bandages . . . I'm not used to that.' He pondered the floor. 'They didn't . . .'

'Bother me? No. Not at all.'

'Good. I wouldn't have liked them to.'

Once the warehouse bar had emptied, they found seats and Edward bought her another drink.

'Only soda water, this time.'

'Yes, I quite understand.' He squinted down at her contentedly. 'Don't want to get carried away. Clear head.' And, having turned away, 'Nice to see you laughing.'

'Hm?'

'I won't be a minute. You take a seat.'

When he came to sit beside her in the still of the room, free from obstacles or constrictions, he began to take his own scale again. His movements became more fluid, graceful.

'Do you know how tall I am, Helen?'

'No. I suppose, really quite tall . . .'

'Quite. Six foot three-and-three-quarter inches. Observers may not be clear on the detail – those extra three quarters – but I'm not exactly a secret I can keep. Helen, I can change my mind, I can turn the inside of myself into absolutely anything. I've taken Quantum Field Theory – the maps it makes for the universe and matter and time – and I've turned it back in to chart the brain that thought it. I've taught myself how to know the answer and let the question find itself. I've made me a genius. But I can't be any smaller than I am. It used to annoy the hell out of me.'

'You look good tall.'

'Haven't got much choice, have I? Thanks, though.' He rubbed at his neck. 'And I'm used to it now. At school I was taller than my teachers, I stood out in crowds at my universities. I stood out. Jesus, I *had* to be a genius so people wouldn't go on about my height. And you know what I actually wanted? Hm?'

'No.'

'To be good.'

'Good?'

'Well, don't sound quite so surprised – it could have been possible. At one point. I wanted to be a good man – the way that James Stewart was good. You know – James Stewart? I think I've seen most of the films that he made, maybe all. Even the one with Lassie.

'Nobody ever noticed he was tall and skinny. They didn't look down Main Street after Destry rode again and say, "Bloody hell, he's a bit tall, isn't he? Spidery. Clumsy, too." No, they all said, "What a nice man." "What a good man." Because he was.

'People loved Jimmy. *I* did. I *do*. Like when he's George Bailey in *It's A Wonderful Life*? Good old George. And *aaaw, the good old Building and Loan*.' He let out an impressively recognisable crackling drawl, then couldn't help a grin.

'That's the only impression I do – practised it for years. That character Bailey, you stick with him, like you do all the time with Jimmy. You want the best things to happen to him, nothing but happiness. When he's down, you stay with him because he might need company and when he's up again you're glad to see it because he makes you feel generous and you believe he *could* have a guardian angel to keep him from suicide and perhaps it'll notice you. Jimmy's special.'

Edward beamed, unashamed.

'You stay with him in that story to the end and it's all good – even the badness is good. Even when he makes mistakes, they're good mistakes and he can mend them.

'I do tend to wonder – if I'm not careful – just how well I would measure up if my guardian angel delivered me into one of Jimmy's lives. I'm pretty sure I wouldn't come off well. I'm not good – only tall.'

He was fishing for a compliment, so Helen thought he might as well get one. 'You've been good to me.'

Edward shook his head solemnly, 'Doesn't count.'

'Why not?'

'Because I wanted to.'

She nudged his forearm and found that she was grinning and frowning without those actions being contradictory. 'All right then, your work does good. When people use the Process, they needn't be hospitalised all the time, or drugged. You let people be happy. And you refused to work for the army.'

'You've been doing your research.'

'Only now and then.'

'That's okay, they can't touch you for it.' He allowed himself a strange, quiet smile. 'And you're right, I couldn't work for the army. But then nobody sane ever could. My God, you can't imagine what they wanted me to do. I mean, they would have loved our Finnish friends – deafening noise, chemical smoke, a sealed white box full of threatening figures – just the thing to soften you up before they ask your life away.

'Seriously – they would try anything. Because they do understand that the enemy they most have to conquer is in between their ears. We all face the same puzzle with that – except that some of us are explorers and some of us are bombers and some of us are speculators on property we do not own.'

'You explore.'

'Yes. But not because I'm good – just because it's the loveliest thing to do.'

Their hands were already loose amongst the glasses on the table-top, it was very easy for them to find each other and fasten, hand over hand over hand over hand while Helen felt a rattle of alarm, like a stick drawn fast along a hard fence. Very far away, her Old Love was observing. Her Maker. She watched her fingers, pale and small in comparison to Edward's.

'Edward, I don't mean anything by this. It's only reall – '

He was nodding before she could finish, 'I know.' He began to lift her hands, 'I don't mean anything by it either.' Steering her up and apart from their table to a point where they could stand, hands now in a knot between them. 'Of course I don't.'

Helen moved through her thinking and was almost certain that she was nothing but concentration and memory and the possession of an open, hopeful mind. He was a good man, despite what he said, and he would give her an answer and that would be all. First the trust to touch each other, that relaxation, and then the answer when she was sure to be listening. That made perfect sense.

'I mainly wanted to make it clear,' He unfastened her hands, only to slip inside them and hold her by the shoulders, 'That you are an extremely good person and in here,' leaning forward now, cautiously, 'In here,' he kissed her forehead, with a moment's release of static energy. 'In here, you have everything you need to get better. In this part of a part of a second, you have it all. That's reality, not wishful thinking.

'Not that I don't like . . .'

Helen, because of a small discomfort she had in her arms, an idea that things should be other than they were,

'. . . Wishful . . .'

pulled him in to rest against her.

'. . . Thinking.'

A button of his shirt was at her cheek along with the slow heat of him. 'In fact I like wishful thinking a lot. Hello, there.' She could feel his voice, burrowing through him.

'Hello, Sorry.'

'Don't mention it. Are you scared again?'

'No. I don't think so.' While her heart lunged against her, amoral and unlikely.

'Good.'

When the audience straggled out from the auditorium again, she and Gluck stepped away from each other smartly and then stood, uneasy within their new distances. Helen thought they should speak, but they didn't.

In the dim interior rock of another cab, Helen was quite aware she was returning to her hotel, but she seemed able to face her arrival and the way time would then press on. The thought of her life, outside and waiting, was no longer impossible. She tried to imagine turning off the light in her room and letting the nothing fall into her head where it could hurt her, but she couldn't believe that as her future now.

Edward nudged her shoulder, 'All right?'

'Mm hm.'

'I've had a good evening, by the way. Thank you. I don't do this very much. Socialising.'

'I would have thought you did it all the time.'

'Then you would have thought wrong. Public faces for public places – not really me. As you might have noticed, I sometimes just want to be offensive when I've had too much handshaking stuff. It makes me grumpy. But of course, I'm such a hound for the limelight, I couldn't walk away and be private – I'd pine.'

'That would be awful.'

'Yes, I pine extremely badly.' He coughed tidily and, when he raised his head again, was serious. 'But that isn't what I want to talk about.'

So now he would tell her, he would give her help. That would be fine, what she came for. All the way to Stuttgart and no stopping her, like he'd said. She would get what she came for and she would be fine.

She turned for his shape in the dark. 'What *do* you want to talk about, then?'

She could feel the press of him looking, holding the look.

'What do you want? Edward?'

'Want? To say the things I already should have. I've spent all night, telling you nothing of any particular use. Partly to have your company . . .' He flinched his head a little. 'But mainly because I don't know what to offer for the best. You should have the best – you're the kind of person who always should. Do remember that, won't you?'

'Okay.'

'I don't have much I can tell you.'

'That's all right.' It was easy to listen in the dark without having to worry how her face might change as she heard what he had to say.

'When my mother died, I was over at UCLA. There was no warning and nothing meaningful that I could do. I flew back home and did my funeral duty for other people, but not for her. My father wasn't there – he'd committed suicide maybe seven years before. Had Parkinson's Disease and he couldn't face the way he'd go. Now I could have helped him with that. If I'd wanted to.'

Helen hadn't heard that edge in his voice before.

'When I went back to the States, all my mourning performances done, there was no one there. No one for me. Before, no matter what happened – right or wrong – my mother was around. I didn't worry her for most of the time, but she was always a possibility of help. I could call her and not really talk about anything, only hear her being herself and that would be enough. I'd put down the phone, sure of what I should do.

'You have to remember, she was the woman who saved my life. Often. My father would have killed me, but he didn't. She got in his way. We both know about losing things, hm?'

As if her presence was part of his thinking, he didn't seem to expect an answer, but she spoke because he sounded lonely. 'That's right.'

'I'm not upsetting you?' His voice sharpened in concern.

'No. Unless you're upsetting yourself.'

'No.' He twisted slightly to face her through the dark. 'For a long time after her death, I was numb; absent but functioning.' Helen nodded without thinking – she knew about that one. 'So I started to talk to my mother in my head. I began to live – far more than I had while she was with me – according to what I imagined might be her wishes. I have to say, we've parted company since. And it was my loss. But that way of thinking about her and getting myself through, is still available to me and would still work, I'm sure.'

'And you think I could do the same with God.'

'You can't have faith if you need evidence. You used to have evidence – that's very unusual – God touching you. Now He doesn't do it. Perhaps that's about faith. Do you call your God *Him*?'

'Yes.'

'*Her* would sound odd? *It*?'

'I know God's not a person, but *He* has always suited me.'

'So you do still believe in something about Him. Start with that. Not that I know anything about this.'

'You're making sense. And I will try.'

'But don't sound like that.' He caught at her elbow, then released her just as suddenly.

'Like what?'

'As if I've volunteered you to walk across hot coals. You're not on your own, you know.'

'You're leaving tomorrow.'

A little silence blundered between them after she said that, as if his absence drew in closer when they mentioned it. She wouldn't miss him, she hadn't known him long enough. He would be leaving her what he'd said, what she wanted; what she'd been looking for. Helen couldn't think how many years had passed now, since she'd last got what she'd looked for. Nobody could just step up and cure her, but he'd done his best and, in this field, Edward's best was the best there could be.

He stretched and then folded his arms. 'Yes. Yes I am going tomorrow, but I'm not ceasing to exist.'

'No, you're not.' Helen was sounding ridiculously glum which was bad of her – Gluck was doing all he could.

'What do you want? Should I promise I'll write?' Now he sounded uncomfortable, which was her fault.

'You don't have my address.'

'You put it on top of your letter. I'm a genius – I notice that kind of stuff. Listen . . .' She found her hand taking his, recognising the heat and depth of the fingers. 'Mm hm, hello again.' They both smiled, their mouths invisible. 'Listen, I saw my mother hurt, physically, by someone else and that wasn't the worst thing. I couldn't bear the ways she hurt herself inside. Every year beyond the divorce, I'd see her cry while I opened my Christmas presents because, yes, she was happy about our being there together and safe – all of that – but she'd also convinced herself that anything she gave me wouldn't be enough. She wanted to be married for me and make a good family. She robbed herself of joy. All the time. Like he had.'

Edward nudged in beside her as his voice fell soft. 'It wouldn't take a Jung or a Freud to work out that I'm never going to like a woman I respect and care for being in emotional pain. I'm going to want to help.'

Helen listened to his breathing and tried to remember the way she would be at home and the proper order of her life. She shivered with a small belief in the disapproval of Something other than herself. Edward shouldn't write to her. It would be bad if he did: good, but bad. She loosed his fingers and rested her palms across her lap.

'You needn't write.'

'I know I needn't. I don't need to do anything. I've worked for decades to reach the point where I can have that degree of choice. So I do what I want to and I want to write. Okay?'

'Okay. But there can't be . . . I should explain . . .'

The cab slowed into the pedestrian precinct where her hotel hid itself. The coloured illumination from silent shop-fronts swept them both.

'Ah, you see that?' Edward pressed to her side of the seat.

'What?'

'*Welt Der Erotik*. A chain of popular Bavarian sex shops. See them all over the place. I'm sorry, I'm changing the subject very badly because we're nearly home. For you. You didn't want to know about sex shops.'

'I suppose I might have – '

'No. I think you might not. Is this where you are?'

'Oh.' She recognised the entrance. 'Yes. This is it. Let me – '

'No. You don't pay for anything. Because this way you've had a nice time and you haven't had to pay for it later. We've established that principle, which I think is good. I'm guessing you had a nice time, of course.'

'Thank you. I did.'

'Good.' He spoke a few words of German to the driver, who turned his engine off. 'Now, Mrs Brindle, we don't have to make this look like *goodbye forever*.'

'But it will be *goodbye for a very long time*.'

'I should think that would look pretty much like forever, though, wouldn't you?'

'Then can I do something I want?'

Something fluttered in the air between them, rocked.

'Absolutely. Do your worst.'

Helen did nothing bad, or worse, or worst. She rested a hand to his shoulder for balance and then executed motions that could be summarised as a kiss, the mildest relaxation of his lips leaving her with a sense of somewhere extraordinarily soft.

Edward scratched his throat thoughtfully. 'Well. I was going to do something *I* wanted as well, but now I'd just be kissing you back and I hate to be repetitive. Thanks.' He searched for something else to say and couldn't find it. 'Good night.' Eyes slightly taken aback by his ending so abruptly, he presented his hand, angled for shaking and she accepted its weight.

'Yes. Good night. And goodbye for a very long time.'

'That's right, but I won't say so, because I do dislike goodbyes. So. Good night.'

They let each other go.

Helen walked herself across the hotel foyer and into the tight, brass lift with the porthole window that periscoped its way up to her floor and to her room and to her self.

Her self wasn't bad to be with tonight, not unpleasant company. She removed her sandals and her skirt, seeing how the heat and sitting had creased it and wondering when she'd begun to get so dishevelled: at the start of the evening, or later when it would have mattered less. Not that it actually mattered, either way.

She took off her blouse. Several available mirrors told her there was too much contrast between her usual colour and the places on her body she'd allowed to see the sun. She didn't look healthy, overall.

With a little more attention, she watched as she unfastened her bra. Her breasts were not like a dancer's, they lacked that kind of discipline, and they were larger. They had what she thought of as a better roundness. In spite of gravity. Probably not to everyone's taste, but then they didn't have to be.

The bra was nice, too – she supposed, a sort of favourite, if she had such a thing – swapped at Marks and Spencer's for one Mr Brindle gave her on a birthday. He'd never noticed the change.

Her knickers were the ones she'd bought at the airport because the airport was where she'd remembered that she'd packed none of her own. If a person has been very tired for a very long time, she will tend to forget things like that – essential items.

When she was naked, the mirror stared back at her until she realised she was thinking of the Seven Deadly Finns and of laughing. The mirror smiled and then looked away. Surely to God she hadn't been smiling like that all evening? That wasn't how she'd meant to be. The mirror slipped back to its grin, it didn't mind.

In bed, she turned the light out and this wasn't a problem.

This wasn't a problem.

Somewhere, a door muttered closed, but there seemed to be nothing dreadful in the quiet between the building's minor sounds. There was nothing like death in the dark. Helen was not tempted to lie and listen to the buzz of blood round her brain and wait for something bad to go wrong. Tonight she did not think forever would come and tell her how large it could be and how quickly she would disappear inside it. Forever would not make her alone, it would just remind her of Edward and saying *goodbye forever* with him which was sad but not frightening. She was determined within herself that there would be no more harm in darkness, only sleep.

There was no harm in Edward, either; no harm in her choosing to not bath now, to not wash him away before she went to bed. Edward was an influence for good, because he wanted to be and because keeping a trace of him with her tonight was bringing her up against the force of Law. She was doing a little wrong, and finding Someone there who would object. A touch of her God was back. His disapproval set a charge in the air, a palpable gift.

Perhaps because of this, she tucked her thoughts in under her eyelids and discovered she had the security she needed to reach for sleep. She rolled close up in the dark, pulled it round her skin and, for one soft second, knew she was all underway, about to be snuffed like a lazy light.

Helen bumped and drifted down through a loosening awareness, before she stepped out and into a fully-formed dream. It was one she'd seen before, but not recently.

Above her was the high, grubby ceiling of her old school's Assembly Hall and everywhere was the sound of the tick of the loudest clock in the world. The invigilator paced. Helen had lifted her head and was resting inside the familiar discomfort of her school uniform – tight waistband, lots of black and blue.

She was sitting her Chemistry Higher, the final paper, the one with long answers that had to be written out. She'd chosen her questions, managed the topics, been finished in good time.

Fifteen minutes left. She was cautiously aware of other heads bowing, shaking, being scratched at with biro-ends.

Twelve minutes left and there was no more anxiety. This hadn't been so bad. She should just check things over now, take it easy and make sure she'd done her best. Her experimental drawings were lousy, but that shouldn't matter much: they would work and they were clear and she wasn't expected to be artistic, anyway.

Eight minutes left and it hit. A tangible, audible, battering terror that coiled and span and folded round and round itself down from her collarbones, to mesh cold through her body and then push an inside ache along her thighs. Eight minutes left.

She absolutely knew. She'd done it wrong. Helen had done it wrong. She was meant to check how many questions she should pick and get that absolutely right; it wasn't very difficult after all: it was printed at the top of the paper for anyone but an idiot to read and one too many answers was almost as bad as one too few, but she had one too few which was the worst. Everything had been fine – now it was the worst.

During her dream, time condensed as it did when she had been, in wide-awake reality, sitting and feeling the sweat from her hands beginning to distort her papers. Trying to avoid any sign of flurry, or any irregularity of breath, she had searched for a question she could possibly answer in not enough time – something even halfway likely. Organic, possibly.

Even with so many years between her and the examination, even deep asleep, her mind could reproduce the horrible wordings of 14a, and 14b, through to 14e.

Part of her then had locked into problem-solving, while her hands had twitched themselves towards legibility. Part of her had been otherwise concerned. Five minutes left and the lick of fear inside her swam into place and fixed her flat to something she had never known before. With the fifth and final section of question 14 still undone, her eyes closed without her consent and the proper force of panic began to penetrate. Rolling smoothly in from the small of her back, she had the clearest sensation of rapid descent, of wonderful relaxation and then monumental tension holding in and reaching in and pressing in for something of her own that wasn't there, but would be soon.

Helen tried not to smile or frown. She steadied herself against an insistent pressure breaking out between her hips and sucking and diving and sucking and diving and sucking her fast away. Four minutes, three minutes, two. A shudder was visible at her jaw.

And then her breathing seemed much freer and she was perhaps warm, or actually hot, but oddly easy in her mind. She slipped in her final answer, just under the given time, before sitting back and watching the man who was her Chemistry teacher collect in what he needed from them all. She wondered briefly what he was like when he went back home beyond the school where both of them did the work they were expected to.

He was a man. She'd been told about men. Men had necessary orgasms which allowed them to ejaculate and have children. Women's orgasms, on the other hand, had been hinted around in Biology as a relatively pointless sexual extravagance.

Helen had very recently decided she was quite in favour of pointless sexual extravagance.

She'd felt strange walking out of the hall, secret, and barely curious about her marks for Chemistry.

Helen's night-time mind was able to observe while the door through which her younger self was leaving gently tipped and shivered and folded down into a small horizon, out of her way. She was alone in a sunlit space now, with something like a fountain for company and a figure far off, but walking towards her and holding yellow papers in his hand. Helen couldn't think why he seemed familiar – he had no tell-tale points to give a clue – still, she knew him. She recognised him in her sleep.

Helen twisted from her side on to her back, one unconscious hand still resting near her waist. Her dream dipped closer, licked at her ear, hard and dark, and said, 'Do not look at the man. Do not look at him unless you have to and sometimes you *will* have to because he will be there. Then you can look, but you must never for a moment think that you want to fuck him, to fuck him whole, to fuck him until all his bones are opened up and he can't think and you've loosened away his identity like rusty paint. Don't think you want to blaze right over him like sin. Don't think you want to fuck him and fuck him and then start up and fuck him all over again. Do not think about fucking him. Think of your intentions and he will see, because they will leak out in the colour of your eyes and what do you think will happen then?'

Helen, warm in her dream, began to smile and the man

and the sunlight across him began to sink and slur away. Thinking of nothing at all, or nothing harmful, she moved towards a very pleasant rest.

'Mrs Brindle? Helen? Hello?'

Her hand had reached for the telephone without the ring of it having fully woken her.

'Mrs Brindle?'

'Uh, yes.'

'You sound groggy, that's wonderful.'

'Who is this?'

'Edward. Edward Gluck. You were asleep, weren't you? And I thought you would be out by now and seeing sights . . . I suppose Stuttgart does have sights – has anyone said? You've slept.'

'Yes, I . . . Professor, Edward – I suppose I must have been asleep.'

'Do you know what time it is?'

'Time?'

'The time of day. No, don't bother looking I'll tell you – two o'clock in the afternoon.'

'What?'

'Two o'clock. Do you feel better? No, you won't be feeling anything, yet. Wonderful. You slept. I'm so glad, really I am. First time in a while, hm? Good. The reason I was calling: I thought we might discuss your diet.' He seemed to be hurrying over a catalogue of topics he might wish to hit. 'The timing of your meals and their composition; there isn't too much available about the dietary requirements of the Process in the public domain. I mean, you won't have read about it. So have lunch with me. How do you feel? Did I ask that?'

'I don't know. I don't – Is it really two o'clock?'

'Ten past the hour. You'll be hungry soon.'

'You're leaving today. You don't have time.'

'Always have time for your interests, Helen, you never

know what they'll give you, if you let them have their head. I'll meet you by Reception at three, no three fifteen.'

'Reception here?'

'Yes, Reception here. Your hotel. Three fifteen. You slept. Well done. Oh, and goodbye. Bye.'

For some time, she kept the receiver by her head and listened to the tone on the line. When she felt sure that Edward's call had happened and that she was awake, she began to feel happy. Happy was the first emotion of her day and a person couldn't ask much more than that. She got up.

Helen stood in the bath and opened the shower, let it roll down her body, nicely cool and good to lift her arms in and turn underneath.

Past two o'clock in the afternoon; that meant she'd been out for more than twelve hours and she felt like it, too, extremely relaxed. She didn't dwell too deeply on her excursions into Stuttgart the night before, but she was glad to admit that the miniature Process she and Edward made together must have set to work. She had been right to come here and had been rewarded with sleep. She tried to think of something thankful she might say to God.

The clean flow of the shower washed her free of any after-taste her dreams could have been tempted to leave. Now she deserved a celebration with the man who had helped her begin to be put right.

Gluck was sitting at the side of the Reception desk, dressed down in blue jeans and a grey shirt. He was more obviously slim today and it occurred to Helen that he might well be quite physically fit, not only active in the brain. He unfolded himself upwards and offered his hand.

'Ah, Helen.'

'Edward.'

'Yes, Edward, you remembered.' He said that in a way that made sure she could tell he was pleased to be Edward with her. Edward would be what he preferred, not Professor Gluck. 'So, good afternoon. You look well. Terrific.'

They went and ate beef with onion gravy and little noodles and extra bread and then something with hot cherries in and Helen was hungry for all of it. Edward observed her appetite and talked seriously, almost formally, about the chemical implications of his work. If he knew enough about her – purely factually – he could work out a programme of general nutrition and supplements that would definitely help her to at least feel more contented for more of the time.

'Are you suggesting anti-depressants.'

'Helen, do I look insane? You know my opinions on that. Those things don't make you happy. They just mean you can't remember you're depressed. Anyway, you're not depressed.'

He looked at her for too long.

'Then what am I.'

'If it wouldn't make you sad to hear it, I think you're bereaved.'

So that was it. Now she could understand how he thought of her. That was good. His phone call, his attentiveness, new gentleness, his eagerness to offer her whatever came into his mind were all because she was God's widow and that deserved respect.

Helen was relieved, definitely mainly relieved. She could now accept Edward's kindness without reservation because what they were to each other had been made quite clear. This was all good, entirely good; in no way disappointing.

He strolled her back towards her hotel through a chain of pedestrian precincts and underpasses, not taking her arm when the crowds seemed to threaten, but somehow suggesting in his stance that he would be ready to do so, if required. Helen reassured him about her enjoyment of the heat, her lack of fatigue and the pleasantness of the lunch they'd shared. He submitted to each of her statements with a steady and caretaking smile.

Edward would go away after this and she would have another rest until the evening and perhaps some room-service sandwiches. He had seen her through the end of her crisis, apparently, and there would be no need for her to bother him any more. No need for her even to write. Today she could think there was mercy beyond her in a place she couldn't see and that her time would pass and she would be content. She would apply herself and look forward to that.

'Here we are, then, home.'

Edward nodded and held the hotel door out wide for her while she stepped inside. He followed and she turned to him.

'That was . . . I do appreciate your letting me have such a lot of your time. When is your flight?'

He shifted his weight very gently towards one hip and glanced away. 'I had to leave the Summit – enough is enough – and I did intend to leave Stuttgart, yes. Then I changed my mind.'

'Why?' Having asked this, she found she didn't want to know.

'I'm not sure. I think I needed a rest. You'll know all about that. When I go back to London, I'll be rushing straight into something. The sooner I get there, the sooner it starts and I want another two or three days to be on my own.'

'I'm sorry you've had to spend so long with me.'

'Oh no, that was just like being alone.' He flinched at himself. 'I do apologise. That isn't at all what I meant.' She let him pat at one of her shoulders. 'I mean you were an absolute relief to be with. Very educated people – no – very educated *academics* are not always very intelligent and certainly not always good company.' He shook his head in almost serious despair at himself. 'And all of this only proves what I said before – James Stewart would have told you the *right* thing there: that you are intelligent and good company. Of course, *I* managed to mess it up.'

'Oh, I don't know. From what I remember, James could be quite charmingly embarrassed. When he did mess up.'

Edward looked out over her head and then let himself examine her, while she examined him. 'Like I said – intelligent. I think I'd better get up to my room.'

She let herself giggle. 'No, wrong hotel. This is where *I* get up to *my* room.'

'I didn't say? I'm staying here now.'

'You're what?'

'Well, I could hardly claim to be leaving Stuttgart if I didn't even check out of my hotel.' He was taking pains to sound plausible. 'Now I'm in hiding. Will you give me away?'

'No. Of course not.'

'Good.'

They rode the lift together in silence, Helen thinking her way through a mainly numb surprise. Edward had chosen to stay here. He must have thought it might suit him – couldn't be bothered to try somewhere else. That must have been it. That made sense.

Edward's floor slid down around them and together they jolted into place. He nodded to himself as he set off away from her, inclining his head round to say, 'Obviously, this isn't the last time we'll meet, but I won't impose. I have a lot here to keep me occupied. I promise.' He seemed keen to be reassuring – she must have appeared more concerned than she wanted to.

'Goodbye, then, Edward.'

He nodded to himself. 'I hope not completely goodbye.' The lift door began to glide shut. 'But I definitely won't impose. See you.'

She didn't reply, the lift having closed against her before she could usefully speak.

For two breakfasts, Helen approached the dining-room

with a tick of anxiety in her chest. She couldn't be sure if he would be there, already picking through the buffet, or if he might emerge while she drank her coffee and gathered her concentration for the day. Nothing would be more normal, people tended to eat their breakfasts at breakfast time, and he would probably come to sit with her because that would be the civil thing to do, but early-morning conversation usually left her in a state of unconditional defeat. She didn't look forward to failing to impress.

As an exercise, she tried to imagine the way she ate breakfasts at home. At home; that other place. She made an effort to think of what happened there. Did Mr Brindle ever compliment her bacon, ask her to pass the jam? Helen found it difficult to remember. There was also something mildly irrelevant about that house, that kitchen, that tired stumble through tea-making and toast and being sure to put the milk in the fridge and the bread in the bread bin and not the reverse, even if you are crying tired, because you don't want to excuse and explain yourself again; when the whole point to your situation is that it does not change and Mr Brindle, you already know, hates explanations.

But now her situation *had* changed. Helen was falling faster and faster and faster asleep. She had unreasonable energy and appetite. When she flew back to Scotland, she wouldn't be able to stop herself looking different. Mr Brindle might not like her different.

'My husband doesn't understand me.'

She practically did say that out loud. As if the snugly breakfasting couples and tidy families would have the remotest interest in the way that her life had been melted down into an unconvincing sexual cliché.

Of course, she needn't have worried, not as far as being joined for breakfast went. Edward either didn't like food in the mornings, or ate it in his room. He was true to his word and did not impose. Edward neither purposely disturbed her nor crossed her path accidentally when she slipped out to visit the gallery, or to buy Mr Brindle a present from the specialist hologram shop.

Helen was aware that if a person was expecting someone, even in an uneasy way, and that someone did not then arrive, a person might feel disappointed. That person might miss the opportunity of finding that someone inconvenient.

Added to which, Helen had a very good reason for speaking to Edward again. She wanted to say how much better she was. She could not do anything but delight in walking for hours without feeling faint, or buying and eating two whole pretzels on impulse and then a slice of apple cake, because the food was there and she was there and she wanted to eat very much. When strangers looked at her, their eyes did not pause for an instant too long, clouding with concern or embarrassment. She was smiling out and other people were smiling in. If there was still only minor comfort from the world beyond this one, she was at least finding a compensation in things present and tangible. It would only be fair to thank Edward for his part in that.

By her third unattended breakfast, Helen began to wonder how long Gluck would be in Stuttgart. Maybe he'd already left and not told her. This seemed unlikely but not completely out of the way. More to the point, she was only staying for two more days herself. Then she would have to go home.

People went home all the time, it was something they liked to do, because home was a comfortable feeling and not just a building they'd lived in before. Helen knew this in theory, but not in experience.

'Edward?'

'Hello?' His voice was slightly cautious and faint along the line as she sat on her bed and wondered about the best things to say in the call.

'Edward?'

Now she could hear him being happy. 'Oh. Hello. It's

Helen, isn't it?' He was happy to hear her. 'How nice. What day is it?'

'You mean you don't know?'

'That's precisely what I mean. When I'm very involved in something, I lose track.' He sounded more preoccupied than brusque, but she was sorry she'd disturbed him.

'No, no. You haven't disturbed me. Thursday already . . . I wouldn't have guessed that. And you're leaving me when?'

'I'm leaving you – I'm leaving Stuttgart on Saturday morning.'

'Then, if you'll forgive me, I won't suggest that I take you for dinner. There are things I have to finish with here.' Helen felt a blunt disappointment nudging in. 'But if you wouldn't mind, if you're not doing anything else, I would really appreciate if we had a drink together in the first-floor bar at something like nine. Or half past. That would do me a monstrous favour, actually.' He was trying too hard again, being too studiously polite. 'I need a break. And I want to say cheerio. And see how you are. Of course. How are you?'

'Well. Very. Nine would be good.'

'That's splendid. I shall aim towards you then.'

'Nine it is.' As she spoke, the hot metal smell of prohibition breezed in about her – a signal that something of God might not be too far away, because even if He was a He, God disapproved of men. Helen had always been taught that, and told not to meddle with them.

But she didn't intend to meddle, so all she had to do was appreciate the clearer trace of Presence in her room.

'Helen, don't go.'

His voice snatched her back to the receiver.

'I wasn't. What's the matter?'

'Well, no, there's nothing the matter. Do I sound as if there is?'

'A bit.'

'Oh. No, I'm only tired. Don't worry. I . . . I wanted to

thank you for calling. That's all. I needed this, really.' He did sound tired. 'One of the hazards of the Process, or of the powers it will release, is an increase in one's capacity to focus on an activity for very long periods. This can be extremely useful, but it can also be extremely like going to jail. I forget I own the pass key. Um, listen, my room is 307, could you knock on my door and come to get me? I'd hate to lose the place again. Help me with that, could you? Hm?'

So at a touch before nine o'clock – it does no harm to be prompt – Helen rode the lift to Edward's floor and walked along a hallway he must have been quite familiar with by now and reached his door and waited. She realised she had no ideas about what to do next.

'Edward? Edward.'

She could hear movement and then a shout. 'Hello. Yes.'

'Well, should I knock, or should I tell you who it is?'

'Never called on a gentleman in his hotel room, hn?' The shout was nearer.

'No.'

'I don't know if,' A lock turned, 'Gentleman is exactly accurate . . .' and the door eased open. 'Anyway, never mind knocking, just come in. Oh, yes, and maybe tell me who you are.' His gaze slithered below her face.

'Me.'

He shook his head slightly as if trying to clear his mind, offered her a nod, a grin. 'Oh. Hello, me. Hello, you. Good. Good.'

307 was not untidy, more like dishevelled. The furniture and fittings made a left-handed copy of her own room, two floors above, but there was a smell of human warmth here, not unpleasant but slightly unexpected, intimate. Edward, who was not dishevelled, more like untidy, waved her towards a seat as he struck out purposefully for the bathroom.

'I *am* ready and I *was* expecting you, all I need to do is shave. Obviously. Sorry. Sit down. Won't be long.'

Sure enough, the abrasive buzz of an electric razor worried into life and Helen waited, glanced around. Edward's desk was mountainous with papers, articles, folders and what she assumed were his hand-written notes. In the same way she tended to look through other people's windows when they left them bared at night, Helen had never been able to resist the attractions of a working table-top.

She slipped over to stand above his papers while Edward continued shaving with what sounded like considerable force. This was where he worked – where he was a genius for real, pacing his mind against itself with no one ahead to stop him and no one behind him to fear.

While taps ran in the bathroom, she had enough time to scan diagrams in heavy black ink, sheets of dense typing and a stack of photographs. She could have examined all the pictures, but the first one stopped her. Initially, Helen tried to understand it and was pausing simply to do that, but then its meaning decoded completely in a rush and she stood and looked and stood and looked because the image wouldn't let her remember that she could do anything else.

The girl had shockingly white skin and made a remarkable background for her hair which shone, oil-black and long enough to rest on her shoulders. A dark stubble showed at her underarms and a fuller shadow glistened between her legs. Her mouth was pursed in something like concentration. Beneath the girl was a man, also stripped but almost hidden, and beneath him was a chair, hardly visible. The girl's weight seemed borne almost entirely on her braced calves and arched feet. There was visible tension in her thighs. Also there was the other thing: what they were doing.

After an indeterminate time, Helen stepped back and to the side and paused, avoiding an opinion of any kind. Gluck emerged: tie neat, cuffs buttoned, cheeks thoroughly cleaned and smoothed. The combination of fresh aftershave and laundered cloth made her think instantly of home and good evenings she could remember having a while ago. This was the scent of being close and then going out to move among strangers and get closer still. Edward smiled and she didn't join him.

When he asked her, they were in the lift. 'You saw those photos, didn't you? On my desk.'

'Yes. No. Only one.' Her left side was against the safely carpeted wall, her right side towards him.

'I thought you had. I'm sorry they upset you. They are upsetting.' He rubbed at one of his eyes. 'I am . . . ahm . . . conducting research into paraphilia, Helen. And a group I advise is trying to treat men who have an addictive use of pornography. They are people who deserve our sympathy, our help.'

'I'm sure.'

'Don't say that, if you aren't going to mean it.' He spoke softly without facing her.

'I'm sorry. I misunderstood.'

'That's all right. Understandable.'

The lift doors opened and she tried not to step out too fast. Edward hung back, eventually being forced on to the landing to save being shut back inside and dropped away. Then he stood and watched her until he seemed satisfied she would hear him out.

'I wouldn't have shocked you for anything. I'm sorry. I was too tired to think straight; I should have cleared the damn things away. They're not even necessary. But please understand, these people need help. We're not talking about recreational use − that kind of relaxation − whatever you happen to think of it. We're looking at a group of men who make themselves almost incapable of sustaining relationships with other human beings in the real world. If they ever have intimate partners, they can't cope. Their jobs come under threat, they lose interest in their surroundings, they don't eat, their lives are centred around a satisfaction they find harder and harder to achieve. De-conditioning can help them to an extent, but they need something better than that. I hope to find that better something.' He rested his palms at both of her shoulders and let her study his face. 'I am sorry. Please. Helen.'

'Please what? I don't know what you're asking me for.'

'Help me not to spoil our night.'

As he dipped his head forward, she understood she should kiss his cheek and that made them fine again, sorted out.

Edward shut his eyes and released a breath. 'Come into the bar and talk to me – so I don't think about all of that pain.' He looked sad tonight and there was a hesitancy, a light hurt laid across the way he moved. 'Will you do that?'

'Yes. I can do that. Anyway, I'll try.'

Edward's third wheat beer was mostly done when Jimmy Stewart decided to put an appearance in. '*Aaaw, you know, I think we should drink a toast to good old Bailey Park.*' Edward was trying to please her, to joke her out of the stillness that fell whenever she thought of leaving Stuttgart and goodbyes. '*Whadaya think?*'

'Bailey Park? You'll have to tell me, I don't know it.'

Genuinely amazed, Edward let Jimmy's drawl desert him. 'Bailey Park. You really don't know? Don't remember? But you're such a clever woman with everything else.'

She felt pleased out of all proportion, but muffled her smile.

'Everybody has blind spots. How are you at choux pastry?'

'Okay, you've got me there.' He couldn't suppress a type of grin, 'Pastry, though, I don't mean to . . . but I can't imagine you. You standing in a kitchen, making pastry.'

'I did try standing in the garden, but the flour kept blowing away.'

'Should have tried the flour bed, hm?' He sipped his drink, trying out an expression that she hadn't seen before.

He was being careful until he could tell if she'd let him be daft. For the first time, she realised he was wary of what she might think.

'Go on, less of your nonsense.'

He peered down at his feet, apparently on the verge of being happy. She tapped at his hand.

'Tell me about Bailey Park. Complete my education.'

'Well, Bailey Park was the housing estate that George Bailey built in *It's A Wonderful Life*. People left their overpriced, rented slums – you never had to see them, you could imagine – and they went to live in the houses that George had built them with the money they'd invested in the good old Building and Loan. It was like a possible Promised Land. Good houses and good people, doing good things – the whole place made the way that George would like it. Good old George. So here's to Bailey Park.'

'You want me to drink to a housing estate.'

'Not *any* estate. *The* estate. All put together with dignity and love. George built it for people. How many things are really *for* people? Can I tell you a secret?'

There was no possible answer but yes.

'I mean it, I want to tell you a secret, Helen. So what you have to do is think if you should allow a man you don't know too well, a man in a bar in a foreign country, to confide in you.' He watched his glass closely, as if it might run away.

'Confide away. It's nice to be confided in.'

'You'll think I'm odd.'

'I think you're a genius.'

'That's very . . .' Gluck gulped at the last of his beer in lieu of finishing the sentence.

'What's your secret. I won't tell.'

'Oh, I know that. Absolutely.' He softened his voice and spoke as if he was describing a sleeping child. 'It's only an idea, not really a secret. Once upon a time, I was trying to say what I wanted to open up within the brain. I could have said that I'd found a way to chart the Field of Thought and to evade both time and circumstance, and explore all the solutions of the world. I've uncovered what makes me. I am a leap of faith, I am a flight. To steal from the language of physics, I am a constant singularity – a perpetual process of massive change. You, too – naturally.'

He lifted his gaze from the table. She didn't know how best to look back at him: an absolutely self-made man.

'I'd been asked to explain myself and the Process, yet again, and I'd even begun to reel off the usual guff when I stopped because something else made much more sense. To me, it made more sense. I wanted to say that our minds were made to give everyone the chance of Bailey Park. The place we take with us, wherever we go – the place that *is* us – we can build it into Bailey Park, we can live in bliss. We have a chance at it, anyway. I have found out a tiny amount about how this can be and I call that the Process, but I know I've hardly begun.'

'Did you say that? About Bailey Park?'

'No. No, the man I was speaking to represented the Pentagon. He wanted me to work within their Advanced Research Projects Agency and – apart from many other terrible things – he was keen that I should teach young men and women how to do terrible things terribly well and without thinking. They wanted to take the pain from the records of war – no more emotional memories, just objectives achieved, rates of success. I don't think the Pentagon understands about Bailey Park. Or bliss.'

'You didn't work for them.'

'Of course I didn't. You know me; I couldn't have. And I'm not an American. That made it easier to refuse.'

'Were they difficult?'

'Well, these NSA hit-men keep trying to shoot me . . .'

'What?' She hadn't meant to sound worried, but it happened anyway, even though he was obviously joking.

'No. I don't do work in America now, that's all. Which is a shame, because I made some good friends there. But

Bailey Park, that's the place.' He raised his glass and she brought hers to meet it. His hand wavered as he set it down. 'I'm so tired. You know, I've just noticed. Tired, tired, tired.'

So they talked nonsense about the Finnish dancers and gently enjoyed each other. Helen tried to frame what she wanted to say – a thorough goodbye and thank you.

'Edward?'

'Helen.'

'I think, it really is time – '

'I know. I was trying to gather my thoughts for a half-way coherent farewell and I couldn't think of anything adequate. Tonight I'm no good.'

'No, well, yes, there is that. Which is . . . it's hard, isn't it?'

'Yes. I would rather not start saying out loud how much I've enjoyed, well – you, basically. Us. If I mention that, I'm admitting we're about to stop.'

'I know. But I want to say thank you. I mean I'm slee – '

His eyes snapped alight. 'I know. You're sleeping. You're coming back to yourself.'

'That's right. Ever since the night with the Finns. I did enjoy that.'

'Except for not eating the meal and loathing the dancers and hating me.'

'I didn't hate you.'

'At the start.'

'I possibly didn't like you very much.'

They began to stand, preparing to finish the evening.

'But you do like me now?'

'Obviously.' They walked carefully.

'Very much?' His words tried to be as weightless as they could – no pressure, no threat.

'I can't answer that.'

'Why not?'

'It would go to your head.' She paused and a beat later, he did, too. 'Thank you for your help, Professor Gluck.'

'Thank you for yours, Mrs Brindle.'

Instead of moving outside the bar and towards the lift, they stood for a little together, not speaking, Helen thinking about her full name and what it meant. Mrs Brindle, married to Mr Brindle and about to go home. Slowly, Helen became aware of a pale, metallic sensation in her limbs. Her face began to feel clumsy and unpredictable.

Edward cleared his throat. 'Come on then.'

Helen reached into her bag, fumbled for her door-key and picked it out, although she had no immediate need for it. They began to walk again.

Staring softly ahead, Edward waited for the lift to arrive and take them in. 'This is horrible.'

'Yes.' She touched him on the arm, quite close to his shoulder. For perhaps the better part of one second, her palm and fingers rested against cloth and she felt him, she absolutely felt him, like a flash photograph taken in skin and expanding around her skull, around her mouth, around her waist and in. She felt him. Here was the curve and dip and warmness of his arm, the muscle and the mind moving lightly beneath his shirt. Here was the way he would look: the smoothness, the colour, the climb to his collarbone, the closeness of his torso and the speed of his blood. Here was the scent of the taste of him. He would taste good, because a good man would. Before she could finish her breath and lift her hand away again, she knew precisely how a kiss or a lick at his naked arm would taste. Good.

'That's us, then.'

'Hm?' She watched the lift doors split apart. 'Oh, yes.'

And they rode up together. Two floors. Twelve seconds. Helen counted them.

'Goodbye, then.'

Helen intended to tell him 'goodbye' back, but he kissed her on the mouth, suddenly, dryly, and stopped her telling him anything. Then the doors began to move and he was moving too, leaving, gone.

In her room that night, Helen bathed and thought of nothing at all. She dried her body slowly and looked in her mirror and she kept on thinking of nothing at all.

At a touch past midnight, her phone rang. She knew who it would be.

'Edward?'

'Oh, you knew.' There was a broad pause. 'I'm sorry it's so late. I've just noticed.' His tone seemed less substantial than usual.

'That's all right. Is something the matter? Edward? Is there something wrong?' She listened while he breathed quietly, but enough for her to hear. 'Edward, what's wrong?'

'Oh, yes. I'm sorry. I shouldn't bother you. It's simply . . . I was looking through this material again and it makes me so depressed. It makes me so unhappy, Helen, to think of it.'

'You mean those men? The photographs?'

'It's all so awful.'

'Yes, but you're going to help them and you know the Process works. They'll be fine. It's normal to be disturbed by other people's pain.'

'Yes, I suppose. Other people's. But it makes me feel lonely, you know? Something about it makes me lonely and I thought that calling you would help. It was a silly idea.' His articulation sharpened. 'I mean, speaking to you does make me feel less lonely, but it's silly of me to impose, to let this stuff get to me.' He began to sound angry with himself. 'I've seen worse. I should just say that I really did enjoy meeting you and that I would be very happy to receive a letter from you now and again. I would like to know how you're sleeping. Hm?'

Helen was growing more awake and able to appreciate his thinking of her – even if it was rather late. 'I will write to you. I . . . do you need? . . . Edward, are you all right now? Is there anything I can do?' There were things she could offer him, naturally, but it was late and her suggestions might be inappropriate.

'I'm fine, really. I've been working too long on one thing, that's all. I'll wish you goodnight.'

Helen didn't answer, knowing he intended to go on.

'Oh but, Helen, it's all such dreadful stuff. I apologise for talking about this, but it really is such dreadful stuff. If I *can't* talk about it, the things don't seem real. If I can't tell you . . . I look at this and the life it has seems . . . I don't know, *more* than mine.'

She heard him change his grip on the receiver.

'I don't know why I'm doing this. I shouldn't, but I will.'

His voice was nearer now.

'I am sorry, but, I have a picture here of a woman with two men inside her. That's what I'm looking at. A picture in a magazine. Her with the two men. Her lips don't really hide the first guy's shaft – the shaft of his prick, which is really quite a size. I'd guess she couldn't take it all in her throat, but this is her ideal position in any case, because these photographs are meant to help us understand the whole of her truth. We have to see the suck *and* the prick. *And* the fuck. Her second companion fucks her anally and, of course, we can see most of him – the part that counts – as well as the lift of her arse, her willingness, openness. He's wearing dark-coloured socks, the second man, he has varicose veins – not bad, but noticeable.

'Have you ever seen two pricks in a woman, up close? I've got pictures of that, too – fucking the arse and the cunt? – it doesn't look like anything you could think of. The penises make one, fat kind of rope that greases and sews right through her. On video, they pulse in and out of time, like something feeding, a fuck's parasite.

'Helen, everything is so clear, far clearer than life. They're here for me to watch them, the two men shoving themselves into pleasure, and the woman having none. She's there to make them come, to make whoever's looking come; that's the entire reason for her, no need to add a single thing. The men can touch all of her, inside and out, but they needn't make her come, they needn't even use her cunt if they don't want to. She's just there to get it where it's put. No pleasure, no fun. Unless, of course, she can take solace from ejaculation for ejaculation's sake. If she does that, then she's a dirty bitch, a slut who deserves every bad thing she gets, even if that includes gang rape at the hands of her camera crew which I know will happen if I turn on a couple of pages, or so. I have looked at this booklet before. She will be used and humiliated by seven men while her mouth has the wrong emotions and her eyes shut down.

'Any sane and normal person would see her condition and wish only to be usefully compassionate. That's the way to be, Helen, that's the way to be. The Bailey Park way to be. Anybody good and with a heart would be afraid to imagine how she must feel. You can understand that, can't you. Helen?'

She was able to say yes.

'I am making sense. I know that. I'm not too drunk to make sense, only drunk enough to let me tell you this. Helen, listen to me. You should listen. Are you listening?'

'Yes.' She can hear an uneasiness, a movement, shaking his breath.

'I want you to find me out . . . You would be bound to and I can't wait. Helen, the girl in this picture, I want to know how she feels. I want to know exactly how she feels.

'I want to know how she feels right up inside, when I'm up to my balls in her, my prick after all the other pricks, after what they've done. I want to have her, too. And she would want me, the pictures make her made that way. I want to be in her while she's raw, while she's open all the way to her fucking womb – and she is opened up, I can see it. I can see everything – the way she's full of it, running with it, her cunt and the other men's spunk. I want to be up her and make her full of me. I want to come. Helen, I want to come. I do. Then I want to see them having her again and we'll go turn and turn about her, turn and turn about her everywhere. Everywhere. I mean there isn't any end to what I want. There is no end, Helen.

'I can't bear the way I always turn out to be. I'm telling you, I'll never get out of this, I understand that. Sometimes I can manage containment, but that's all.

'I can't help you any more, Mrs Brindle, I'm the wrong man for the job. I'm the wrong man. You'll get better – '

She knew she was going to hang up, but the sound of the receiver falling still gave her a kind of jolt. Gradually, she discovered that she felt very peaceful, not needing to do anything: to cry, to move, to remember the edge in his words and the heat. She would turn out the light now, to calm herself and dream. Decisions could be taken in the morning, if there were any to take. It seemed there might only be one and that it was taken.

At about two a.m., the phone rang. She counted to twenty before it stopped and the silence sucked in around her again with a hissing throb. The noise hadn't disturbed her, she hadn't been asleep.

Mr Brindle didn't like his present much.

'What's this?'

Really she should have given it to him before dinner, because then the overbaking on the pie-crust wouldn't already have made him annoyed. It was strange how quickly she could drift out of practice with pastry and baking – a few days off and her presentation began to slip into collapse.

'What is it?'

'A hologram.'

He was gripping the picture's frame with both hands, angling it forward and back, but staring at her so, of course, he couldn't be able to see the image change. 'I know it's a hologram, I've seen them before. I mean what is it supposed to be. I can't see a thing.'

'I'm sorry I went away.'

'I'm not talking about that. I'm talking about this: your present to me which doesn't work. If I want to be angry about your running off across Europe with your lunatic sister and to hell with me, then I'll be angry about that. I have free will. That's what you tell me, isn't it?'

'Yes.'

'Well?'

'I think it will work where there's more light.'

'And?'

'She needed to get away.' Mrs Brindle compounded her lie, her original lie, the one that would follow her around now until she either forgot to feel guilty or forgot the truth. And, then again, a lie compounds itself if a person only lets it take its head. 'The divorce and everything – she needed a holiday.' She held her face calm, her eyes unwary and offered Mr Brindle a taste of her perfectly honest shame which he could interpret as he liked: a response to her failed obligation, hidden transgression, contemplated adultery. God knew which.

'I'm not talking about your sister. I'm talking about this. Not that there's any point. It isn't working.'

Mr Brindle set the picture down next to his uncleared plate and gave her the chance to take both her offences away. The hologram would have to be disposed of with the bad pastry, but she hoped she would have more luck with the summer pudding and the lightly cinnamon-flavoured cream. Mr Brindle always enjoyed that and it looked wonderful to serve, all the different colours of red, the new season's fruit that made her kitchen smell of berry-picking and being much younger than now.

She sat back at the table and watched him tasting, examining, turning the white cream and the bleeding fruit together into something spoiled and pink. If she'd been sticking to the Process and its dietary advices, she couldn't have been eating this. Instead, she would have bought the supplements and trace elements suggested; the ones that were too numerous to be hidden successfully anywhere in Mr Brindle's house.

Mr Brindle began to eat steadily, contentment in a shine across his forehead and his lips. Mr Brindle hadn't been angry about her trip yet, but probably he needn't be tonight. Later would do. When he handed her his bowl, he wasn't frowning. He even rubbed his index finger over the back of her hand.

Because she had been away and he might have thought about that, thought about her not being in any way available to him, he might ask her to be with him tonight. Not that they didn't share a bed usually, but he might have recalled the way they used to commemorate their sharing of occupancy. She wouldn't deny him. A refusal would be unwise and he wouldn't be demanding, not more than once. They would try to read each other, and then discover again they were written in two different languages, were quite untranslatable. Their intentions would subside, or rather, Mr Brindle's intentions would subside. After an hour or so, she could leave him and come downstairs to anticipate a morning made hopeful by the simplicity she planned into her daylight hours.

★   ★   ★

Her days at home after Stuttgart could seem so much like her days before that Mrs Brindle often managed not to think about her trip. The Process, she had abandoned. Her collection of clippings about its inventor, her articles and notes were all underneath the liner paper in a kitchen drawer, but they might as well have been thrown away. At some point, she *would* throw them away but, at the moment, having to touch them might remind her of a man and what he did, and generally her life was freed from that.

Freed until dark. In the hardest place of the night when the same old fear of dying slipped over her in a fast, loose slither, when it breathed at her – then Edward was there, too. Curled on her side, with her face against the burn of the carpet, she shut up her eyes and was shown and shown again her age and maximum possible time remaining, the losses and degenerations that were seeping through already to cloud her life, and which would end in no more than a memory of the lies she told and the darkness in her thoughts. Lies and thoughts of Edward would harden in her like old blood, and death would hollow her out into nothing but a soured and stiffened echo of herself.

She would be all bad because of Edward – the battery-acid drip of Edward – the patient and poisonous shadow that showed her the way his forehead led his body when he turned, gave her the scent of his hand left in her skin and the impossible, racing feel of him that eased close with his breath on the telephone. And all of this was completely her own deliberate fault. She was harbouring the parts of him that stung, in under her eyelids and next to the prickle of appetite under her tongue. She couldn't balance her books for this, or for a holiday that was a lie and that was so much to do with the Flesh of a man and so little to do with the Spirit and the other Love she'd lost.

Alone after sunset, she was nothing but wrong ideas: wrong like they were again now, when a part of her wanted to say that if God didn't mean her to think in the way that she did, then He shouldn't have made her able to. God ought to be fair. If His divine intention had been to keep her inside His laws, He should never have left her to cope with things alone, or have teased her with a few days' respite before slapping her down again. She had been by herself and very tired for too long and not even saints could always manage that.

Mr Brindle had a habit of telling her about saints.

'Suicide is suicide. They murder themselves and then everybody paints their portrait, names their bloody kids after them.'

'They're examples.'

'Crap.'

'They are examples.'

'Okay, fine, they're examples. So you have thousands of examples of how you're supposed to behave and how you're supposed to think and all of the rules you're supposed to follow. So why don't you go to church any more? Hm?'

'You know why.'

'Aye, you're right I know why. I know fine why. You came to your senses. Creeping round here like Mrs Fucking Jesus . . . I didn't marry that. Giving me that wee fucking Edinburgh smile every time I fucking swear.'

'That's not – '

'What? True? You wanted me and you got me and now you've to fucking live with me when *I know you*. You're fooling nobody. "I've lost my faith, I've lost my faith." You never bloody had any. You're forgetting, I saw. I saw the way you were, home from your piss-hole bloody church. I saw the colour in your face. I knew. You only ever went there for a come. Sweating with your eyes shut, kneeling – you were having a fucking come. I know. You only knelt because you couldn't stand. Then God couldn't get it up any more so you left him. Right? Right?'

He didn't always get so angry, there'd been something on his mind that time and then she'd been stupid and tried to explain herself to him, to talk about what was between them and growing thicker and filling the house until it was difficult to breathe when they were both inside. Everything she'd ever read about disagreements and about marriages had told her that she should explain and she had tried. Wrong night, that was all, she'd picked the wrong night.

'Right? Right?'

Mr Brindle had been holding her by the wrist, really lifting her by the wrist until she was standing and walking, stumbling beside him from the living-room into the corridor, into the kitchen. She spent a lot of time in her kitchen; it was the part of her house which felt most like a home.

Remembering when Mr Brindle had opened the drawer was hard. Perhaps she hadn't seen, or had only heard the scrape of the wood and the clatter of the contents inside, or she could have been too confused to notice anything except that Mr Brindle was still shouting and that shouting always made her feel confused. Or as if she would cry. Sometimes it made her feel as if she would cry.

When he put her hand in the drawer, she thought he was looking for something and turned to his face. Mr Brindle was smiling in the odd, tight way that people do when they are nervous or embarrassed by someone's pain.

Of course later, she would find this caught in her memory, because Mr Brindle had been embarrassed by *her* pain, which didn't arrive at once, but was on the way.

She listened to the shutting of the drawer and watched the effect of his effort shudder across his face, followed by a moment of stillness, almost puzzlement. There was a hot numbness in the fingers of her hand. Mr Brindle dropped her wrist and stepped away, observing.

Then Mrs Brindle wanted to sit down, except that she didn't because she also wanted to be sick and she had a quite bad headache which made her need to rub her temples. She tried to lift her hands and discovered that one wouldn't lift. It was stuck. A burst of nausea and a white, high sound happened when she pulled on her arm and then she looked at her fingers, the four fingers of her right hand that were already a slightly unfamiliar shape and bleeding and a little hidden by four flaps of sheared-away skin. She could see the light of one of her bones.

While she fainted, Mrs Brindle was still figuring the whole thing through, so that when she turned back to consciousness, she knew what Mr Brindle had done. He had taken her hand and closed it in a drawer. She had made his damage worse when she wrenched her fingers free without understanding where they were.

Mr Brindle was kneeling on the floor and holding her round the shoulders, trying not to look at her bleeding, but slipping his eyes down and sideways all the same. He told her that he was sorry and she nodded and fainted again.

It would have been best to take her to the hospital, but instead Mr Brindle called their doctor and then drove to the surgery. Her pain was an intimate thing between them which they didn't need to share. Mrs Brindle listened while her husband talked about a horrible domestic accident and she then sat extremely still while her doctor explained that two of her fingernails would have to be removed. He would first give her ring injections – appropriate for fingers – which he hadn't practised since his student days, but he would do his very best.

Mr Brindle waited outside while the needle went in and the scalpel cut and the blueing nails were tugged amazingly, easily away. She thought for a moment how softly she was put together. Then her wounds were dressed, splinted, turned into plump, clean fabric. Afterwards, the doctor looked for a long time at her face, but she couldn't tell him anything, even though both of them knew she wanted to.

Funnily enough, the kitchen hardly ever reminded her of that day. Mr Brindle had cleaned her blood off the drawer himself and she would have had to study it carefully to see the denting in the wood. Now it was only the place she kept her tea towels safe: soft, clean, fabric things.

Edward had been able to hold her hand and find nothing strange about it, because it was fine now. More than two years of healing had made it useful and strong again. She didn't brood on what had once hurt it, because there was no point. But she did sometimes remember what she had thought of while she listened to her nails come away. Mrs Brindle had considered how deeply she believed that marriage was a sacrament and that no one should act against a sacrament. Mr Brindle did not treat marriage sacramentally. This meant that, in many important ways, she was not married to him.

This was a bad thing to think, or an odd thing to think, but not un-useful. In a way, it made her feel free enough to be able to stay and lie beside Mr Brindle at the start of her nights, hearing the rustle of his hairs against her sheets. Inside she was free. She was staying and lying and knowing that she was free and not married to him.

Then Edward sent a postcard.

When he had almost become a person who was more in her mind than in recollections of reality, Edward got in touch. Five weeks after Stuttgart he wrote to her, on the whole of one side of a postcard that showed a view of night-time London and was sent inside an envelope.

Dear Helen,

For a while I thought it would be better not to write, but then I was sure you wouldn't write either. That made me sad. I am so sorry for being irresponsible. I thought you deserved the truth about me when you'd told me the truth about you. Now I think I thought wrong.

> *I hope you are well and happy Helen. Tell me if you are*
> *not. I repeat my address below in case you have lost it.*
> *Do tell me if you are not,*
>
> *Edward.*

Helen put the card in her coat pocket and went out to walk.
A fine summer was finally breaking and dusty rain fell out of
an almost blue sky. It didn't bother her. Inside her pocket,
she ran her thumb across the gloss of the photograph and
then the polite friction of the writing surface; a postcard
in an envelope, because all of the writing was for her and
she had a husband and Edward had perfectly understood,
without being told, that Mr Brindle did not know about
him and that Edward should not help him to find out.

She tried to think of what to do and couldn't. An uneasy
tiredness dropped close in around her and she took another
turn away from the house and then another again and there
was no way she could write back to Edward and no way she
could not.

Helen walked and discovered new details in herself. As
far as she understood her God and His opinions, He would
think it was bad for her to be tempted but worse for her to
be disappointed that she hadn't given in. Nevertheless, she
was sad that she had no hope of escaping the straight and
narrow way and now that she'd resisted temptation, what
little of God had returned to her was receding. God no
longer needed to keep her from urgent sin and, because
He didn't want her for Himself, He'd left her alone. He had
abandoned her again and never explained Himself, never
said why, that's what hurt her most.

She was beginning to think that relationships were possibly not her strong point. She couldn't manage one with
God, or with her husband; she didn't like her sister and her
parents were both dead. That only left Edward and all of
her books – including the Good one – would advise her
against him. He was not well. He'd admitted that. He

had tastes with which she could not agree and which didn't even seem to please him, only to have power in his life. His not wanting to like what he liked made him a less than hopeless case but, nevertheless, Helen knew that damaged people often sought each other out and fell in love with their mutual diseases, to the detriment or destruction of their hopes and personalities. There were whole books about each part of that progression and the misfortunes of those trapped in repeating behaviours and bad relationships. Helen was attracted to a sick man; she was therefore sick. Edward was attracted to Helen; he was therefore sick. Helen was even sicker for knowing he was sick and still wanting him and yet, oddly, she felt very well for somebody so sick.

How was Edward attracted, that was what she didn't know. It was none of her business, but she did want to know. He hadn't said why he was writing, or hadn't said clearly.

Without noticing, she had made her way back to her gate. Mr and Mrs Brindle's garden gate that defended Mr and Mrs Brindle's garden, around Mr and Mrs Brindle's domestic home. Soon she would stand in their garden, sheltered in the lee of the house and tear up the card with its envelope and burn them both, the powdery rain still falling about her silently.

She buried the ash.

Dear Mrs Brindle,
  Dear Helen,
  I won't do this again. Having received no reply from you and having waited this reasonable while, I became unable to provide a sufficiently definitive explanation for your silence. I write now because another silence on your part will allow me to know that any explanation is no longer relevant. Or rather, that I am no longer relevant to you and should develop a little silence of my own. The rest of this letter

will be about that so perhaps you need not read beyond this point.

Of course, I hope you do. I personally am curious. I can't help reading anything once I've started. But then you know that. I can't help most things once I've started. I can work the Process for anyone but myself.

So I have resorted to the standard, really rather brutal methods that might be suggested for my reconditioning. The brutality appeals to me: seems suitable and good for the satisfaction of my self-disgust. In case you were interested, I look at my pictures having injected myself subcutaneously with 6mg of Apomorphine. The injection causes nausea unrelieved by vomiting, at least in theory. This means I should associate my sexual obsession with nausea, rather than orgasm. No carrot, all stick. I watch my videos while sniffing valeric acid – vile stuff – and once again hope for successful results. These rigmaroles seem to be taking effect, they undoubtedly make me feel more lonely than I have in several years. All the old friends going.

I do intend to become more normal.

That sounds alarming, doesn't it? Like some terrible per- vert whining. Really, I simply want my free time back again, my time for hobbies and work and the people that I like.

I want to be able to stand full in your eyes without what I might describe as shame. I wish I could put that more convincingly, but I can't.

All of which has little to do with your difficulties and a great deal to do with my self-obsession. I have been reading on your behalf, you know. Here is a quote for you 'Ne demande donc pas la foi pour pouvoir prier ensuite. Prie d'abord, et la foi inondera ton ame.' Someone called Grillot de Givry, with whom you might identify. He suggests, if I can presume a translation, that you don't ask for faith to pray later, but pray first and faith will flood your soul. This sounds quite encour- aging and is several hundred years old. I'm sure you've read him already; I'm sure I'm being no help here. As usual.

Actually, what I am doing is talking too much because I am nervous. I thought I should tell you something, that's all. On the fourth of next month I will be in Glasgow. There's a little two-day thing going on up there which I might attend. Equally, I can stay away, if I'm told to.

If you don't write and give me a yes or a no, then I won't know what to do.

Unfair of me to say so, but true.

Edward.

'I didn't think you would.'

Edward appeared happy, but his mouth was tense. She thought it seemed tense. The over-illuminated air of the hospital canteen eddied round them as colour-coded human beings went to and from their curing and quieting tasks. Helen noticed she could taste, increasingly clearly, other people's panic and exhaustion and her own confusion, welling in. When Gluck stood up to meet her, he'd shaken her hand, very formal and far away. But when he caught at her eyes, he didn't seem formal, hardly even polite.

'Um, didn't think I would what?'

She couldn't read him, not clearly, not yet.

'Write. Of course. That's why I'm here.'

'You wouldn't have come anyway.'

'No.' They caught themselves perusing each other and stopped at once.

'Really?'

'Yes, really.' His voice sounded thin and vaguely petulant. 'Sorry, I didn't mean to be abrupt. I'm not making a good impression and I do want –' He clawed between his collar and his neck with one hand, 'Sorry. Look, let's walk. I've had more than enough of this place. I should never have suggested we meet here. I might as well have dragged you out to the local abattoir; dignity and privacy, meat-hooked. Oh, I don't even want to think about it. Let me . . .'

He elbowed forward across the table, trying to slide inside his own anecdote. 'You know they had therapeutic rabbits here?'

His face seemed very slightly thinner and very slightly afraid. She nudged at his knuckles, just to say *hello*. He chanced a smile. 'Rabbits.'

'Rabbits?'

'Mm. Lots of them. Participating patients could have one of their very own to care for, be fond of, give a name to – as you do.'

They were both smiling now, they'd remembered they could do that.

'Nice.'

'Yes. Then the last time they had a conference here, the caterers screwed up. No food for the Sunday evening.'

'Don't tell me.'

'Oh, yes.' He sneaked in a whisper at her ear, the heat of it bleaching the meaning away from his words. 'The psychiatrists ate the therapeutic rabbits, every one.'

Then he dodged back, apparently uneasy again.

'Let's go.' She tried to sound calming while remembering the bludgeon and tease of his breath. 'I mean, would you like to go?'

'Yes, thank you. And if the shrinks want to burn me in effigy while I'm away, I am quite agreeable. They're exactly the types to believe in that kind of thing. Voodoo specialists. Sorry. I'm not going to get annoyed again. I'm going to leave.'

Edward stood up and dragged his chair aside loudly, frowning down at the furniture that hemmed him in. Helen moved over to join him and rubbed at the small of his back.

'Oh.' He sounded on the verge of pain. 'That's . . . thank you. But – '

She stopped before he could tell her to.

'No, don't stop.' Edward lightly took her hand and replaced it, stood while Helen rubbed again and tried to think how she had done this un-selfconsciously.

'Edward?'

'Yes.' He faced forward: scanning, challenging the room.

'Are you all right?'

'I'm . . .' He reached his arm to lock it round her back. She stopped moving, just held. 'I'm all right, yes. I am simply too angry, having spent a whole morning surrounded by drug-company reps.' He kept staring out, but slightly increased the pressure of his arm about her.

'You know what I put down as my hobbies in *Who's Who*?'

'No.'

'Laughing at Classical Ballet and drug-company reps.'

'I see.' That sounded a stupid response, but she'd never met anyone else who'd been put in *Who's Who* and she'd never held Edward before, not for this long. Stupidity was all she could muster.

'This room is full of them: reps. So we shouldn't really stand like this . . .'

'Why not?'

'It will make them excited.'

'They get easily excited?'

'They lead extremely sheltered lives. I mean, look at them – not exactly the faces of men who get lucky.' He lifted his arm with a final, jingling brush at her spine. 'Not that I'd know. How are you?'

'Okay.' She thought she wouldn't move away from him just yet, because she wouldn't be able to touch him this way again.

'No. I said "How are you?"' He finally faced her.

'Tired.'

'I stopped you sleeping again, didn't I? Because I am a stupid bastard and sometimes it shows. I shouldn't have – '

'I came home. I don't sleep at home.'

'Okay. But you look well, though. Trust me, I'm a doctor. You do.' He dipped in and kissed her cheek, retreating before she could make any response.

They left the hospital together and walked the straight and Great Western Road, in towards the Botanical Gardens and the town. Artfully displayed interiors posed through drawing-room windows and Gluck was mainly silent, although sometimes impressed by the sternly grey perspectives of Calvinist pseudo-classical façades.

'This is all very nice. Not like London.'

'No, not like London. This is bad old money, but with good old style, because it's Scotland. We have style.'

'You're a Nationalist?'

'No, a realist. It's just true.'

Helen stumbled through her mind for useful things to say and noticed they were practically trudging now – this was too long a walk to be welcoming or sociable. She was getting it wrong, so many different kinds of wrong.

Gluck inhaled hard, 'I do apologise.'

'What for?'

'The mood I'm in. Mental hospitals make me very uneasy . . . well, furious. Which is decidedly unwise – they're the one place where no one should seem to be in imminent need of sedation, and I always do. And it is . . . not good to be with. Very unattractive and I'd rather be . . .'

'Attractive.'

'Well, now you mention it . . . Probably. Something like that.'

'You are attractive.'

'Now I didn't say it because I wanted you to – '

'I know. That's one of the reasons you are. Attractive. I'm sorry, I shouldn't say.'

'No. Quite likely you shouldn't.'

Edward began to walk a touch ahead. She hadn't thought until now that he must have been slowing his pace down to hers.

Every time a bus churned by, Helen wanted to apologise for its noisiness, for the intrusion, for the fact that it destroyed whatever atmosphere they might have been creating. Not that any atmosphere she could think of was actually taking shape. This was her home territory, she ought to be able to welcome him and be entertaining about a place he'd never visited before, but she couldn't. She hoped for a light inspiration that could kick off some safer, smaller talk, but nothing came. The skin above her eyes felt sensitive and tense.

'Ach God, this is awful. Oh, I'm sorry.'

She discovered she was holding Edward's hand, soft around the curl of his fingers. They had reached a standstill and he was looking at her flatly, his mouth tight.

'Oh, I didn't mean to say – I hate trying to make conversation. I think if you have to make it then you shouldn't be bothering. But I want to make it. I mean I think that I do want to talk. I don't know what to do here, Edward, do you know what to do here?'

Edward freed himself from her and then slid his hands up to touch either side of her face. He held her along the jaw and beside her cheeks, fingers mildly chill as they slipped to the start of her neck. His pressure was firm but trembled slightly. Hard under her breastbone, a type of fluidity seemed to break out; it lurched and then sparked away into a heightened, untrustworthy peace. She watched him and he watched her, because they were fixed in a position where they could do nothing else, although this was almost unbearable. When Edward spoke, Helen focused her attention on his lips to steady her concentration and found this didn't work. He had good lips.

'Helen, we've forgotten we know each other. I think that's all. No, it's not. I'm afraid that I seem disgusting now – because of the way I've behaved today – '

'No, really – '

'Then because of Germany – what I told you – what I do – and I find that I care about you more when I can see you than I did when I was thinking about you and I don't want to be disgusting and, Jesus Christ, Helen, I'm only a genius, I can't be expected to cope with this. With being confused,' He rubbed his forehead, 'I don't like to be confused.'

'I know how you feel.'

She touched his hands for the sake of touching them and at once he let go of her face. That seemed a shame.

'Look, I was going to drag you off to the Gardens . . .'

His hands tugged down against hers as she lifted them, the

palms and thumbs and fingers, all made alive and in keeping with the proportions of the man.

'The Gardens up ahead there . . . and I'd have made you look at the squirrels when they're really just rats with a perm and cheeky to boot. I think we shouldn't do that. I think I should go home.'

'Really?' He was trying to be unhurt, just the way he'd tried not to notice when she said *home*. He didn't understand about her home and how she and Mr Brindle would define that word in ways that disagreed.

She squeezed and tickled at his palms. 'That was in the wrong order. Sorry. I'm going home because then I'll come back out again. Right at the corner on this side of the street there's a big hotel with a bar. You'll find it no bother and I'll see you in there at . . . I will try to come and see you there at eight o'clock. If I'm late it means I couldn't get away, so don't wait. I'm sorry to be so uncertain. I will try.'

'I understand.'

'How was your sister?' Mr Brindle was watching the Saturday sport on Mr Brindle's TV set, from Mr Brindle's chair. 'Still depressed?'

'Yes. She's not doing well.'

Although hardly anything was different in the living-room, Mr Brindle made it untidy, surly, and somewhere she could only intrude.

'She needs to take herself in hand. She can't go through life expecting to be helped all the time. Even if her sister does have her heart set on playing the fucking saint.'

She could be sure he'd hardly moved since she left him after lunch: sitting, sunk into the scrappy jeans and the sweatshirt and the stocking feet. He was wearing white socks. One day at home for white socks without slippers and they're done.

While she moved across the kitchen, she began to call through what she needed to say.

'Would you mind – '

'What does she want now?'

'I don't have to.' She filled the kettle, switched it on, came back to lean in the doorway and stare at the back of Mr Brindle's head.

'You don't have to what?'

'Saturday night on her own – it makes her feel lonely.'

He turned to her, 'And it won't do the same to me?'

'I don't have to.'

'Ach, go on. Why not. Why not.' He waved her over with his hand until she stood beside him and he could loop his arm in tight round the tops of her thighs. 'Will you be late? You don't need to be late.'

'No, I won't be late. I don't have to go.'

'I can watch the film. It's decent, for once. Give her my best. Ho, ho.'

'Yeah, right.' She stooped down to kiss him and was sure, as her lips read his cheek and she smelt sleep on his skin, that she was betraying him. To kiss and betray. She would never have thought herself so far beyond help, but there she was, bending to him with a biblical condemnation like cold leather at her back – kissing to betray a trust.

Mr Brindle glanced up to her, smiling, and stretched to give his own, answering kiss.

Helen was dressed for visiting her sister who was not in Glasgow and could not be visited, this meant she was not dressed for Edward, or even for the hotel bar. She felt indelibly ugly as she waited for her vision to adjust from a rather beautifully violent sunset to an interior gloom. The last time she'd had to pause like this, obviously searching for someone and at risk of disappointment, she'd been no older than twenty. Perhaps she appeared to be faking an elaborate absence of partner that would be the beginning of a come-on to the room. She knew there were glances evaluating and probably discounting her already as she tried to turn smoothly and take in all the tables where Edward might be. She was slightly late; he might have gone.

At least no one she knew ever came here, it was safe. No one she knew – she couldn't argue with that. Mr Brindle had made sure there really was no one she knew: only the paper-shop man and the butcher and all of the other people she paid out Mr Brindle's money to. She couldn't remember when she'd given up the struggle of trying to stay friendly with the last of her friends. Whatever they'd been able to give her was never worth what Mr Brindle made her pay. Some of the churches had called sometimes, but not recently.

'I'm sorry, did I give you a start? You looked right past me twice.'

The bar turned back to its various preoccupations and she let Edward lead her aside towards the furthest wall. A ridiculously piercing light made a tight hoop on the table-top. If they leant forward, their faces were bleached blank, or troubled with odd shadows.

'I'm late.'

'I know. I was just going.'

'Were you?'

'No. I was just preparing to spend a very long night getting maudlin drunk on my own. Tell me about how you are, Helen, all about that. Did any of what I suggested help?'

She had expected he might be angry when she told him that she'd abandoned the whole of his Process and gone back to her nights spent with death. But Edward was only sad. From time to time, she would mention a detail from her home or from the particular style of living she had made and a shiver of discomfort would close Edward's eyes or make him stare away. He found her life far more unpleasant than she could.

If he asked her questions, they were gentle, but precise in a way that meant she answered them without evasion or concealment. Perhaps for as much as an hour, he was with her in her thinking, as if they were dreaming together, or of each other.

When she had no more to say, he let her watch him while he made her a part of his work, an element in what was the brightest and closest part of him. His expression died away to something more than sleep, a lonely consideration that took the colour and the pupils of his eyes and deepened them together into one, dark thing that saw and saw and saw. His voice sank in his chest, solid and low. He ripped pages from his notebook, covered them in tiny, regular print and gave them to her. He asked her to repeat certain instructions and orders of action and she did so, as if she were taking oaths of allegiance to a country they intended to create. Last of all, he made her laugh.

'That's better. I don't mind being serious, but I draw the line at solemn. And I'm tense enough as it is. Don't want to mess up again.' He paused for an unnecessary breath. 'There's nothing else I have to suggest, but at least now I can feel I've done my duty properly.'

Helen dropped her head while her smile couldn't help squeezing down into something grey. 'I didn't know I was a duty.'

He reached immediately for her hand, but then didn't touch it. 'You're not. See – I'm messing up already? *That* was my duty, but *you* are not and now I can talk *to* you, instead of *about* you. I mean, I could have written you a letter with all this.' He prodded the pile of notes with his finger. 'Couldn't I?'

'Mm hm.'

'But that wouldn't have been as good.'

'No.'

'Look at me. Okay. Now shall we enjoy ourselves? Would that be the right thing to do?'

Helen sat at rest while a swipe of vertigo pressed through her. She no longer had any grip on the right thing to do.

She had no idea of anything but what she wanted, and what she wanted was not an idea. Considering what might stop her from doing wrong, or what might make her hold on morality even more precarious, she said, 'You could tell me about you.'

'How do you mean?'

'We've talked about my problems . . .'

He eased out half a sigh. 'I said in my letter, I've been trying all the nasty old tricks I've just spent my morning preaching against: drugs that make me sick, foul smells, electric shocks –'

'Shocks?'

'Helen, if I thought it would help, I'd sit and watch mucky videos while beating a steel mallet off my head. Any unpleasant stimulus will do. The trouble is . . . do you really want to hear about this, because I may enjoy telling you in a way that I should not.'

'I don't believe that.'

'Because you believe in confession?'

'Because I think you're trying to be different. And maybe . . . I'm curious.'

'Curious. Well, then I should tell you everything, of course.' There was a brittle line in the way he said that. She'd forgotten how easily she could hurt him and how little she wanted to.

'Not that –'

'No, no. You're curious, that's fine.' He stared at the table and began a sharp, low monologue. 'So I should start with what? Number of times I come in one day? An average day? Six. Everything else has to fit around that number: where I go, how long I can stay, what work I can do, what excuses I make to slip away, what possible material I can get that will still have an edge, that will still manage to stimulate me when I've already seen every bloody thing there is. Have you ever sat up late at night when you should have been marking papers for a third-year exam and watched a

German Shepherd licking Pedigree Chum off a cunt before fucking it? Good film, terrific reviews – if you read the same papers I do.'

He wasn't being angry with her; she had to bear in mind that he wasn't being angry with her.

'Or the guy who loves to fist them, gets in there up to his wrist, has a preference for cunts and doesn't mind the blood. Or actually, I beg your pardon, he *likes* the blood and I *don't like* any of this at all, but I have to have it because anything else doesn't work any more. I watch men shoving Perrier bottles where the sun will never shine and part of me hopes that the bottles don't break, but only a small part, because the rest of me is watching. I always have to watch. No matter what.

'Even if it hurts. Do you know how many times I can wank before it starts to hurt? I know exactly, but that isn't where I stop. Some drug addicts in withdrawal, they have the same problem. I've written monographs on it: the fascinating phenomenon of forcing yourself to shoot your load over and over again, even though every time you touch yourself it makes you want to scream. Still, I wouldn't wish to exaggerate, that only happens every month, or so.

'And I am trying to fight it, I'm doing my best with the aversion therapy . . . Aversion – that's a joke. I'm going through all the steps, every spell and potion for de-conditioning success, but I already loathe what I do. I can't hate it any more completely and I still don't stop. Jesus, I'm even starting to like the electric shocks – I associate the charges with being about to ejaculate. Still curious?'

'Of course, if you're going to be angry, then you won't be anything else.'

'What?'

'Mr Brindle does it all the time: gets angry. It's something people do instead. I don't know what he really is, but he gets angry instead. I think you don't want to be ashamed.'

Edward wrapped his arms tight around his ribs, exhaled

and inhaled again. 'Ten out of ten. Ten out of ten. You might want to add in that I would also rather not be afraid. Obviously I am.'

'Why.'

'Why?' His voice sounded tiny, surprised. 'Because I don't want you to go.'

'That's . . . something good.'

'It might not always be.'

'Mm hm.'

'And I need you. You're one of my cures. The best of them, in fact. Pain and nausea I know about – I know all about – but if I can talk to you, I remember it later. When I open up a magazine, when I put in a video, I remember you and I can't . . . I get too ashamed. It's good. To be humiliated.'

Edward rubbed at the back of his neck, then reached for her hand again, took it and pulled it smoothly along the table-top. Helen sat very slightly nearer while he rubbed his thumb across the root of her fingers, worked into the shallow fold of skin behind the knuckle and inside the tidy dark of her closed fist.

'You wouldn't believe how easily it started. I was fresh back from America, very young, very promising and I didn't have time for a person to be in my life. I was busy building myself into a genius and finding out how easy that could be and there was so little space for everything necessary, I quite frequently went without sleep. But then again I have never been devoid of feelings – sexual impulses – I've always had what most people have – the desire to be with someone. I've often wanted to love.

'I'd never thought that buying people, hiring them, would be a way forward for me; not because of scruples, I was just scared of diseases and of being caught. The books, the magazines, I could use them according to my schedule, they seemed perfectly convenient and unshameful. Naturally, at that point I didn't quite realise I'd end up having private carrier's lorries arriving to dump shifty, plain, brown packages, addressed for only me, at every house and research establishment I would ever be associated with.

'It has to be a private carrier, you see – Her Britannic Majesty's mail won't deliver my style of literature – the illegal kind. It comes under the same regulations that prevent you from posting shit. Obscene and Offensive Material.

'My life is neither wild, nor exotic, just massively embarrassing.'

He grabbed at his glass and found it empty, this appeared to puzzle him.

'Did I drink that?'

'Yes, I think you did. Edward, you want to change, that must make a difference. You'll find out how to do it and it'll work. You're a genius – that's what you're for.'

'Yeah.' He frowned at the buttons of ice left in his tumbler, shook them.

'I wish I could help you.'

'You *do* help. Really – you are already helping me. I came up here without any kind of dreadful material and I've been okay. I made it. That's . . . more than twenty-four hours since I looked at anything.' He searched her expression to see if she understood. 'I haven't done that in years. Obviously, it doesn't mean too much; I could remember enough to see me through, if I tried.' She watched him frown to himself and wished he needn't. 'But I haven't tried. I've been . . . quieter. I've been thinking about you, instead.' He brushed her arm quickly. 'I mean of what you would think, your disapproval. I should have asked you if I could, though, shouldn't I? If I could think of you?'

'It's your mind, you can think about what you like in it. And I did say I wanted to help.'

He kissed at the top of her head. 'You're good, you are.' His face seemed terribly lonely, with a light of hunger to it. 'Anyway, this may sound quite unimpressive, but I walked all the way through two different railway stations today and I didn't buy a thing. And bear in mind that when I'm travelling I do make a habit of buying things in this particular area.' He breathed out a dull laugh. Moral turpitude governs my travel arrangements far more effectively than any tourist agency. In Europe and America, I take an extra bag – for reports and research, that's supposed to be – but I bring it back home full of filth, my favourite. Customs hassle me sometimes, that's all.

'In Britain, I have a weakness for railway stations. Well, they're so romantic,' He didn't smile, 'And they're where I started out, because they're ideal. They have everything waiting for me: *The Story of O*, true-life sex crimes, pathology with pictures, *Justine*, top-shelf magazines you can buy in armfuls because no one knows you and no one cares and any possible disapproval will not stick. These places are nowhere, they don't count, so I can be anyone I want to – be disgusting – be quite openly what I am.'

'You are not disgusting.'

'It's kind and completely unrealistic of you to say so.'

'Edward, please.'

He laid his hand above hers and she felt him warm and then the cool of him lifting softly away. She heard him clear his throat to speak, to murmur in close at her cheek. 'In Glasgow today I went from the platform and into a taxi, without even looking for the bookstall, not a glance. My hotel doesn't have a soft-core channel. I did check. I don't think you *have* any sex shops that I could search for. So I'm fairly safe. No.' He paused and let her cheek touch the shape of his mouth. 'I'm very safe – you're here. So I'll be good.'

She eased her arm in round his shoulders because she needed to and it also seemed the proper thing to do. Edward leaned back against her. She felt it when he exhaled, understood the sudden flex and rub of his neck. The surprising weight of his head rocked against her.

'Tired?'

'Exhausted, actually.'

Helen enjoyed how comfortable and comforted she was with this man in an almost-embrace, with the shift and the change of his bones, his breath. An emotion resembling fear prickled at the small of her back, threatened, then withdrew again.

'It's odd.' Helen wasn't speaking to make sense, only to be speaking, to keep some limitation between them, a boundary of words. 'It's odd.'

'You can say that again.' Edward tried a chuckle and then they both rocked inside it together long after the sound had gone. 'You did, though, didn't you? Always thinking ahead.' The back of his neck rubbed against her again, at home with her in a sleepy, disturbing way. 'Oh, Helen. You're a good person. What are you doing here with me?'

She turned to meet his stare but couldn't hold it. 'I'm being where I want to. And I'm not all that good. I just don't often do what I want.'

'Is what you want bad?'

'Sometimes.'

'What kind of bad?'

Something bloomed at the back of her thinking like an unpredictable pilot light. 'I don't know.'

Although it was very gentle, very milky, she could feel Edward's voice shake low and solid against his ribs. 'You must know, it's what you want.'

Helen tugged her arm from behind him and sat forward to the table-top. 'When I was at school, I used to read up on the sexual diseases. They were so correctly frightening; things like syphilitic aneurysms, I never forgot about them. If you had bad sex, wrong sex, then your blood vessels would balloon up in your chest and finally burst. You would explode inside because of badness; because of men and badness and that seemed absolutely fair.'

'You only get syphilis from someone else with syphilis.' He was making an effort to sound authoritative. 'I mean that's a . . . fact.' But he ended in a stagger of consonants. 'An absolute . . . Hmn.'

'I know, I'm just saying that when I was young I was always afraid that even if I thought too much about it, about men, I'd balloon. Everyone told me how terrible sex was and how men might do anything and I would wonder about that anything – what it would be like – and then I would worry that I'd burst.'

'But you didn't. You can't have thought bad enough things.'

'I suppose not. There's time yet, though.'

'True. And I'm a bad influence.'

'Yes.'

Their silence surprised them, left them undefended, suddenly. Edward rubbed lightly at his arm and watched her face.

They thought for a moment and then they agreed themselves into a kiss, the open-mouthed soft and hard kiss with him she now realised she'd very often thought about. For some considerable time, they were both lifted up in far too much breathing and in her touching the gallop of pulse at his throat and the soft heat at his collar and the whole, continuous shape of him while they touched – Edward not incautious, not discourteous. They did not hurry, only ached towards each other, in the grip of babbling neurones and unruly electricity.

'Well, then.' Edward smoothed against one of her breasts very slightly as he moved to close his arms on her again; the accidental but un-accidental nice experiment. 'I had hoped – ' He sighed slowly so it would catch in her hair, 'You must tell me what we're going to do. Helen? Are you still here?'

'Yes. Yes, I'm – You're very . . .'

'So are you. Tell me. What do we do?'

248

Her hands met behind his spine and she held him as if he might print himself under her skin if she gave him enough of her pressure and her time. She couldn't, didn't want to speak.

'Helen. Please tell me. Either way.' Silence licked between them. 'It's no, isn't it?' The way he said it, she understood he'd been prepared for disappointment and understood that he deserved much better, but that she couldn't give it him.

She had to look at Edward very clearly, so that he would know she was telling the truth. 'Everything would have to be different and it's not. That's the only reason . . .'

'Does everything matter?'

'Don't make me argue. Please. I can't.'

But Edward didn't make her argue, he shook Helen's hand over-gently and was too polite and telephoned for a taxi to take her home even though he was a visitor to her city and must have found that slightly difficult. When he came back to their table, she saw, really saw, how well he'd dressed and made an effort for her and she wanted to make efforts back and not leave him unhappy, not leave him.

'I'm sorry, Helen. Again. Intellectually, with people I can be . . . I can out-perform anyone. But I know I'm not good at touching.'

'That isn't – '

'That's fine. I know. Don't worry.'

He worked himself into his coat, struggling slightly with one of the sleeves. When she reached to help him, he stepped aside. 'No. It's okay.'

Of course, she was too late home.

Helen scrubbed and laundered out the reek of Edward E. Gluck, the untouchable tang of herself with him. Only her jacket remembered him clearly, she couldn't make the time to dry-clean it, or had no wish to find the opportunity. Still, even there his scent faded; the pitch and throb at her stomach when she moved the cloth died quite away. The impossible had no shelf-life, couldn't last.

Cooking was the thing now – a blessing, perhaps literally. Mr Brindle was a highly particular eater, always had been. It was necessary to please him, but beyond that basic requirement, Helen could find a certain self-expression and an occupation for her time. Her choice of menus came to rely on increasing allowances for preparation. Overnight marinating, standing, resting, proving, reduction and clarification – they all encompassed a type of waiting, a business that need not interfere with thought, or the active avoidance of thought.

A clever choice of dishes might see her washing up the breakfast ruins, Mr Brindle having duly gone to work, and then inching out the whole day with tiny exercises in perfectionism. Happily, her efforts were rewarded with fairly consistent success and she could feel that she was doing her best, making a go of it, of Mr and Mrs Brindle, of them.

Her peace at the dinner table was bought in little accidents. Helen gave herself more time to work, but also became more careless. Her concentration was poor and she was continually burning herself with pot lids, sugar syrup, steam. Opened cans and the good knives she had bought a long time ago – as an investment and as things to make her glad – slashed at her palms and fingers. She used the bright blue colour of dressing recommended for kitchens, because they cannot be lost in foodstuffs by mistake. Mr Brindle made her change them when he was in the house. He did not want a wife whose hands were ridiculous.

But he did want a wife. Mr Brindle had taken to touching her more than she could remember he ever had. At times when she could not expect it, his arm would thump in around her waist, or he would pad up behind her and palm at her breasts. He never approached her at night now, never in their bed, but his sudden presences started to soak their home. He was like a flood. Helen would wake on the living-room floor and have to stand immediately to have her head safe above the flux and drift of something. Mr Brindle spoke no more than usual, but left a new kind of silence, washing in behind him whenever he left her alone. The arrangements of her furniture slid towards the cramped and the uneasy, the submarine.

> Dear Helen,
>   No more aversion — total abstinence. Much more to do with the Process: 'more gentle and more terrible', as I do tend always to say.
>   This is my first day. I shall tell you of any others.
>   I won't lie.
>   One day. Twenty-four hours.
>
>   Love, Edward.
>   And thank you for your help.

Love. A small word like scalpel or a pocket knife. She'd never been able to write it down and she couldn't tell from the writing whether Edward did it easily.

Another enveloped postcard. She didn't burn it. Too much water about in the air, it would never have caught.

Sinners were supposed to burn, but here she was drowning instead, sinking in something that pounded up fast at blood-heat into what was already her standing pool of a house. She had never realised she was like this, had never been this kind of woman in her life. The World and the Flesh and the Devil, they were all supposed to tempt, but the Flesh had never troubled her before. Helen was not used to thinking of her own flesh and the way it would ask inappropriately for the flesh of someone else. Helen hadn't known about undersea nights, layered with the salt ghosts of lip and tongue and touch.

> Dear Helen,
>   Seven days.
>   Thank you.
>   Love.

Mr Brindle fed avidly, but never grew fat. Only dense and quiet, like a low-tide rock.

> Dear Helen,
>   Almost slipped away there, but didn't.
>   Eighteen days.
>   Love,
>   Edward.

If God was God, then He could see right in through her, as if she might just as well be a window or a Russian doll made out of glass. If God was God, He stood outside of time, so that everything she'd ever done was stacked up inside her for him to count like chips she'd used to back the wrong number, the wrong bet. God knew her complete, the finished facts of all she'd do until she died, and she was either forgiven now or she was not and that was the way it would be and had been, forever and ever, amen. Whatever she did, God had watched her already, doing it.

Now and again, as she thought of Edward, Helen's good fear, her God fear, would tease and dazzle back towards her. Wrapping chicken thighs in smoked bacon, she had paused and understood that yesterday when she stood in the same place and stared through her ghost reflection in the same window, she had been deep in her usual, stable, lack of faith. Today she was convincingly afraid. She heard the falling sheet-metal din of Heaven's terror on all sides, shivering and slicing with the wonderful clarity of God and then, like any storm, it passed.

> *Thirty days.*
> *Dear Helen,*
> *A whole month.*
> *I am happy. Hope you are the same.*
> *Love,*
> *Edward.*

Mr Brindle did not like his Greek honey pie. There was too much salt in the pastry which had been correct for the recipe but not for his tastes. He didn't shout at her, only asked for a piece of fruit and a glass of water to clean his mouth. She went and fetched them as quickly as she could, thick currents tugging and struggling at her legs.

> *Helen,*
> *I celebrated my month the wrong way.*
> *Back at six days now. Think I have learned from this.*
> *I let you down, didn't I?*
> *Sorry,*
> *Edward. And love.*
> *You deserved better. I know that. I will try.*

Coincidences and earthquakes, they were acts of God. People didn't make them happen, they happened to people. If Edward was meant to happen then Edward was an act of God. Perhaps God disapproved of her staying here and only *thinking* of Edward when *being with* Edward was God's will.

This was difficult to think about. Helen polished the windows with newspapers and vinegar because they left no streaks and combed out the fringes on the Chinese rug they'd bought when Chinese rugs were still expensive. It was hard to imagine that Edward was God's intention. She would have been pleased to do God's will, obviously, but then thinking how much she might want to would make her restless. Helen found she could be impatient to serve God.

'I've been meaning to ask you . . .'

Helen was rinsing the last of the soap-suds from the kitchen sink. Out in the dark of the garden she could see the box of yellow brightness that pressed down across the grass from the lighted window. She watched as Mr Brindle's shadow joined hers and then swallowed it.

'Ask me?'

'Mm.' His chin settled in heavily at her shoulder while his hands stooped and caught at the hem of her skirt. 'You don't mind, do you?'

'What?'

'This.' He dragged up her skirt in one hard motion, turning it out like a sleeve, so it gathered up high round her waist. Then his weight forced back against her again, covering her with the cloth that covered him and taking the balance from her legs. Something tumbled in the cupboard under the sink.

'You don't mind. Open your blouse. No, I'll do it, you're tired. I can do it right.'

She felt the first, hot tug. Buttons chattered everywhere on to different hard surfaces. She tried to remember where she heard them fall, so she could find them later and they wouldn't go to waste and Mr Brindle ripped at the cloth of her blouse, dug his cold, blunt fingers under her bra and wrenched it up, squeezed at her, squeezed again, enjoyed a twist.

'Is he out there? Does he watch the house? Where does he live?'

'I don't know – '

'Shut up. Can he see me now, in my house, touching my wife, having my wife? Can he see? Answer me. Can he see?'

There was no point in saying. 'Who?' There was no point in saying it, she knew.

'Who? *Who*? Who do you fucking think.'

She felt the fumble and a shearing, unlikely pain.

'Edward. *Eighteen days and love* Edward. *Touching my wife in the street* Edward. *Get her back for another fuck later* Edward.'

A final, hauling cut and release, the scratch of a raw nail from his finger.

'Feeling better? That's the way you like it, isn't it? With the knickers off? Did you smell them after the last time? I did. You cunt.'

There'd been another night, years ago, when he'd hit her more. Then, Helen knew she'd done nothing, hadn't understood at all and so she'd been able, in a way, to defend herself. This time, she couldn't resist him, couldn't find the strength, because she was at fault and whatever happened, it was meant. God's will.

Lying on the linoleum in the wet of something, she kept still. To keep still was important. Invisible. She thought about invisible.

'Cunt.'

She felt him open her and spit.

'Cunt.'

She felt the beginning of the kick.

He usually stopped because he was tired, not because he wanted to.

'What's the matter? Helen?'

'Nothing.' She hadn't thought she'd ever use his number. 'I'm fine.' Even when he gave it her, the hurt behind his eyes had told her very clearly that he didn't believe she would call. 'I just wanted to call.'

'Well, that's . . . thank you. I'm very glad.'

Her breath was coming in hot gouts. There was a plan she'd made for what to say, but it was slipping.

'That's all right. I wondered . . . I wondered . . .' The sentence failed her.

'Where are you? And are you okay, you don't sound it. Where are you, Helen?'

'Here.'

And then she cried. It surprised Helen how very seldom she cried, but when the feeling was on her she did it a lot.

Edward wanted to come and get her, but she made herself able to say she would go to the underground station at Gloucester Road and he could meet her. He said that wasn't too far to his house.

Although she had no doubts that he would be there, she worried he'd be late, or that she wouldn't see him, or would take the wrong way out. If he wasn't right on hand and ready to be recognised Helen knew she would start crying again and people who cried publicly in London were always mad; changing guards and ravens and the homelessly mad – that was the capital. Helen didn't want to be homeless or mad.

At the barrier she concentrated on lifting her bag ahead of her and feeding her ticket through correctly and on looking up only at the very last point she could.

Edward.

Edward making this home.

Edward making this safe.

She was taken by a liquid feeling that pained her while it pleased.

Edward, already sidling through the crowd, cautiously

tall, rummaged at the top of his hair with one hand, indisputably there. He lifted her bag away from her, took her arm and was ready when she swung in and held him and was able to hold her back.

'Hello.'

'Hello.'

He was so much more of himself than she had remembered, even though she had tried to remember him well.

'Welcome to Bailey Park.'

Helen felt him rest his mouth against her hair and knew that people were walking round them, thoroughly inconvenienced. She didn't feel guilty a bit.

Outside there was a dry, grey, bite in the air and unfamiliar leaves, big like crumpled sheets of brown paper, were softening the pavement. They walked to Edward's home, side against side, cradling each other's waists because for two people walking together, this is the most comfortable way to proceed.

'I won't consider it.'

'I have money. I mean, I'll be able to get some. Tell me a good place to stay, that's all I need.'

'Helen, you don't have any money, be sensible. You can be here.'

'That's not why I called you.'

'I know that. There's a room you can sleep in, *will* sleep in, and I will trust you, if you will trust me to do nothing but sleep. I'm hardly going to creep up on you in the dark – not one of my vices. If that's what was worrying you. I can't think of anything else, unless you just . . .' He burrowed his hands in each other uneasily. 'You've come here because I'm your friend. I hope. I help my friends. *Aaaw, come on, Helen. Let me help you out and do like Jimmy would – I've never hayd the chaynce before.*'

'No, leave Jimmy out of it, I'm talking to you.'

'Then let me be here for you, because I want to. Be here for me.'

They weren't really arguing. The words were like an argument, but they didn't mean one.

'I can't.'

'Do it anyway. There are so many other things you can't. You want a whole life full of *can'ts*? Maybe this is one you can. Come on, it's harmless. Me too.' Edward seemed to consider smiling, but then didn't want to risk it. He left the room instead, fumbling as he closed the door, and she knew he had gone to make up the bed where she would sleep.

She sat in Edward's living-room and listened to him scuffling softly in and out of other doors, opening drawers and bustling, moving inside a flat that was totally his. Everything here was built up and covered with years and years of Edward, uninterrupted by anyone else. He smelt of his flat, she realised, and his flat smelt of him and she was breathing easily, liking the taste of him in her lungs. She was coming up for Edward's air and finding it familiar and still. This was a good, soft place. Her hands, clasping tight to each other, were lit by the slightly disturbing high and wide window that still held the sky she'd seen behind him in one of his photographs.

At rest and with an emptying mind, she remembered how much she ached: because of the bruising and confusion and most of all with holding on, with clinging as hard as she could from the inside, so nothing of her personality could fall out of place. The concentration she had needed to force a way through the journey south had left her almost hypnotised with exhaustion. Sentences and images looped and repeated inside her skull, cut loose from any sense.

Slowly, she stopped trying to look all right. Mr Brindle had been careful as ever to leave her face unmarked, but if she really wept, the hurt would show and now she wanted it to. Mr Brindle had made the pain, but it was hers and she could do what she wanted with it at any time.

'Oh, don't. You don't need to. It's fine now. Unless you want. It's okay if you want.' She hadn't heard Edward come in and couldn't think clearly how long he'd been gone.

Helen bleared up at him while he stumbled forward and patted at her. One of his hands was holding something. 'I made toast.'

For some reason this let waves of sobbing break up through her. She listened to herself. She wouldn't stop.

'Well, it's all . . .' He clattered the plate down on the table and tried to lever his arms in about her. 'Toast is all I make. Helen. Helen?' She knew he was beginning to lift her, but couldn't help. For a moment he rocked her forward 'It's all right. You know it's all right.'

They scrambled against each other, Edward making for the sofa until they hit it and fell. For a long time, Helen was aware of being against him, his pullover and solid ribs. She touched him from inside a fog of her own noise.

Edward held her until she was quiet, until the sky in the window had bruised into an overcast night.

'Helen. Helen? You're not asleep?'

'No.' She swallowed. Her throat was raw. 'No, I'm here.'

'Good. And I'm here, too. No.' She turned and met the quiet tension in his arms. 'Don't move. Just lie. I want to talk to you – it's nothing bad.'

He began to kiss across her forehead, sometimes brushing away her hair because that was a good thing to do. 'I wanted to say.' he punctuated himself, 'That you.' with regular, 'Are exceptionally beautiful.' tiny pressures of mouth, 'And that you have.' and breath. 'A beautiful brain. I was incapable of saying this properly before. Because I can be almost terminally inarticulate when it comes to people. You know how I am – I do get it right, but only eventually. I count myself lucky that you're so patient.

'And now I have a duty to say that, inside here, in your mind, there's no limit to you. You are your own universe.

260

Your own happiness. They could dye you with silver nitrate; you'd be your own photographic plate. A picture of the roots into your soul.' Edward paused, nuzzling her hair.

'Networks. And webs. And branches. Layered. Woven. Spun out of need and hope and, um, love. Love.' The word caught at something in her blood. 'You're free, Helen. You've always been free. If God made your mind, then that is the way that he made you. Now you're to stay here as long as you like. Nothing bad will happen, do you understand?'

'Okay.'

She knew that when she spoke, her words touched his throat, the open button at the collar of his shirt and his neck.

'Whatever has, will . . . whatever happens, our mutual conditions are not at fault. That is to say, I can't second-guess God, but if I'd made you, I would wish you to be completely yourself and not necessarily perfect.'

Her eyes stung out of focus and she shook her head against him. 'It's all gone wrong.'

'Oh, don't say that. Please. Not when you're here with me. This is the point where it starts to go right. Don't try to stop it. We can be safe here and . . . we'll have fun or something. Talk. You can have this. You don't have to pay for it – no more than you already have. You're not a bad person, Helen, not sinful. I don't think we even understand sin – what we commit and don't – we can't judge. We just should collate our total information, be complete and act for the best. We're for the best. We, meaning me and you. What do you say?'

She said yes, because she felt yes.

'Thank you, Helen.'

'Why thank me?'

'Because you came to me.' She tried again to sit up and this time he let her. 'I mean thank you for knowing you'd be welcome. He grinned up at his ceiling and then down at her. 'All the way to London with no guarantees . . . That Mrs Brindle, she's a determined woman and she does get what she wants.'

Helen thought of what she wanted and Edward's eyes stammered shut while his hands wrestled quietly with each other. '*Aaaw, yagodda see, I wish a was a little bit bedder at making folks feel okay. No practice.* James Stewart would do this better.'

'But he wouldn't be the same as you.'

Edward flushed mildly and began a contented frown. 'Better luck next time.'

'No thanks.'

The cold toast was still on the coffee table, untouched. Edward stirred, 'Well, I'm going to . . . If you would like to see your room. I don't know . . . are you tired?'

'Absolutely.'

'Good. That is, you'll sleep, which is good. Will you?'

Helen nodded. Stood up and apart from him.

The room he offered her was lined with shelves and heavily curtained and carpeted. The small sounds she made unpacking her night things; coming back from his orderly bathroom that smelt so remarkably of his skin; undressing for bed – every tiny impact and footfall was damped down, softened to silence. He had given her somewhere insulated where she couldn't help but be at peace.

Their first breakfast developed the easy shape it would always have while she was there.

'Toast.' Edward pointed at the toast plate in case she found it unfamiliar and seemed to wonder if he read his newspaper next or talked.

'It's all you can make.'

He let go the paper and smiled. 'Well remembered.'

'You only told me last night.'

'Nice to be remembered, though. Toast is, in fact, not

absolutely everything I can make. It's nearly absolutely everything.'

'Good. I can cook. But I don't like to.'

'Fine. That's fine.' There was a tremor in his hand. He noticed and rested it under his chin. 'Sleep?'

'No thanks, I've just had one.'

'Fine. Good.' He leaned his chair back recklessly. 'Well, I'm going to do some work now, since I have time to do that again. If you –' Feeling himself unsteadied, he swung into the table again. 'You should treat this as where you live, as home. Do what you want. Bearing in mind that I'll take you out to eat. If you want to be taken . . . I won't *make* you eat . . . that is, obviously you *will* eat . . . but not necessarily with me. It's not a problem, um, evidently. In fact the only one confused here is me.' He sighed lightly and began again. 'If you do want to go with me, to eat, then we can co-ordinate times and things; it would be more efficient that way.' He felt forward for the butter knife, something to distract him.

'Why did you put me in that room?'

Setting the knife back and numbly making sure that it was straight, 'I know, I know. It *is* the spare room, it simply isn't all that spare. It's always been where I keep the stuff – everything's in there. I do apologise.'

'It's like . . . a library . . .'

'I know. It's not good. You could stay in my study instead.' He examined the palm of his hand with sudden concern. 'I should have mentioned . . . And now I have to say that I am making use of you – of your presence – because it keeps me out of there. Not that I go in there any more, in amongst the muck. I'm behaving.' He checked her eyes. 'I am. But if you're there, even if you've *been* there, it will make me feel safe. I slept safe last night.' He borrowed a glance at her, then blinked away. 'But I should have asked your permission, I know.'

'I slept safe, too.'

'Oh. Well, good.'

'How much is there?'

'How much . . . ?'

'How much muck.'

'Oh, as much as you could see. Four walls, from ceiling to floor: videos, magazines, books.' Edward seemed anxious to be comprehensive, keen to be humiliated with absolute accuracy. 'There are some originals of *The Oyster* and *The Pearl* from when I was kidding myself this was all about art – bloody expensive stuff and no good, because Victorian tastes are not quite mine. Porn gets dated, like anything else. Which all helps me to side-step saying that I don't exactly know how much. I counted the videos once; there are seven hundred of them, seven twenty, something like that, but that's as far as I got. The act of cataloguing tends to become secondary. I start off alphabetical and then I go astray. I get too absorbed in my work.' He was trying to keep it light, but his eyes weren't managing. 'No self-control.'

'You have control now.'

'I try. Seeing it all offends you, doesn't it? I mean, the titles are bad enough. I'm sorry.'

'I was surprised, that's all. It helps you if I'm in there?'

'Honestly?'

'Of course.'

'I don't want to put you under pressure, but yes, it does.'

'Well I might as well stay there, then. You're the one who'd have the problem being in there. I don't mind.'

Edward twisted out a smile and rubbed his cheek.

'But why haven't you thrown it all away?'

He spoke with the air of a man describing an incorrigible friend. 'Will-power.' He rubbed his cheek again. 'I decided I would test my will-power by keeping my temptations within reach. Otherwise they're hardly a temptation, after all . . .' His eyes searched the air above her. 'Obviously, if my will then fails me, I can get really disgraceful pretty much instantaneously.' Edward examined her expression almost surgically. 'I know, I'm fooling no one, not even me. I know exactly what I'm like. I only ever assume the moral high ground to get a running start for my descent.'

He huffed out a breath with something approaching relief, still bewildered by himself, but more content. 'Positive action must be taken, I realise, I just can't take it yet. I do live in hope, though – I'm back to nearly a month without a slip and some days I don't even think of wanting it. Eventually, I'll be able to chuck it away. And I'll do the chucking, no one else.' His mouth tensed. 'By then I might have worked out how on earth to dispose of it. I can hardly stack it all down at the bottom of the stairs and wait for the bin men to come. If that isn't a slightly over-appropriate verb.'

Edward began a stretch then faltered, stopped. She wanted to touch him a little and thought about how.

'Oh, God.'

'Edward? What?'

'Oh, God. Helen. I didn't – '

Helen had pushed up her sleeves, as she often did. She had forgotten the scratches on her forearms, the random bruises, the finger-grip imprints. The marks were dark, ripe, full of blood.

'What did he do?'

'It's all right.'

'No, it's not fucking all right. What did he do?'

She really didn't need him to be angry on her behalf, Helen was perfectly able to manage that herself, if she chose to; she was a determined woman, after all.

'What did he do?'

Edward was starting to frighten her and she couldn't allow him to. He was starting to shout.

'He found one of your postcards.' She didn't say that to blame Edward, only to make him be quiet and just let her forget it again. 'That's what he did. He found your card.'

'Oh, Hele – '

'You'd have watched it, wouldn't you? If I'd been a video, you'd have watched.'

Edward almost reached for her, but then let his arm withdraw. He closed both hands over his head and said nothing.

A person who is scared and angry often strikes out inappropriately. Helen wished that she didn't conform so perfectly to type.

They were civil to each other after that, but they didn't exactly speak. Edward shut himself into his study for most of the day and she dozed, watched children's television and found it stupidly moving, then dozed again.

'Hello.' Edward knocked at his own living-room door.

'You don't have to do that.'

'Well. I don't feel comfortable. I don't know what I should do.'

'Yeah.' Maybe she should go. A sinking, greyness in her limbs made her think she should go. But there was nowhere that would have her, or nowhere she could have.

'Do you . . . should you see a doctor?'

'No.'

'You're sure?'

'It's happened before, I never went to the doctor then.' She heard Edward snap in a breath and force it out again.

'You're right about me. I will watch anything. You're quite right. But I do have to know it's not real. Jesus – real people frighten me. And if it was real pain . . . Helen, I grew up with that. My mother, I saw what Dad did to her. Or if I didn't, I heard it, I saw the marks. It was my fault then and it's mine again now. I was stupid to write to you.'

'I didn't tell you not to. I didn't want to tell you not

to. You didn't do this; you weren't there.' There was an uneasy pause that she wished she could leave unbroken. She couldn't. 'You were stupid to write to me?'

'The way that I did.' He moved to stand beside her chair, very still. 'I had to write, but I shouldn't have done it that way.'

'Don't let him make me angry with you. I don't want to be. You haven't done anything wrong.' She leaned until her head could touch his arm. He let her be close, but didn't move closer. 'Do you think we'll work, Edward. Do you think I can be here?'

'You need somewhere to stay and I need you with me.'

He rubbed at her ear with his thumb and forefinger and she heard the shingly, seaside rush of sound close beside her eardrum. When she was a girl, she'd loved that noise. It was private, something no one else could ever listen to. For a moment he squeezed slightly and she caught the thrum of his blood, or her own.

'Helen, my work keeps me busy, but it's lonely when I stop. Especially now, when there's nothing else here. I would need you, even if I didn't . . . You know. If I didn't feel for you.'

'Will we work, though?'

'I don't know.' He tried that again, to make it seem hopeful. 'I don't know. That's not something I'm professor of. But I think we'd be good.' This time, he'd sounded mainly sad, so she kissed his hand.

At first, Helen worried, imagining how they might be and what they might have to do to each other if they didn't take care, but the slow days they made together left her nothing but settled and calm.

She listened to Edward at night, his orderly pattern of preparations for his bed and sleep, and she rested in her room with his videos and books and was secure and undisturbed. She felt her conduct and presence here were justified, were all right, and her memory started her life with the day she stepped up from the underground at Gloucester Road. Glasgow wasn't hard to keep out of mind.

Helen came to believe she was good and could have good things. She didn't deserve them any less than other people she could think of. Edward was right, if she accepted all the facts about herself – the ugly and the clean – she understood who she was precisely, all the time. She hadn't done anything bad since she'd known her own nature and its controls. She had come to no harm and had been offered the chance to change away from what might be called sin.

There was always the possibility of sin with Edward. Undoubtedly what she felt for him was love, she admitted that, but her love need not be expressed in ways that were wrong and had to be paid for. She was learning how much salvation there was in the passage of time; it could reform passion into friendship and let her live here, growing well and strong. Her sleep was obedient and prompt, her dreams unmemorable but happy, and if her God was watching she couldn't feel it and couldn't feel His loss.

Edward pursued his work, sometimes shouting in his study, emerging and pacing, then diving back again, but with an underlying air of fixed content. He began to make sentences involving the word *we* and talked about taking pains with his appearance because this made him feel clean and as if he were leading an upright life.

'Come and see my study.'

Helen was newly back from buying milk, her face and hands anxious for the warmth of the flat. The warmth of home.

'It's nothing very interesting, but I thought you might like to see.' He held the door for her, which was something he liked to do.

Only one wall was occupied with shelves. The other three were covered in photographs, drawings and picture postcards, fixed over each other like scales.

'They're lots of little slices through my head – the things I like to remember. I can focus on one picture and it will fire off through the whole day. It's a sort of music; so I can sit in here with an old friendship playing, or a nice day, or a good argument. I occasionally like to argue.'

Helen was more interested in his dark, monstrous desk and its huge computer. 'I thought you didn't approve of them.'

'Computers? They're things, instruments, nothing to approve or disapprove. I have a problem with the people who use them. The person who uses this one is me, so I like it fine. And it gets me into the Net. I love the Net. It carries proper information, facts with added emotional interference, irrelevancies, passions, general human subversiveness. People keep overrunning the machine and so it's full of Completed Facts and nobody in there has to forget *what* they are – human. They may forget *who* they are, but anyone can be lost in thought – thought is a very big place. Every day, I make a point of feeding the Net with new things conventional programming would not like: ethics, nonsense, morality.'

'And I thought you were working in here.'

'I do that, too. Honestly.'

He looked so suddenly earnest, she had to rub his shoulder to make him smile.

'I know. You work hard, I'm sure.'

'I'm sure also. Sadly, the Nobel people don't agree. Not this year.'

'Oh, I'm sorry.'

'I'm not. Not this year. I couldn't spare the time.' He brushed her with a soft glance, 'They'll have to give me one in the end. But back to morality . . .'

'Yes?' She noticed a beat between them, a flicker of something that quieted again.

'There is, of course, very human and understandable *im*morality on the Net. My printer could stay active, day and night, discharging uncontrolled configurations of anatomy. I could spend all day in here, having virtual sex. The screen's radiation makes you sterile but the text still makes you come. Neat, isn't it?' He didn't smile.

'And is that what you do?'

'No. I've never tried sex on the Internet. Not because I disapprove – '

'Obviously.'

He pinned her with a tiny look. 'Yes, quite obviously. I have never gone in there because I know I haven't got the strength of character to ever climb out again. I do harmless things in cyberspace: talk to colleagues, work. I spend my days at work. That's what I wanted to report. That all is safe and well in here.'

'Um, good. Well done, then.'

'Yes.'

She felt very much as if she should shake his hand now, but didn't.

Edward appeared happy in a tentative way, grabbed a pencil from his desk and put it back down again. 'Mm hm.'

Helen's time gently expended itself in reading or walking, playing the tourist. At first she was unsettled by the air of satisfaction she noticed in so many of the people she passed in the street. Faces and bodies moved under a thin but unmistakable sheen of health. The shops that were closest to her calmly charged ridiculous prices and sold ridiculous foods while their staff seemed to appraise her and find her an introduction they did not wish to make. Locked gardens and high windows and craftsman-applied paintwork were all wadded in with a cool lead-and-smoke-flavoured air, only occasionally coloured by the stench of crumbled drains. But her new district's little brushes with squalor and the repetitive fuss of its prettiness gradually eased into normality. A person can grow used to anything. Helen learned that when she ceased to care about it, the city – like God – receded and let her be.

Sometimes she wished she had money to spend on Edward's house – to buy an ornament or picture that he wasn't expecting – but then, as he said, he didn't actually need any more than he had. Helen did no housework at all, not even the toasting of toast. Edward's cleaning lady looked after the house twice a week, taking care of everything but Edward's study and Helen's room – the two places she was asked not to disturb. Because she never saw where Helen slept, she made assumptions, but Edward and Helen did not. They made a point of dressing fully for breakfast and rarely kissed.

'Forty-eight days.'

Sometimes, he would pop through at supper-time and clear his head of work before he went to bed.

'That's a long time.'

'Yeah. The fillings in my back teeth are fusing.'

'What?'

He flopped into an armchair. She liked that none of the chairs belonged to anyone in the flat. They could both feel at ease sitting anywhere, although she did prefer the sofa, because it allowed her to stretch out and lie. She was getting lazy. Or comfortable. Sleeping and reading paperbacks and going out to eat – it made a comfortable life.

'No, only joking. Forty-eight days. Wouldn't have believed it.'

'How do you feel.'

'Great.'

'And more generally? All this?'

'Great.'

'Anything happening you don't like?'

'No.'

'Anything not happening you would like?'
They both laughed instead of saying anything.

Their dinners with each other were different. She looked
forward to them more.

'Well?'

'I don't know. Would it be enough, Edward?'

'For me? It would be perfectly enough for me. What about you? That's what I'm asking. If it's going to be . . . I don't want to do something wrong and I might because I don't know my way . . . around. You know I don't.'

'It'll be, it'll be fine.'

'Well, yes. I hope.' He ran the curl of one finger down the slope of her cheek until the muscles in her back began to shudder. 'Fine would be what I was aiming for. I haven't exactly studied the area properly. Not in a way that would help.'

They were making Horlicks in the kitchen which seemed quite entertaining in a nicely pointless way and was also something for which they were both in the mood. She watched him stirring the milk and laughed.

'What? Am I a bad stirrer?' He looked worried happily, 'What?' then just worried, 'What?'

'I think . . . I'm not sure . . . what I think.' She stood by him and squeezed his free hand around her wrist, her pulse. 'Nerves.'

'You feel frightened. I hope I don't – '

'You don't frighten me, I'm just nervous. Or . . .'

'What?' He danced his thumb down to the heart of her palm and left her with a broad need, drumming in the length of her arm while his eyes worried at hers. 'What.'

'It might be nerves and – heartbeat-raising things . . . those sort of things.'

'Thank you for being so specific.' Again his thumb grooved a charge into her veins.

'Expecting – you know.'

'Expecting.'

'Me expecting you.'

'Ah, well, yes. That would do it. Quite possibly.'

'That's the same speed, but not the same thing. And I'm . . . I don't know.'

Edward turned up the gas and put her hand where she could reach her fingers in beneath his jaw so that she could understand the kind of time his blood was keeping. This meant she also touched his voice.

'After this, then. Shall we?'

'Yes, that would be – definitely, yes, fine. Hot milky drinks, though . . . they're meant to make you relax? Should we – '

'To make you sleep, actually.' He watched her, peered clear inside her mind and tickled there. Her fingers felt him swallow once. 'I should think we'll keep lively somehow.'

'That's not unlikely, yes.'

'Listen, it won't be anything we don't both agree.'

'No.' And she turned him to herself and held him because of wanting to and because she was scared. They both slipped inside a kiss, waited a slim moment while he caught her tongue between his teeth and then opened for her again, milk-sweet.

'We still have to do the Horlicks.'

'Mm mh.'

She felt him, hard in at her stomach and ribs – something to call down a murmur of sin.

'What should we do? If we're thinking of – '

'Moving on to other things? Well, I think it doesn't matter if the milk hasn't absolutely boiled.' He lifted the pan experimentally, his unoccupied arm fast around her waist. 'Do you understand about Horlicks?'

'As far as I can tell, you've been managing fine.'

They didn't know where to start: which room would be best. The kitchen and the study were too unwelcoming, the bathroom wouldn't do, her bedroom was full of his past, his bedroom was his bedroom and would lead to things.

Living-room.

He drew the curtains, although the flat was far too high for anybody to see in. You never could be too careful, though and, anyway, Helen had stayed nervous of that window, its hungry size, and Edward didn't want her to be nervous, not now.

'I'm okay.'

'You're not worried?'

'I'm not worried.'

'Because I'm right here . . . well, obviously – that's what this is all about – me being here with you. Helen, you'll have to forgive me if I sound . . . if I stop making sense during this. It's only that I'm getting pre-occupied. With you. I want me to be with you.' He adjusted his grip on her back. 'Really, I think I should go and sit down over there.

'I'll be right here. Well . . . that's why we're both . . . It's only me, though. I won't change, because I want me to be with you.'

But they still clung against each other, as if they were saying goodbye. Something was pouncing in her chest and panic was shining the length of her bones.

He perched on a chair and sat rubbing his jaw and looking beyond her shoulder. Helen had thought of sitting, but that didn't seem quite the right thing, so she waited as she was. She stood and braced herself against herself and the roiling need that was stroking the meat between her ribs and then dipping its head clear inside her, striking a light. It seemed superfluous that she should move in any visible way.

'Helen? Should I help?'

'No.' He mustn't touch her, that would make things go wrong. 'No. I'll start now.'

She could hear him watching, while her fingers tried to unmuzzle her buttons, but she didn't look up. The best thing to imagine was maybe being in a changing-room at a shop. That would be the calmest option she could think of and he hadn't asked for a performance, only that she be undressed and that he could see.

The air shivered against her. Every slip of the cloth, each release, first followed her habits of motion and then altered beneath the press of observation.

She bent forward and carefully re-learned the weight and motion of her breasts. They were waking up. She stood to catch her breath, to be more displayed, and found that she could watch Edward watching, while her body met his eyes. He sipped in a breath. She stepped out from the last thing that hid what she was and gave him what she wanted, or at least what they'd agreed.

There was a certainty in her now, cold and unchangeable and planted in the opened flutter of blood at her heart. She was naked in the eyes of God. Raising her arms and setting her hands at the back of her head, she could feel His terror drumming under her womb.

Edward's face was lovely in an unfamiliar way and almost grave. His lips were parted, his gaze one unified, unfillable depth. Black. He blinked gently with a little frown. 'Helen. You are beautiful.'

His last word tingled against her stomach and she felt she might cry.

'You're gorgeous, that's what you are. Gorgeous.' He murmured, making her strain to hear him, making her whole body listen in. 'You needn't say, but I would like to know – maybe you could nod or shake your head – and tell me. Are you wet? For me?'

The question which makes its own answer. If she hadn't been, it would have made her; but she had been, so it made her more.

'Oh. That's nice. Thank you. I have to . . . I have to step outside for a moment, you know? Maybe, if you sat down. I'll just . . . be back soon.' And he walked around the edges of the room and out of the door.

Without him there, she felt foolish, even slightly angry, but mainly alone. The leather of his armchair felt peculiar to her, cold and unpleasantly animal. She crossed her legs at the knee and stared at her dark reflection in the blank of Edward's television screen.

He came back and faltered to a stop when she faced him.

'I'm sorry. I didn't want to do something that would offend you.' He studied her face. 'Are you all right? I didn't want to leave you, I know it was the wrong thing to do.'

'If you had to go . . .'

'Yes, I did.' He sat again, not so far away that she didn't notice he smelled of soap. She was beginning to be cold.

'I know we said I wouldn't touch you and I do understand that. You are a person of principle and there are things you can't allow. I am not your . . . we're not . . . able to. But I did think – you're so far away like that. Don't you feel far away?'

'I suppose.'

'Might I hold your hand?'

Helen let him have that: a small, formal contact they could have exchanged in the street. Either they'd already done far too much and were lost – might as well do anything now – or this was the way they'd control themselves and be reminded of how they could and could not proceed.

'I love you, Helen.' Before she understood the words, hot shards of how they felt were carving through her, every way they could. 'I do. I've thought a lot about it and I do. I don't want to frighten you or hurt you.'

Helen had no reply, so she kneaded his hand.

'I thought I might . . . This is nothing you couldn't let me do, or I wouldn't suggest it, but you don't have to. I thought that now you'd done this for me, I could do something for you.' He studied her patiently, giving her nowhere to hide. 'And something for me, of course.' He brought out a small pair of scissors from his pocket. 'I would like to cut your hair. If I could.'

'My hair?'

He let his gaze fall against her, so that she would feel it

where he meant. 'Not on your head.' He nodded rather formally to the ache that was folding her back to her spine, made his proper introduction to her body. 'There. I want to take care of you there. I don't have to, absolutely I don't have to, but you've let me see – and you are wonderful to see – if I trimmed, then I'd . . . see more. Will you? Let me? I promise I'll be careful. God, I'll be careful.'

It was only when nothing was left to stop her but her conscience, that she found how small and liquid her conscience was. Edward pressed it and it poured away as she saw the metal shine of the scissors coming and liked to think how cool and odd they were bound to be.

A man should never touch another man's wife. The wife should not let him. If she moves she must not move to meet another man's touch, unless she has a failure of conscience and, even then, she has the moral law.

Without morality's prohibition to protect her, she will be stripped down to her soul and the empty fault inside it. She will feel the long, tight haul of the man being near her and the need swinging in her blood and she will move to it because she has no mind, no choice. The steel shock of twitching blades and the curiosity of fingers, they will be all she is.

Kneeling low, Edward snipped her in close to the skin, taking pains at the slick of her lips. Helen watched her body being shorn back younger and opening under something hungry and new. When she came, Edward held his blades steady, but not far away and watched her with complete attention, watched right through her as if she were a wet perspective drawn on herself.

Then he talked to her: a nervy monologue that whispered in under his work. 'If you're very still . . . really very still, that's it. Perfect. You are perfect. Completely. Just extremely nice.'

She trusted him. No matter what he did, she would still trust him. No matter what he asked, she would allow and the thought of that covered her with a dull, sweet fear. She was finding out who she was. For months, her imagination had already known that he would be terribly steady and calm against her and terribly soft. She had faith in the way that he was and would be, and it would be so hard not to stay with him now, even though she was completely certain that he could do this and things like this any and every day. There would be no standing that. She would become the kind of woman who would want him to do everything they could think of and who would love it.

Edward had been speaking for a while without her listening, because she was only holding herself still, beneath the ebb and flurry of his breath.

'I can't look at you and think of the pictures. This just isn't like them. They always end up the same way. I hate that. They always end up reaching inside women, reaching here.' She rose a little to meet his description. 'It's as if they were looking for something, just kind of searching around.' His words landed, tepid against her thigh. 'They always fumble at it like a jacket pocket, or something – the crack where they lost their spare change – and this isn't *like* that, this isn't *for* that.' A thumb-stroke at her newer, sleeker self. 'This is not a thing. This is you. But for the pictures, in they go – the same move for every possible occasion – checking for standard dimensions, getting a good grip.'

Edward was keeping busy, fervent, while Helen felt herself slipping below his obsession.

'Then when I watch the women grab the guys' dicks and I look at their wrists, the action of their wrists, and they might as well be gutting fish – get the guy hard and toss him off with the minimum effort, the greatest efficiency. And you know this is something they've done a thousand times before, come after come after come. Repetition. When it's real it doesn't repeat. It's fresh. It's lovely. Beautiful.'

He halted and the sudden lack of motion stung up through the muscle of her back. 'This'll never be the same.

I'll be learning you forever.' And once again, the clipping: thorough and methodical to clear the way.

Edward didn't have to tell her, she quite understood; he was making her look like one of the women in his films, like what he must want, a body pared down to its entrances, a splayed personality. But even her disgust yawed and clamoured for more of him when he was finally done and drew his hands away, because inside herself she *was* like the women in his films.

Edward rested back on his heels, glanced at her with a type of helplessness and let his head drop. 'I am going to stay here. You should get away to bed.' He seemed unsure of where to put the scissors now. 'Nothing happened that was bad, did it? And we agreed – all of it. I, um, know you've been very good to me already. But if you didn't mind, I would watch you walking out. If I could. The way you are now – to look at you this way would be wonderful.'

He paused, folding his arms and possibly waiting for Helen to speak, even though he had removed her from any thought of words.

'Tell me if I've pleased you, Helen. You've pleased me. I mean, I've never been in a . . . similar position.' He raised both hands to his mouth, breathed what he still had of her, and then bowed his head. 'I'm very happy. I want you to be happy as well. You're better than anything else I know. Are you happy.'

'Yes.'

Helen stooped extremely slowly to gather her clothes, precisely as he asked her to and then she left him.

Edward told her, 'Thank you. Thank you very much.'

In her room she climbed straight into bed, still stripped and still echoing with Edward, and she curled on her side and was private too late, her knees close up to her chest. She was not happy.

Helen did not expect to sleep, but down into uncon-sciousness she went, tiny cuts and strokes of horror mum-bling at her as she fell.

A garden caught her; a warm, flat green place with soft trees and bushes and the high, close buzz of insects on every side. She was naked, but as soon as she noticed this, lizards began to drop from the undulating branches above her and flattened themselves across her skin. They covered her surprisingly well, but were chill to the touch and when she walked she could feel their claws tear at her minutely.

She passed an empty cave with a stone at its mouth and felt all the lizards raise their heads to look at it respectfully. While she brushed them back down into place, she caught sight of a bearded man, digging in one of the flower-beds with a narrow metal blade.

The gardener raised his hand in a sort of blessing. 'Hello, Helen. Your lizards are doing well.'

'Yes.'

'Would you like to see my heart? It's sacred, you know.'

'Yes, I would.'

He opened his shirt firmly with a shower of loosened buttons and then let his arms fall aside to unveil a plump, glossy heart, winking and panting moistly through his parted ribs. Something glowed and wormed inside it like a lightbulb element.

'I could bless you with all of my heart.'

'Could you?'

'Oh, yes. But underneath the lizards, there's nothing to you any more. A blessing won't do any good – you're past saving.' He smiled beatifically and Helen tried to stop herself from staring at his chest wound while it trembled and sucked, inviting. She felt sure that if she could touch the heart it would forgive her and she would be saved.

The gardener stood, poetically casual with his arms still wide, as if he might be embracing something large she could not see. It was a simple thing to step forward while he eyed the wavering trees and to reach her hand inside him. The heart nuzzled her palm and let her touch the urgent ribbing of its veins. If she could hold it for a tiny while, then all would be eternally well, but as soon as she tried to grasp it, the heart ducked away from her and she knew this was in case her badness made it burst. Then slippery and hot, like the mouth of meat-eating plant, the gardener's wound began to close and clasp around her in a massive, insistent bite. It shattered the bones in her wrist with a long, creaking snap, while the heart hid itself, now entirely beyond her reach.

The hot plumes of pain she dreamed lancing up her forearm, lingered momentarily as she woke into the silence of her room. Almost as soon as she remembered where and how she was, she realised her door had been opened and a figure was close to her bed. She lay, hypnotised by probabilities and the weight of their approach.

Edward.

Of course it was Edward, there was no one else for it to be. His soap, his toothpaste, his warm washed body; she could not help but breathe him in completely. Then a brief kiss, lightly clumsy, delivered above one eye and he padded away, sneaking the door shut behind him.

Helen lay on her back and peered up at nothing with her arms folded in across her breasts because that felt correct. This way she could check how solid she was, how much of her was really here. As she moved her muscle and her skin, the places where Edward had touched her felt different and light, but underneath was the dirt of her thinking. She would have left her room and gone to Edward and talked with him about what was on her mind, but she couldn't ask Edward for advice about leaving Edward.

That was why she had to go. She had to leave.

Helen was being emptied of all but the terrible things that she wanted to do. She was fading away. Odd prayers had already begun to ambush her, full of insistent requests she'd never intended to make, prayers that knew she would be disappointed when a man left her bedside after only a kiss.

So in the morning she should go. She should make her usual breakfast and read the paper and have marmalade and toast and do nothing to cause uneasiness or alarm. She should try to wonder aloud again how a man of such undoubted intelligence couldn't manage not to slop his saucer full of tea when he knew it made drips on the tablecloth eventually.

'I know, it's because I'm not awake.'

His eyes were vaguely puzzled as he spoke. She had intended only to tease him, but had sounded bad-tempered instead.

When he finally left for his study she caught him by the arm and, at once, he leaned towards her without resistance, naturally letting her kiss him on the mouth as though this was a long-established part of their morning routine. His grin, the half-halt before he turned to the doorway and the nervous rub of his hand at his hair were the last things she saw of him, which made her glad because they were all very good to remember, very like him.

Helen left Edward's flat as she might have for a visit to the museum or the park and took herself to Victoria where the coaches are. With money that was Edward's, and for which she was sorry, she bought a ticket to Glasgow and then waited in the waiting area until it was time to go.

'Helen?' Mr Brindle sounded – how did he sound? Not angry. Almost afraid.

'Yes, it's me. I'm coming back.' and one more time, to convince herself, 'I'm coming back.'

'When?'

'Now.' Silence washed back at her from the receiver. 'I wanted to say . . . if you would let me come home, I would be there in half an hour.'

'Let you?' His words were softening and softening, she could have mistaken him for someone else. 'Let you? Come back. You really will? I thought . . . what I did . . . I thought. Thank God you're back.'

'You don't believe in God.'

'Thank God you're back.'

The house made her ashamed. Mr Brindle had kept the place neat, perhaps only a little more tired than when she left, but still, it compared badly with the Kensington flat. Helen realised her tastes had been changed. She had come to expect the kind of simplicity expense can sometimes lend to things. Helen had stayed with someone who led the life of a wealthy man and who could afford to be careful of quality and design. Material things hadn't mattered to her before. They did now.

'I tried to be tidy.'

Mr Brindle escorted her doggedly upstairs past rooms she already found too familiar. Bathroom, boxroom, bedroom. Outside the bedroom, Mr Brindle stopped. He was keeping his distance – possibly finding her mildly repellent and she could understand that. Frowning towards her, he mashed his hands into the pockets of his jeans: very old jeans he wouldn't normally have worn around the house unless he was doing some type of dirty work. 'Cleaning up. Dusting. It was like, it was a way of thinking of you.' Everywhere smelt mildly of his sweat. 'That thing that happened . . .'

Helen found she could meet his eyes quite firmly until his gaze withered away. He didn't like it when she watched him.

'That thing. I lost my temper. You know when I lose my temper . . . I don't mean it.' She watched. 'I won't do it again. You shouldn't have just gone, though. I worried . . . your sister, she didn't know . . . I won't do it again.'

He nodded and retreated towards the head of the stairs, wiping his hands down the front of his shirt and Helen knew she did not believe him. Even if he didn't think so, he would do it again.

Inside the bedroom, the mirror of the vanity unit blinked at her slyly and there was nothing she could touch or see that didn't seem ready to trip, to leap, to start up the process of making her pay for every piece of every wrong that she had done. She had come here to submit and Mr Brindle would do God's will to her, even though he was an atheist.

There was, undoubtedly, the problem of her being a weak person in so many ways. She was susceptible to doubt and hesitation. When she opened her case to fetch out her bits and pieces, the atmosphere of that other place, of the flat, swam up to tug at her and make her current course of action seem confused and difficult to take. Almost all of her wanted to be in Kensington and maybe only lying on the sofa and feeling nice, at ease, and expecting that she would see someone she was very fond of quite soon, if he wasn't already there with her. She wanted to be comfortable. She had always wanted to be comfortable. Helen didn't like to be hurt. She enjoyed it when good things happened and she could show they pleased her.

When she'd been in that flat on her own, sometimes she'd put on the radio in the sitting-room and not exactly danced, but wriggled and bobbed, when she'd felt so inclined. Even if she hadn't been alone, it would have been okay that she'd done this and not something she needed to worry about. She had forgotten how much space in her mind the worry had to occupy, it was already burrowing and smothering every image she was holding inside when she wanted the freedom to remember incidents and people she cared about.

'Helen.' Mr Brindle was shouting from downstairs, although moderately loud speech would have been perfectly audible. 'You going to be up there all night? You're home now. Okay?'

She abandoned her case on the bed, still full.

Mr Brindle was calm when she joined him in the dimness of the living-room. He sat in his usual chair, watching a documentary about something to do with crime, and was not especially fatter or thinner than before, but made out of something very minorly different. His flesh seemed more porous and less convincing.

'Sit down. You travel far? Tired?' He didn't look at her.

'Not really. No.'

'Fine. You'll sleep in the spare room. Sheets and stuff are out.' He didn't look at her at all.

'Yes.'

For an hour, the television jabbered recklessly between them. They did not speak again, or draw the curtains, or turn on the lights. Helen watched the room coagulate around her under shrapnel bursts of light.

Whatever he was planning to do with her would clearly involve a wait. Helen knew that tomorrow Mr Brindle might consult with the men he worked beside, or ask opinions at his pub on what he should do and how he should feel about his wife. The influence of like minds could very often make him angry with her, even if she had not.

Helen, because she could be so easily frightened, had hoped there would be no wait and no opportunity for her to break and run away to softer things again. Still, nothing was wasted in God's economy and the time she was being offered could be put to use. She might be able to prepare herself.

But this particular part of her waiting – waiting in the fluctuating dark with the television noise and no hope of distraction from the man and the name and the telephone number she could not think about – it was no longer bearable. 'You know – '

'What?' Mr Brindle must have been pausing all that time, ready for when she would speak.

'I just thought I would go up now.'

'Well I won't be long behind you.' He made a small, breathy laugh, either out of nervousness or disgust. 'Not long now.'

'Fine. Good night.'

She didn't attempt to kiss him because that would have given him the chance to turn his head away.

Mr Brindle had done well for her in the boxroom. The old wardrobe had been emptied and then refilled with a tangled heap which was all of her clothes. A small stack of paint tins occupied the corner furthest from the unmade bed. The carpet had been hoovered and the walls were penitentially bare. He had left her sheets and blankets and a small electric fire to annoy the damp. When she switched it on, it clicked and rang and produced a fine, acid burning of dust.

All right, God. I'm here. What do you want me to do? Be my shepherd, be my father, let me know what I should do.

She stopped, didn't open her eyes, but called a halt to herself. Her breathing raced towards a strange anticipation. She listened and could hear the jump of her heart. Careful, now, be careful – this could be nothing, wishful thinking and nothing more.

Helen was kneeling, because a person at prayer is intended to kneel, as a signal of humility and respect. Body kneeling, hands folded, eyes shut – all of her curled and closed to keep out this world and permit its better replacement to enter in. To enter in. For years she had knelt and protected the vacuum that she was, her absence of the convincing and the convinced.

She needed to be very careful and still. As she might be if she hoped to touch a nervous bird.

She should consider the degrees of pain. She should recall the degrees of pain that emptied prayer had caused her over time. To accept her loss of faith and fall silent in defeat had been a relief, but then a burden. God knew, she'd tried to be rid of it. God knew where that had got her, too.

And then a brief stab of inspection dropped through her. The house seemed to lurch around an axis and return almost before she could think. Quiet again. But an ordered stillness, packed and immanent, laid itself down on the backs of her legs like sweat, near as live hands cupping her face.

All right, God. I'm here.

While she opened her mouth to breathe, an inward rush took her and squeezed to her spine. This time the sensation dissipated as gradually as smoke in her veins.

Helen opened her eyes and the boxroom was unchanged. She couldn't think what she'd expected.

A sign.

Stupid.

Might as well hope He might leave His umbrella behind.

And it wasn't even that He'd been here. Not that. Only that He was close.

Close. The kind of word to make a person cry without knowing it. Close. A movement of hope behind glass.

Father, I'm here and I don't know what to do.

After that the speed of everything went wrong. Helen performed what tasks she could remember were called for about the house, even performed them over again, and was still left surrounded by abandoned hours. Walking out to the park, the shops, up and down the stairs and corridors, made no impact on her energy or pace. Every morning Mr Brindle left her and every evening he returned and she had no sure way of judging what had passed between those two directions – it could have been a minute, it could have been a week.

Maybe not really a week, she didn't think they'd last a week before it happened.

'Cunt.'

Wednesday evening, meal over and at every point satisfactory, but then she'd tried to bring him a coffee in the sitting-room and dropped the cup. Her hand had forgotten itself. Mr Brindle heard the impact of the china and the liquid as they came apart, stood and watched for a still moment as the dark, wet heat sank into his rug.

Then he stepped forward and slapped her. 'Cunt.' Slapped her in the face where it would show because he wasn't being careful any more.

Nothing followed, but in Mr Brindle's eyes, Helen saw the sharp start of intent, before he could pack it down again. Naturally, she was afraid, but she tried her hardest to accept that her fear had meaning; it was part of her process. It would make her soft and open, the way she had to be.

Because each night she would kneel and be raced towards the increasingly completed fact of God. Larger than understanding, deeper than death and time, He would hood down over the house like snow, patient and immeasurable.

Father.

So the time drops by you like blood then eddies with uncertainty and after days of waiting you still wait, discovering the way this feels cannot be unbearable because you bear it. You are not yet fully prepared, you have to remember that. This final interval is here to make you ready and complete.

Praying becomes all you do, it ribbons around you while you move in the world and tells your life out and up to that Watching, that anatomising Stare. You step from daily fear to fear until the sun sets and the house begins to move in time with the nasty itch in your husband's hands. Not long now.

Friday night. Twenty-two hours gone out of the twenty-four and you're kneeling, again kneeling, in the room he's given you and you hear him on the staircase and in the corridor and this time, like every other time, something important tears up under your ribs when he passes your door without coming in.

Your husband doesn't come in, but you know that tonight isn't over because you've changed; there's nothing left of you to say; you've let God see it all. Not that you could have believed He didn't fully know about every layer of tissue He's asked you to peel away. The point is, you had to tell Him and He had to hear. This was your part of the process and your Father who art in Heaven, but who is also much nearer and much more terrible than that; He will forgive you now.

Forgiveness. Feel it pick you back down to the child, take you off your hinges and clean you to the bone. He's here, your Father who is tender like a furnace and who will hold you for eternity, if you would only ask and He can make you ask. He can make you go through fear into somewhere else entirely.

It is something like half-past ten when you go to Mr Brindle's room, the bedroom you at one time shared. You are aware of a lightness in your hands and limbs, the tiny noise of your feet and the press of black air against your flesh, your cleaned and uncovered self. Second-hand illumination seeps out around the doorframe. To be at this point already, so quickly, you hadn't expected that.

Turn the handle, open the door, absurdly prepared for it to be locked or for the bogey man ghost to leap out and take you at once. Walk in, gently, because you are standing at the edge of nothing and you don't want to slip. Mr Brindle is sitting up in bed, staring at a paperback which you have the time to recognise as one of the detective stories that he likes. Crime: nothing else caught his interest as intensely, and what does that say about why he married you?

Magically slowly, he lifts his head.

He does not make a sound.

There is a slither of confusion in his eyes and he glances away but has to, in the end, come back to you. Your body is balanced, naked, and breathes fast from the top of its ribcage, as anxious as any discovered animal, and Mr Brindle's mouth thins to a stroke while he reaches your eyes and you offer look for look and beat him. Then you feel the precise ignition of his anger, just as he helps himself to the rest of you in a long, falling glance and sees what you need him to see.

You are not as he remembers, not quite. He moves his head a scrap to the left and examines again. Not the same. He is finding out what Edward has done to you and what you wanted Edward to do to you and enjoyed, and you can think of Edward now, very clearly and with love. There is nothing to stop you thinking whatever you like.

Now Mr Brindle understands. You have been sheared in tight to yourself, to your nothing-but-sex, and each of the questions he chose not to ask you and the hardest assumptions he most liked to make are proving inadequate.

You are turning and walking back out at an even pace when you hear Mr Brindle rip himself up from the bed.

The knowledge of him behind you and on his way scalds

from the back of your neck to your heels, but you will not run or even rush. There is a bang of complaint as the door cracks round against the wall and shudders in again. Mr Brindle beats it away. He's in the corridor.

You have nearly reached the boxroom. He is closing on you very fast and now makes a sound which swipes you off balance as if it were a blow. You have never heard a noise like this from a person before: a high, long howling that jars with every impact of his running feet.

You make the room, halt and enjoy for an instant the impression of being safe, of an objective successfully reached. Then Mr Brindle hits you, the whole of him hits you, drives the use out of your lungs, and you fall with one hand reaching down ahead of you to shield your face.

'You didn't die.'

'Yes, I did. I felt it.'

'No. You didn't die.'

Helen opened her eyes and saw the unfocused shine of a metal counter while somebody's hand adjusted the bend of her knee. She knew that she was dead and they were laying her up on one of those special tables they had for autopsies. It was very unfair to be doing all this while her mind was still inside her body.

'Leave me alone.'

'We will in a while.'

A different hand drove a spark of hurt so hard into the bone of her leg that it exploded her understanding along with the table and the room.

So Helen was cut loose and floated for a time she did eventually calculate but never quite believed. Small pieces of reality would swim out to meet her and then sink from sight. She became accustomed to the notion that her body was being kept somewhere, lying in uncomfortable clothes inside a bed. The rest of her was mainly unwilling to be anywhere, having an idea that any kind of definition would involve it in the guaranteed discovery of pain.

Her hair was stiff and sour-smelling when Helen moved her head and at night people took her blood pressure all the time when she was so tired that the grip of the cuff on her arm made her weep. She was unconvincingly thirsty and could not remember if she had ever been given a drink.

Sometimes the gardener seemed to come and talk to her with his heart – the heart liked her now, it was warm and insistent against her fingertips.

'Helen?'

'Yes.'

'What were you going to die for?'

'You.'

'I never asked you to.'

'I guessed.'

'Helen, did you think if you were meant to die, we would even consult you?' He smiled when she couldn't answer him. 'Have you touched my heart?'

'Yes.'

'Has it touched you back?'

'Yes.'

'Then go away and be satisfied.'

A woman arrived to polish the floor under all of the beds and Helen woke for long enough to take the scream of machinery back down into her sleep. Beyond every dream or darkness, Helen watched and watched a sort of dance where Mr Brindle twirled her body so that it banged and cracked and splashes of light appeared with colours in time to his beat. As their finale, she would spin against the wardrobe and tug it down to cover her and keep her safe, or to let its weight finish the death Mr Brindle had started for her, she couldn't be sure.

'So you don't remember.'

Helen frowned, cautious. Without any warning, she was conscious and apparently taking part in a conversation.

'You don't remember anything after that?'

She was staring up at a policewoman with a soft expression and no hat. The policewoman frowned so Helen said something which felt correct.

'No. No, I can't remember anything.'

'He telephoned.'

'Who? Did somebody call me?' Hope suddenly thumped at her, but she explained to herself that Edward wouldn't call – she had left him and not said why, not said anything because she had to come to Glasgow to make things right.

The policewoman, rather than giving an answer, was shifting her weight and glancing across Helen's bed to a policeman. He pursed his lips and dropped his head forward in a way that might have meant he was nodding consent, if you knew him very well. He was trying not to move or

296

be distracting; supportive but invisible, that's what he was aiming for, Helen could tell.

The policewoman gave a nod of her own and began, 'Mrs Brindle.' She cleared her throat. 'No, nobody called you. Your husband called us. That night, or at least, very early that morning, I think it was . . .'

'Two fifteen.' If you want to know the time, even an invisible policeman can't help but tell.

'Two fifteen. He called us to, to turn himself in. He thought he'd killed you. You were under the wardrobe when we came.'

'I didn't die.'

The policeman gave his sleepy nod again and very quickly patted her hand, as if he was scared he might catch himself doing it. 'No. That's right.'

Another small cough and the policewoman continued, 'When we arrived, Mr Brindle was relatively lucid and rational.' This had the sound of something that was already firmly written down. 'He let us in and told us where you were. An ambulance was called. He expressed, I'm afraid, no relief when he was told you were alive. At this point he informed officers present that he had taken a large number of paracetamol tablets some considerable time before.'

'A very unpleasant way to die.' The policeman offered, almost consolingly.

'Yes. That's . . . Yes. Any treatment offered after internal damage has been done can only be a sort of management. They made him as comfortable as possible. This must all be very shocking. I am sorry. His brother has identified the body that – '

'Won't be necessary. You won't have to.' Again the pat at her hand.

They seemed very gentle, these people from the police, and anxious to only ask and say what was absolutely needful. She had the impression they might have sat by her bed before, or perhaps they had met when she was under the wardrobe and not thinking but still listening – perhaps the sound of them was familiar. She would have liked to tell them how she felt. Certainly, they seemed keen to know her feelings and ready to help if she was unhappy. But she wasn't unhappy – she was awake and she was alive and those were two such remarkable things, she had no room for any more.

The policeman gave her a quiet smile as he and his companion finally stood. 'You'll be numb, that's what it is. You'll be numb – these things, it's how it happens.' He nodded a great deal while he said this, but watched her as if she were a problem that might not be solved conveniently. Both the police then left her alone to work out the finer details of herself, because they had everything they needed and, even although they were obviously pleasant, they had other duties which, most likely, called.

Helen lay and watched the light fall impeccably from the neon strips above the ward and thought that moving her eyes and paying attention and saying sentences and all the time being careful to make no savage or even tiny movements of her head was far too much to be doing at the one time. A rest was required.

Something very easily accomplished. In years to come, she could see herself emerging as a champion sleeper: started late in life, but now an eager narcoleptic, a woman who liked to be able to leave any situation simply by strongly favouring the interior of her own mind, safe behind darkened eyes. Night, night.

When her new dream was steady and she could stand and look about her, she knew at once where she was: in the kitchen of Mr Brindle's house.

'What are you doing here? You're upstairs, dead.'

Mr Brindle was sitting on the floor in his dressing gown. He turned his head up to glare at her and she saw dark matter begin to purl from one of his ears. He scratched at the side of his face in irritation, but seemed otherwise quite normal, perhaps overly pale. His voice hadn't changed, it still had enough edge to make her seem shorter and weaker than she was. 'Go back upstairs.'

'I'm not dead.'

He smiled slyly, sensing a trick ahead. 'You will be.' A sudden cough distracted him. His lips were turning blue. 'You'll die and be nothing, like everyone else in the end.' He wiped at the sides of his neck and examined the rusty stains across his fingers. A great deal of him was leaking away as Helen watched.

'Today I am not dead. You didn't kill me. You couldn't. And I let you try.'

'All right, then, I killed myself. I know I killed someone.' Another cough. 'So it was me. I'm dead. What'll you do about it?'

'There's nothing I can do.'

'You aren't going to pray for me? Like a good Christian should?' A laugh bubbled in his chest but couldn't emerge.

'Oh, I'll pray for you. I can pray now – about anything. I'll pray because I'm able and because it will help me. And because I know you'd hate me to.'

He smiled, a sheen of blood dulling his teeth. 'Cunt.'

After that the dream clouded over and she sculled out into something smooth and aimless that allowed her to feel rested and content, even when they came to take her blood pressure again.

Mr Brindle was dead and she was not. Sometimes God was really very obviously good. You didn't have to understand it, you just had to accept – God was good. He did well. He gave her things she was not expecting.

Like the sight of an anxiously tall figure walking softly down the ward, his concentration on the floor. Not a dream and not a mirage: a man with an extremely severe haircut, wearing a long grey overcoat and a very red scarf and putting his hands in his pockets and taking them out again, as though they could not be comfortable except in motion. The scarf made her close her eyes for a moment, it was so bright.

'Helen. Helen, are you awake?'

'I'm awake. I've got a terrible headache, though.'

'I should think you do – you have a fractured skull.'

She blinked up to see Edward folding his arms and tilting himself away from the rest of the ward while he tried to pull in a smooth breath. The muscles in his jaw ticked with an effort at control, but still he started to cry.

'Shit.'

Helen tried to reach and touch him and her attempt sent the walls and ceiling spiralling. She lay back and let the vertigo subside. 'I've got the headache – you don't have to cry.'

He fumbled for a chair and lifted it close to her bed, all the while repeating quietly, 'Shit, shit, shit.' and rubbing the heel of his hand across his eyes. 'Why the hell did you go back there?' He sat. 'Was it me?'

'No.'

Taking her wrist, 'Was it me?' and then letting her slowly move her hand to set its fingers round his thumb and grip. 'Did I upset you?'

'No. I had to get back here and sort things out.'

'Sort things out? He could have killed you. You must have known that. Couldn't you even have phoned?'

'You would have come and got me. You would have done the right thing, but it would have been too soon.' Edward didn't speak and pulled his hand away from her.

Helen thought of God. It was important He was here for this. If God was God, of course, he would be in each of her bruises and her water jug and anything she could think to name – but she needed His help to say what she must.

As soon as she opened her attention, Something monumental began to pour in. A sense of humour must obviously be amongst the everything that God had – for years she'd needed to hear from Him just a little and now He was determined to be deafening.

'Edward? I can't turn my head to look at you, I get so dizzy. You'll have to speak to me. Please. I am sorry I hurt you, I didn't want to.'

'No, you only wanted to hurt yourself. What were you thinking of?' His words choking out, breaking. 'Jesus, I come up here and I find the house empty and then the neighbours say what happened, only they don't really know what happened . . . I thought I'd go mad. Helen, I could have got you, I could have been here in time. He never would have hurt you if I'd been here.'

'I know.'

'I would have stopped him.'

'I didn't die.'

'You could have.'

'But I didn't. I got through. I was taken through. I mean, I'm *alive*, Edward. I believe in Something – or Something believes in me. And I believe in me and I can do any and every living thing a living person does. I am alive.'

He drew his chair in with a scrape that made her smart. The smell of his hair, his sadness, his skin, was an astonishment as he leaned in to set his voice neat beside her face.

'Helen, I intended to come here and be . . . acceptable. I couldn't be where I should have been to help you and I know that what I did made you go away.' She tried moving her head to disagree and he kissed the rise of her cheek. 'I want to tell you all the things that a good man would, all the right things, but you know I'm not good.'

'Tell me, anyway.'

'I can't. I can only say what I want and that's frankly quite inappropriate.'

'Tell me, anyway.'

'Helen, I want you to be alive with me – the whole

301

completed fact of you with me. I want to do that. God, I got so lonely down there. Because I can't do what I used to any more – the films, the magazines – and I'm telling you, I gave up fighting it and tried and it didn't even matter, because I couldn't do it, couldn't even begin. I just missed you. There's nothing I can do about missing you. I haven't got anything when you're not there and I don't know what to do with me on my own, with myself.'

She felt him press his forehead into her pillow and lifted her hand to touch his neck and then the tight trim of his hair.

'Helen, I should go. They said I wasn't to upset you.'

'You're not. Tell me something.'

'What?'

'How do I look?'

He lifted his head and blinked at her. 'How do you look?'

'Yes. Tell me.'

'Um.' He began a kind of frown. 'Just now?'

'Just now.'

She heard him pull up a breath to speak with and then stop. Then he breathed again. 'Do I have to get this right? Helen? I mean help me, I don't know what you're asking. I love you. Can I say I love you? I love you.'

She felt that. It washed along, snug under her skin, slow and heavy and more than enough to stir up the pain in her bones. She held him by the wrist with as much strength as she had, 'Mr Brindle never told me how I looked. So I want to know. And I love you.'

'You . . . ?'

'Love you. How do I look?'

'Well, you're – Really?'

'Yes, how do I look?'

'Um, you look lovely. That bastard – he didn't stop you being lovely. Your nose is a bit . . . He broke it.' His hand smoothed light on her forehead, catching a hair back into place. 'I would have killed him. Murder has no possible justification, I believe that absolutely, but I would have killed him if he hadn't killed himself – I would have. Sorry.'

She felt his face grazing above her, breathing her in.

'Helen? That thing they've given you to wear, I wouldn't – I don't think it's very nice.'

'I'm a mess.'

'You're a lovely mess.' He surprised himself with a laugh that ended dangerously close to something else.

'Oh, well, I've never been a lovely mess before.'

'It won't happen again.'

'I've been a *mess* . . .'

'No. You're still doing better than me. Listen, you may not be able to see this, but I am in no way at what we might laughingly call my best. Shaving this morning, I don't know, I can't have been thinking – I look as though I've tried to cut my head off. Blood everywhere.'

'Don't let the nurses see, they'll keep you in.'

'I wouldn't mind staying.' He paused to let her think about that. 'Helen, could I bring you a different night-dress tomorrow? If I came tomorrow . . . I could come tomorrow. I live here. I have a flat, I'm renting a flat, that seemed to be the thing . . . I mean, would that be useful? Something more comfortable for you to wear?'

'That would be good of you. Thank you. I'm a si –'

'I know what size you are, Helen. I know exactly what size you are.'

A porter wheelchaired her out of the hospital because her walking was strong, but her balance much weaker, and she represented a risk of accident to herself. Edward loped, or occasionally had to trot beside her. She was being discharged to his flat and his care which made this feel like a fixed prescription, as well as a choice on her part. There was a good solidity about the plans for her immediate future. Edward had admitted his qualifications in matters of the brain and friendship and the proper authorities had accepted him as a person who was fit to have charge of her. In spite of, or perhaps because of his doctorates, the ward sister had given him a checklist of contra-indications for cases of head injury.

GROWING DROWSINESS OR CONFUSION

WEAKNESS OF AN ARM OR LEG

VOMITING

LEAKAGE FROM THE EAR OR NOSE

SEVERE HEADACHE

'I've had a headache for a week.' Sitting in a rented flat and drinking badly-made tea and thinking she is more fond of her city now than she has ever been and that the autumn sky through the window is of the very best colour in a blue eye and good enough to break your heart.

'For a week.'

Edward is busy being pleased. Helen's sister bought clothes and cried and looked at him as if he might very well be a monster and he was still pleased. Whatever he does or does not do, he cannot help being pleased. At the moment he is smiling at Helen in a way that means he will be slightly deaf, because he is not listening a bit.

'Headache. Me.'

Now he is concerned, but also pleased. 'Not a severe one.'

'How do you know?'

'I'm a doctor.'

'You're a professor.'

'I had to be a doctor first. Does your head seriously hurt?'

'No, doctor. I just wish it didn't spin.'

'I know, that'll wear off, though. Your balance is out of whack.'

'You don't say.'

'Oh, but I do, I heard me.' And he takes her temperature the way he is meant to at regular intervals, especially at night.

Helen thinks of him at regular intervals, especially at night, and she grows more well. She walks without help, she can bear to read print, they take her stitches out. For the very last time, she talks to the police and all they discuss is no more of her concern. There will be an inquest and she will get through it because Edward will be there.

One evening she sits in the best of their flat's remarkably purple armchairs and eats a hot meal with Edward. The people that Edward telephoned have cooked it, but he puts it on the plate.

'So it's edible, at least.'

He starts their washing-up and Helen follows him in to make a pot of tea. They both enjoy their tea. When she fits herself behind him as he works at the sink, they both sway slightly under the impact of what they are because they haven't touched this way since Kensington. She slips her hands in round his waist until they meet above the buckle of his belt. He leans in to her, only lightly and she can feel all of him live, 'Are you sure?' and each of his syllables rubbing and snuggling in. 'We don't need to hurry.'

'What have I got here?'

'Me.'

'Mm?'

'Edward E. Gluck. The E is for Eric. I don't want to rush you.'

'I know.'

'But I will have to in a minute, if you don't stop. I'm only flesh and blood, after all.'

'I know. That's what I want.'

'Is it?'

'Yes. It is.'

Which takes them to her room and to the drawing of her curtains and to a kiss which is so interesting they are unable to move on for quite a while.

A person should not undress another person while that person is undressing them.

'I'm sorry, it's because of the dark – if you could do that button.' Edward does have extremely large hands, which are not always un-clumsy.

Helen is finding it difficult to co-ordinate speaking with the everything else that is happening everywhere. 'Different, isn't it?'

'What?'

'Clothes. Going from the outside in. Someone else.'

'Mm hm. Different and much better. Oh, God. No, I'll do that, because it's . . . Okay, you do it, then. But – '

'Ow.'

'Sorry, I did say . . .'

They stand and clasp each other woodenly and Helen thinks they are afraid of breaking or of the roaring of their skin or of the fact that they have exactly what they want, that they are holding it.

She walks him to the bed and they cover each other up, carefully and entirely, and begin the gentle, strenuous fight to cling and be still and kiss and move and touch every place when there are acres of places, all moving and turning and wanting to be touched. Edward's skin, she could never have fully imagined how completely satisfactory Edward's skin would be. And he has a good weight, the right weight, something she can move to take.

'Can I?'

'I wish you would, yes.'

A stutter of hands and there he is, the lovely man. In.

'Jesus that's –' The other stutter, the big stutter. 'Oh, Helen. Oh, I'm sorry.'

'No, stay there.'

'But I've – '

'I know.' She can feel the twitch of him, the slight withdrawal. 'Stay there, though, I like you there. And we have ages, we have all night, we have years. I'm taking it as a compliment.'

'I was hoping it would be.' He coughs, relaxes, sinks on to her. 'Not exactly the demon lover when it comes to flesh and blood.'

'From what I've read, I shouldn't worry, we'll be fine.'

'From what you've read?'

'Self-help books, they cover everything. I've gone through most of them.'

'And you've read about this.'

'About all kinds of things.'

'You're as bad as me.' She feels him twitch again.

'I came across sexual information in the course of my general reading.'

'Really.' Twitch. He is smiling in both possible places.

'Yes, really, and sometimes I wanted to read about men. I wanted to like them, because often they seemed such a good idea and not the way I'd been told, or the way that I'd found them to be. I mean, they go wrong; any kind of person could go wrong, I understood that, but then I'd see a man walking or tying his laces, or something, queuing in a shop and he'd be so lovely and clear . . . He'd be the way a woman couldn't. I'm a woman and men are made to be particularly not like me. That is such a good thing. Like men swallowing . . .'

'Swallowing.'

'Yes. Have you ever watched a man swallow – absolutely nothing but that? It's incredible. You've all got that high adam's apple and it moves so fantastically well – like it's happy and buoyant and vulnerable and working just the way that it should be – and the jaw's got a proper edge and there's that bit of friction. With men you get friction. They can really be a quality design.'

'I'm glad you approve.'

She rests her mouth near his throat and he swallows for her. 'Mm hm, that's it.'

'Well, I'm a man.'

'I know that.'

'I swallow like a man.'

'But you swallow like you, too. And you have your kind of man's chest. When you stand up, it's at that right kind of an angle, that clear line – no breasts.'

'What about my angle now?'

Helen licks his neck and closes her eyes while his body gives a gentle jump and hers answers it. 'It's a good angle.'

'Anything else, while you're making a list?'

Her hand makes a slow reach down to where it wants and he shivers up for a moment to let it through so it can hold him.

'These would be on the list. These are the best. Very nearly the best.'

'You be careful with them, then.'

'They're gorgeous, they feel gorgeous.'

She explores while Edward stretches full awake. 'Oh dear.'

'What?'

'You didn't read that in a self-improvement book. Unless it was a very good one. Oh, dear.'

'If you don't like it, I can stop.'

'Don't you dare. You have no idea of how many nights, of how long I've been thinking of your hand doing that, and of me being here and inside you and doing this with you, and this.'

They begin doing this, and this, Edward talking them through.

'Oh, God . . .

'That's nice . . .

'I think . . .

'If we . . .

'Make it slow . . .

'This will . . .

'Turn out . . .

'Fine.

'Oh, yes.

'We're Fine.

'Love you.'

'I love you.' and so she does.

Her thinking is beginning to steam over, but Helen knows precisely who she loves and precisely Who has let her love him.

'That's it.'

'No, that's it.'

Oh, yes, so it is.'

They're almost away now, almost one and the same thing and not a thought between them except for, 'Edward?'

'Hm?'

'You have really large feet.'

'Feet?'

'Mm.'

'Now she tells me.'

'You do.'

'I'm very tall.' Bright at her ear, breath and sound and Edward being pleased to sound mildly offended. 'Didn't have big feet – I'd fall over. We wouldn't want that.'

'No, we wouldn't want that.'

And, having nothing more to say, Helen lets herself be. She is here and with Edward as he folds in around her and she around him and they are one completed motion under God the Patient, Jealous Lover: the Jealous, Patient Love.